Fatal
Love

Books in the Tom Stone series by Michael Patterson

Playing at Murder
Deadly Retribution
Ring of Truth
Death or Honour
Fatal Love

Fatal Love

Michael Patterson

Crescent books

First published in the United Kingdom in 2019 by
Crescent Books Publishing

ISBN 978-0-9569798-8-9

To my father-in-law, Jack. It was an honour to have known you!

Chapter 1

While DS Milner was reading him his rights, Commander Jenkins didn't take his eyes off DCI Stone once.

'You really don't know what you are doing, do you?' Commander Jenkins asked at last, in a surprisingly calm tone, but nonetheless with a look on his face which bordered on contempt. He didn't wait for a reply. 'You just couldn't wait. I told you that I would soon be retiring.' He paused. 'This will soon be revealed for what it really is. A vindictive witch hunt led by an attention-seeking, delusional and renegade police officer. What is almost as inexcusable is that you have also now involved other, more junior officers in your scheming obsession.'

Moments earlier DCI Tom Stone had announced he was arresting the commander for perverting the course of justice, as well as encouraging a third party to commit a crime. This was related to a case DCI Stone had recently been working on. A case which involved two deaths, indirectly caused and deliberately covered up by Commander Jenkins, a senior officer within the Metropolitan Police Force, and Charles Cope, currently a government minister in charge of UK security. Cope would also be arrested before long.

Commander Jenkins now turned his attention to DS Milner. 'And you, whatever your name is, might not know it, but you've just ended your own police career before it has even got started.'

Milner didn't respond. Instead, he simply said, 'You are now to accompany us to the station, where you will be formally charged.'

In the face of Commander Jenkins' obvious attempt to intimidate him, Tom couldn't help but admire Milner's assertiveness.

'Does the Commissioner know about this?' asked Commander Jenkins, this time in a less aggressive tone of voice.

It was Tom who replied. 'He was informed a few minutes ago by one of my officers.'

A thin smile appeared on Commander Jenkins' face. 'So you hadn't told him? Have you even considered the consequences of what you are doing for the Met? It will be a PR disaster for the force.'

'Or a triumph,' replied Tom, albeit not too convincingly.

Chapter 2

Later that same morning Tom was seated in the Commissioner's office. There, along with Sir Peter Westwood, were DCS Small and Tom's immediate boss, Superintendent Howard Birch. Unsurprisingly, given the media interest which would undoubtedly be generated, Sir Peter had convened this meeting as soon as he had become aware of Commander Jenkins' arrest.

'I thought we had all agreed,' said Sir Peter, looking directly at Tom, 'that Commander Jenkins and Charles Cope would both relinquish their current roles at some point in the future.' He glanced at Superintendent Birch. 'I've already taken the liberty of briefing Superintendent Birch concerning the evidence you have compiled against the two of them.' He then returned his gaze to Tom. 'Anyway, what changed?'

'What changed?' repeated Tom, having anticipated this question. 'What changed was the fact that a concerted campaign, designed to discredit me, was being conducted by someone in a senior position within the force. I suspect strongly that Commander Jenkins and possibly Charles Cope were at the forefront of this campaign. I was just about willing to accept that they would, *at some point in the future*, leave their respective positions, but when this happened it changed things completely. Suddenly, rather than Commander Jenkins and Charles Cope being the guilty parties, it had become me. You must have seen all of the media coverage relating to the Emmanuel Aphron case?'

This was a murder case which Tom had just concluded. During the investigation Tom had come under an increasing and at times quite vitriolic personal attack. An attack which, as far as Tom was concerned, could only have been orchestrated by Commander Jenkins in an attempt to discredit him and therefore protect the commander's position.

'You say that you suspect Commander Jenkins and Charles

3

Cope were involved,' said Sir Peter. 'You know, however, that suspicion is not the same as evidence. Unless you have that evidence there is no way this would actually get to court, let alone secure a conviction. You must have known that.'

'Of course I did, sir,' replied Tom, 'but what was I supposed to do?' There was a momentary silence before he carried on. 'I took the view that simply letting this happen was not an option. I didn't, and frankly still don't, care what happens to me. I came to the conclusion that it was better to finally put a stop to all of this. My only regret is that I didn't do it much earlier.'

Another brief silence followed. This time, though, it was Sir Peter who spoke, in a surprisingly positive tone given the circumstances of their meeting. 'Incidentally, many congratulations with the Aphron case.' He paused. 'At one stage it didn't look too good for you, did it?'

Tom redirected his attention towards DCS Small. 'It didn't. Especially when DCS Small informed me that he was taking me off the case, due to the increasingly negative coverage about me in the press.'

Before the tension could increase any further, Sir Peter said, with a slight laugh, 'Well, thank God you beat him to it. I'm sure DCS Small is mightily relieved that you solved the case before it happened.'

By now all three were looking at DCS Small, waiting for a response. That response, when it came, was surprising and had the effect of immediately reducing the tension.

'Well, yes,' he said. 'It wouldn't have looked too good for me, would it?' He shook his head. 'I think I owe you an apology, Tom. I should have trusted you. But, I'm afraid, at the time I was more swayed by speculation and innuendo, rather than the evidence available. It was an error of judgement on my part. I do hope this doesn't damage our relationship irretrievably.' He paused. 'If it's any consolation, I have offered to resign.'

'Which, incidentally, I have not accepted,' said Sir Peter, quickly.

DCS Small held out his hand towards Tom. For the briefest of moments it was unclear what Tom's reaction would be. Finally, though, he too held out his hand and said, 'I suppose it's possible I might have done the same, if I had been in your shoes.'

4

'Good. Well, at least that has been sorted out,' said a clearly relieved Sir Peter. 'Now, how are we going to handle the Jenkins situation?' It was not missed by all of the others that his previous, formal reference to Commander Jenkins had now been dropped.

'I understand lawyers for both Charles Cope and Commander Jenkins – and this is highly confidential – have already applied for their immediate release,' said DCS Small. 'I don't know, at this early stage, if they are likely to be successful. But I'm sure we will soon find out.'

'Release?' asked Tom. 'Do you mean on bail?'

'At this stage, we really don't know,' Sir Peter said. 'I understand, due to the security implications, this is now with the Home Secretary. In the meantime, let's do everything by the book. The very last thing we need right now is for it to fall down due to an administrative or technical cock-up.'

'It's not a cock-up. It's starting to look more like a cover-up,' said Tom, anger once again in his voice.

Sir Peter didn't immediately respond, instead waiting for Tom's anger to dissipate. When he did speak, however, it was in quite an assertive manner. 'There will be no cover-up whilst I'm in charge. As I said, we do everything by the book.' He then added, in a friendlier tone, 'You look tired, Tom. My strong suggestion is that you take a couple of weeks off. You need to recharge your batteries and be ready if this does come to trial.'

'*If* it comes to trial?' asked Tom, emphasising his first word. 'Why on earth would there be any doubt?'

It was DCS Small who answered. 'The thing is, Tom, when you covertly recorded your conversation with Commander Jenkins you did so using police equipment and without the appropriate approval.' He paused momentarily. 'I can totally understand why you did it, but Commander Jenkins and Charles Cope's lawyers are likely to have a field day with this. I don't need to tell you that, in past cases where this has happened, any recordings have proved to be inadmissible. In fact, in a few cases it has been deemed to be illegal.'

Once again everyone was looking at Tom for a response. When he spoke at last, it was, perhaps, not the response they were expecting.

'I don't care any more,' he said, almost in a tone of resignation. 'You have my evidence. I've arrested both of them. It's up to you to now do with it as you wish.'

There was an extended period of silence whilst everyone took in what Tom had just said. Eventually, Sir Peter said, 'Tom, I can sense your frustration. All I can say is that you have the total support of all of us in this room.'

It was clear to everyone that a *but* was about to follow. It didn't take long.

'But,' he added, 'I have to warn you now, the fact this has potential national security implications will inevitably mean that it will be taken out of our hands. After that, I can't really say what the final outcome will be. I'm sorry, but I'm only trying to be open and honest with you.'

'Well, at least someone is being honest,' answered Tom, with a hint of sarcasm.

It was DS Birch who next spoke. 'Why don't you take some holiday leave? You've certainly earned it. I'm not sure what else you can do anyway – at least in the short term. Emotions are understandably running high right now. A few weeks away from all of this, I'm sure, would help. There's also the distinct possibility that news of the arrests will leak out. If that does happen then the press will be all over you.'

When Tom replied it was in a surprisingly calm and concili-atory manner. 'You are probably right. I do feel physically and emotionally drained.' Realising what he had just said, he quickly added, 'That doesn't mean I'm ready to be put out to grass yet, though. I've still got a few years left.'

'Okay, that's all agreed, then,' said Sir Peter. He looked directly at Tom. 'Yes? Agreed?'

In truth Tom had never really enjoyed holidays. In fact, over the years, he had come to realise his commitment to the job, ahead of his family life, was one of the reasons why his marriage to Anne had failed. Right now, though, he genuinely was feeling tired and drained and could see the advantages of taking a short break.

Nonetheless, it was with something less than total enthusi-asm that he answered, 'Agreed.'

Chapter 3

'So, what happened?' asked Mary, almost before Tom had set foot through the front door of their house. It was later in the evening and, unsurprisingly, Mary had been on tenterhooks all day. Although Tom was not the type of person who readily showed his feelings and emotions, she had, nonetheless, over the preceding days, recognised the signs suggesting a build-up in his stress levels. Of more concern, though, were the clear indications of his inner turmoil.

Tom and Mary had been together for a couple of years now, with Tom moving into her house in Bagshot just a few months earlier. Initially, it had been agreed that this would be a temporary move, allowing Mary to take better care of him during his rehabilitation. During an earlier investigation, Tom had been shot by the son of a criminal he had previously arrested. Whilst his injuries were not life-threatening, they had necessitated regular physiotherapy, together with time for rest and recovery.

The temporary arrangement had, however, turned into a more permanent move, and in fact Tom had recently even put his own house, in Staines, onto the market.

Tom and Mary had originally met via a dating website, something which Tom, even now, could not quite believe he had actually subscribed to. Although he'd had one or two brief relationships since he and Anne had divorced, the truth was that he hadn't entered into them with any great enthusiasm. It always seemed as though his career, somehow, had managed to get in the way.

Indeed, this was probably the reason why his marriage to Anne had failed. Even the birth of their son, Paul, early into their marriage hadn't changed his priorities and, in retrospect, that was probably the final factor. Anne and Paul had subsequently emigrated to Australia and, over the years, contact had been lost completely.

7

Recently, Tom had begun to think more and more about Paul. With those thoughts, though, came an increasing sense of guilt and shame. Guilt about the reason for the marriage breakdown and shame that he hadn't even tried to find out what sort of life his son had made for himself in Australia.

When Tom and Mary had met, he had undoubtedly been at the lowest point of his career. Although, at the time, he was only in his early fifties, he felt much older. His enthusiasm and energy levels had reduced appreciably, and it just seemed, both to himself and to his colleagues, that he was simply passing time until he could retire. Looking back, he could now see how he had been in danger of descending into a sort of spiralling paranoia. He no longer seemed to be assigned to any of the more complex or interesting cases and, worse, felt his colleagues, some of whom he had worked alongside for many years, were all too aware of this and had started to feel sorry for him. During his career, he had always looked forward to going to work, but at this time he had begun to almost dread the thought. He spent most of the night awake, thinking these thoughts, and then spent his work day looking for details that supported his pessimistic mental narrative.

The one good thing that had come out of this period of his life was that, for some inexplicable reason, he had decided to subscribe to the 'Never Too Old for Love' dating website, and it was through this that he had met Mary.

Coinciding with this personal milestone, his career had suddenly taken a dramatic turn for the better. He had become involved in one of the most high-profile serial murder investigations of recent times, almost by accident, and it was largely due to Tom's contribution that the case had finally been resolved, resulting in him becoming a media celebrity. More importantly, as far as he was concerned, it had renewed his love of policing.

Since then his reputation had continued to increase, especially as he had been brought back into some of the more interesting cases, which provided him with the opportunity to demonstrate his true investigative skills. In fact, his professional reputation had never been higher. But his natural wariness was never far away and he knew that what could go up quickly could just as quickly come down again. This defence mechanism, he knew, was an integral part of his personality and, in many ways, had served him well over the years. Experience had told him that there was always something, just around the corner, which he might suddenly crash into.

Perhaps he had crashed into it already. There was a real danger that, by taking action against Commander Jenkins and Charles Cope, he had destroyed his career. Mary had known his intentions and the risks, but, to his surprise, she still gave him her unconditional support.

'Did you do it?' Mary asked now, before Tom could reply to her first question.

'I did,' he answered in a matter-of-fact tone.

'Well?' she said, the inflection in her voice making clear her impatience.

By now they were both standing in the kitchen. 'Of course, Commander Jenkins made all manner of threats. In fact, he even threatened Milner.'

Tom had 'acquired' DS David Milner at the time of his career low. Then he was just a young and raw detective constable who had still to get his hands dirty in any real policing. But that was soon to change as his career shadowed the improved fortunes of Tom's own career revival, and it wasn't long before they had developed a strong relationship of their own.

It was a relationship which, despite Tom feeling uncomfortable about it, had gradually extended outside work-related matters. Tom came from the old school where work and private matters did not mix well. Notwithstanding this natural wariness, he had become very fond of Milner. In fact, he sometimes felt that perhaps he was starting to see Milner as a substitute son, especially given his lack of contact with his own one.

Mary had none of Tom's reticence. She had an outgoing personality by nature and was never embarrassed to show her true feelings and emotions. She had instantly taken to Milner and these feelings had become stronger in the immediate aftermath of Tom's shooting, when Milner had provided emotional as well as practical support to her.

'Threatened David?' she repeated with genuine concern. 'I didn't know he would be involved in the arrest.'

'Well, that was never my intention, but he insisted,' answered Tom. 'In fact, I'm glad he was there. I was proud of him. He wasn't fazed at all – or at least he didn't show it – when he served the arrest warrant.' There was a very brief silence before he added, with a slight laugh, 'But don't tell him I said that.'

'So what happened then?' she asked, declining to respond in a similar jocular vein.

'We arrested him and took him down to the station, where he was formally charged. At the same time Charles Cope was also being arrested. By now, though, I would imagine both have been released on bail. No doubt there will be a lot of legal toing and froing between the prosecutor's office and their defence teams before they are formally charged. I'm not now convinced, though, it will get that far.'

'Why on earth wouldn't they be charged?' asked a genuinely shocked Mary. 'After all, the evidence is very clear.'

Tom briefly told Mary about his meeting with Sir Peter, DCS Small and DS Birch. 'They are right about the unauthorised use of the wiretap. Even though there is a clear admission by Commander Jenkins, it's highly unlikely that it will be used. If I'm being totally honest with myself, I knew that at the time but couldn't think of any other way to get a conviction.' After a brief pause, he continued. 'Perhaps that's the problem. I just wasn't thinking straight at all.'

'But, if it does go to trial, will you be involved?'

'As I was the lead officer, accumulated all of the evidence and coordinated the arrests, I think that's an absolute certainty. In fact, I would be very upset if I wasn't.' A brief silence followed as Mary took in what she had been told and the possible implications for both of them. Before she could say anything else, though, Tom spoke again. 'But, if that happens at all, it's not likely to be for a while yet. In the meantime it's been suggested to me I should take some leave. So that's what I intend to do.'

Mary's face immediately lit up. 'That's wonderful. Given what you have been through the past few weeks, I think you've earned it.' Tom could sense that her mind was now in overdrive, and this was confirmed when she added, 'Perhaps we could go away somewhere. It seems ages since we were able to completely get away just by ourselves. I'll ask Sharon if she could look after the shop whilst we are away. I'm sure she wouldn't mind.'

For a few years now, since her husband had died, Mary had owned and run her own florist's business in Bagshot. It was something which she enjoyed, not least because it enabled her to have her own independence. She also liked to be in the company of other people, and this provided a perfect opportunity. Tom, on the other hand, was not naturally a mixer, much preferring his own company. So far, in their relationship, with one or two exceptions, this had not been a problem, although both were increasingly aware that this might not be the case in the future.

Tom, hearing Mary's suggestion, immediately realised, notwithstanding his dislike of holidays, that it would be churlish in the extreme to disappoint her. 'That's a good idea,' he said, with as much enthusiasm as he could muster.

Mary smiled, moved forward and took hold of his hand. 'You look tired and a bit tense. Why don't we see if we can relieve some of that tension?'

Chapter 4

It was eight in the morning and Tom was seated at his desk, back at the station. Immediately in front of him were DS Milner and DC Gary Bennett.

'Welcome back, sir,' said Milner. 'Did you have a good holiday?'

'Wonderful,' replied Tom, confusing Milner, who wasn't used to such obvious positivity from DCI Stone. 'And thank you for asking, Milner.'

He and Mary had returned from their holiday a couple of days previously. Mary's son had an apartment in the Algarve and, as it wasn't being used, had offered it to them. The weather had been sunny, but not too hot, and they had even spent some time walking together. To Tom's surprise he had actually enjoyed it. Well, at least the first week. He had a notoriously low boredom threshold, and two weeks away was about as much as he could endure without his boredom turning into something that he might regret.

'So tell me what has been happening whilst I've been away,' Tom said, making it clear that the discussion of his holiday had now finished.

Given their involvement in the arrests, Milner assumed that this was what DCI Stone would be most interested in. 'Well, it's more about what hasn't happened,' he said. 'It looks as though both Commander Jenkins and Charles Cope were released very quickly, and since then it's all gone very quiet. Nobody is saying anything.' Milner looked in the direction of his colleague. 'And both DC Bennett and I were asked to sign a notice which prevented us from speaking to anyone about their arrests.'

Tom interrupted before he could carry on. 'You say *asked*. Were you given any choice?'

'Not really, sir,' Milner replied. 'It was made very clear that we didn't have any other option.'

Tom remained silent for a while before asking, 'And have you mentioned it to anyone else?'

'Of course not, sir,' answered Milner, slightly aggrieved that DCI Stone even had to ask the question.

Tom gave him a searching look. 'But you've just mentioned it to me.'

He could see the immediate shift in how Milner held himself, clearly embarrassed and uncomfortable. Before Milner could respond, Tom spoke again, in a much more conciliatory tone. 'It's just that I want you both to one hundred percent comply with the order. These things are taken very seriously, and it could be a career-ending situation if you don't stick to it religiously. No one knows – least of all me – what the final outcome will be, so let's not worsen things by shooting ourselves in the foot.'

It was DC Bennett who next spoke. Gary and Tom went back a long way, allowing him to ask questions which DS Milner, even though Milner was Bennett's superior, perhaps couldn't. 'Sir? Have you also signed it?'

'No, I haven't,' Tom replied, 'although I suspect it will only be, now that I'm back, a matter of time before I'm asked to.'

There was an uneasy silence as each of them considered where all of this was leading. After a while Tom said, 'Okay, let's all park this. In the meantime, tell me what has been happening. What are you both currently working on? I'm sure that our local villains haven't all been on holiday as well.'

Milner, obviously having anticipated this question, turned to face DC Bennett. 'Why don't you update DCI Stone on what's been happening?'

Although DC Bennett had known Tom for many years, it was only recently that he had joined Tom's team. Like Tom, Gary Bennett was from the old school and, based upon his experience and years of service, would have expected to have made Detective Sergeant by now. That he hadn't was due to a combination of factors, not least the fact that he had recently suffered from debilitating work-related mental pressure and stress, which had affected both his professional career and his private life. It was Tom who had helped him through this difficult period and brought him into the team, working directly under DS Milner.

Under normal circumstances this would have proved to be

an untenable situation. After all, Bennett was a lot older than Milner and had vastly more experience, ingredients which were likely to cause resentment. The fact it had succeeded was partly due to Milner's awareness and sensitivity to the situation, but mainly due to DC Bennett's obvious gratitude that he had been given another chance and was back working as part of a team.

'Nothing too exciting, sir,' said DC Bennett. 'Well, nothing compared to the Aphron case. Just the usual assortment of burglaries, drug offences and miscellaneous alcohol-related incidents.' He paused momentarily. When Tom gave no response, he carried on. 'We also had a missing person called in.'

There was something in DC Bennett's tone which caught Tom's attention. 'That's not unusual. What's so different about this one?'

'That's what I thought,' replied DC Bennett. 'But when I started to look into it there was something which just didn't ... well, seem right. Just an intuition, really.'

'Well, intuition is sometimes the most important part of police work,' said Tom. Over the years he had come to trust his own intuition, or antennae, as he preferred to call it. It was not included in any police manual, but, with increasing experience, it had always stood him in good stead. 'So what is your intuition telling you?'

DC Bennett referred to his notebook. 'Glyn Burton was reported missing about a week ago. So far, unfortunately, we haven't been able to make any real progress in finding out what happened to him.' He looked up at Tom. 'By now you would have thought that we would have had some clues as to his whereabouts. But there's nothing. It's as though he's vanished off the face of the earth.'

'But, as you say, it's only been a week,' Tom said. 'Is there anything unusual in his background which has caused your antennae to start buzzing? What, for example, do we know about Mr Burton?'

'Forty-six years old. Married, with two children. Lives in Richmond. Clearly very well off. I went to visit his wife myself. Not the sort of house any of us could afford, unless we won the lottery.'

'I'm assuming you have checked hospitals.'

'First thing we did, sir. No record of any unidentified man of his age and description having been admitted to any local hospital. So we have extended the search further afield. We are still looking for his car, and there is also no trace of his phone.' DC Bennett glanced at his notebook again. 'He rented a flat in the City. We went round there almost straight away. But there's no sign of him being there since his disappearance. I spoke to a few people who lived in some of the nearby flats, who all confirmed that they hadn't seen him recently. One of them did, however, mention how he would sometimes come back with a woman.'

'What? The same woman?' asked Tom.

'Recently, yes. Quite well-to-do, according to the neighbour, but apparently there were one or two different ones prior to that.' DC Bennett gave a slight laugh. 'When he told me I couldn't work out whether he was being judgemental or just envious.'

'What did Mr Burton do for a living?' asked Tom.

'This is where it gets interesting,' DC Bennett replied. 'He is something to do with the City. He has his own company. Well, a partnership actually. Financial advice, wealth management, pensions. That type of thing.'

'Is there any chance of suicide? Did he leave a note or anything similar?'

'Nothing, sir. I asked around, but the people I've spoken to all say that he would be the last person to kill himself. It seems like he was a larger-than-life character. He clearly enjoyed the socialising part of his job. Nothing I've heard about him would suggest a suicide. But, of course, you never know.'

Both Milner and DC Bennett remained silent, waiting for a response from Tom. After what seemed like an age Tom finally spoke.

'So that means he's missing either because he wants to disappear or because someone or something has made him disappear.' Another pause followed; this time, though, it was mercifully brief. 'Let's assume, for the time being, at least, that he intended to disappear. It could be, of course, that he has just left his wife and gone off with someone else. Perhaps the woman he has been seeing recently. Or it could be that, alternatively, his business was not as successful as he would like people to think. After all, his particular profession can often be as much about image as substance. No one would want to hand over their money for investment to a person who looks as though they are just about to go bankrupt. You mentioned a business partner. Have you spoken with them?'

'Yes, sir,' replied DC Bennett, once again referring to his notebook. 'Craig Blackwell. Forty-two years old and living in Hampstead. I haven't been there but looked it up. Again, it's quite an expensive area. They've been partners for about ten years. Apparently, they both worked at the same company – again, something to do with the City – and decided to leave and start out on their own. They have an office in the east of the City and it was there that I met Blackwell.'

'How did he seem? Did he give you any indication that there were any issues between them or any business problems?'

It was suddenly clear to both Milner and DC Bennett that DCI Stone was taking a real interest in this case.

'I did ask him about their business, but he didn't give any indication that things were difficult either personally or professionally.' DC Bennett paused. 'But you can never tell with these types of people. I would imagine that putting a positive spin on everything is second nature to them.'

'I'm guessing that you didn't like him, then,' suggested Tom.

When DC Bennett answered it was with a surprising amount of emotion. 'Not really. Personally, I wouldn't trust his type as far as I could throw him. As far as I'm concerned, encouraging people to stash away their money in dodgy tax-saving schemes should be banned and anyone found guilty of doing that sent down for a long time.'

Tom let out a slight laugh. 'Well, at least we now know where you stand on this issue. Perhaps if we were wealthy we would also use these schemes. Anyway, as long as it's legal, everyone has a perfect right to do whatever they want with their own money.'

'I understand that,' answered DC Bennett. 'But that doesn't mean that I have to like him.'

Milner then decided to join in the conversation, partly to take it in a different direction. 'And what if he didn't intentionally disappear?'

'Well, then, Milner,' replied Tom, 'we are talking about some sort of accident or worse. Do we know who the last person was to see him?'

16

It was DC Bennett who answered, this time without his previous emotion. 'As far as we know it was his wife Jane. Apparently he regularly plays golf on a Sunday morning. She said he left as usual, but returned earlier than normal. He then spent some time in his office and, when he came out, according to her, he seemed to be very angry, saying that he would soon have to go out again. When he did leave, that was the last time she saw him.'

'Do we have any idea what had brought on his anger or where he later went?' asked Tom, more in hope than expectation.

'I'm afraid we don't,' replied DC Bennett, 'although we do know that his wife received a text from him, at about 4.30 pm that same afternoon, to say he still had to meet someone else and he might not get back that night.'

Whilst Tom was thinking through what he'd just been told, Milner suddenly spoke. 'Do you really need to get involved with this, sir? As you said, it's possible he's just run off with another woman. I'm sure DC Bennett and I can handle it. You must have lots of other things to do. I suspect you have hundreds of emails to go through.'

Tom's initial expression suggested a degree of annoyance, but this was quickly replaced by an ever-widening smile. 'I've only been away for a couple of weeks and you are now telling me what I should be doing. Just as well that it wasn't any longer, otherwise you might have moved into my office.'

In a strange way, Tom was actually pleased that Milner could now say such things to him. It was another sign of his increasing confidence. But he wasn't about to admit as much to Milner.

In any case, he wasn't worried about catching up on his email. His approach to emails was very simple: ignore them as most were 'just for information', usually so the sender could cover their own back. If there were any which needed action, then he'd soon find out via the old-fashioned way, i.e. a phone call or face-to-face conversation. Ninety-nine times out of a hundred this strategy worked. On the one occasion it didn't, well, he would just have to handle the consequences.

'It actually seems just the type of investigation which would ease me back into things,' Tom said. 'And anyway, I agree with DC Bennett about it being unusual. I can't quite say why, but it's just one of those feelings that I occasionally get. But, if you feel that it's not, then, of course, I will defer to your vast experience.' Tom was now clearly enjoying himself and, as he glanced towards DC Bennett, he could see a thin smile appearing on his face.

Milner's response surprised both of them. He simply shrugged and said, 'Well, it would be foolish to ignore your feeling. That's agreed, then. I'm sure both DC Bennett and I will appreciate your involvement.'

Tom couldn't work out if Milner was playing him at his own game but decided that this was probably the appropriate time to end it. Milner was getting too good at giving as good as he got. 'Right. Why don't you and I start by going to see Mrs Burton? Sometimes a fresh pair of eyes works wonders.'

'When do you want to go?' asked Milner.

'Let's go now. The sooner I get back into proper policing, the better,' he answered. 'Give Mrs Burton a call and see if we can meet with her. I'm sure all of those emails can wait a bit longer.'

Chapter 5

Later that same morning, Tom and Milner were seated in a large room. From here they could see the River Thames below them. Different types of craft were either moored by the side of the river or making their way along it. As the sun reflected off the water it gave the impression of an almost perfect early winter's day.

DC Bennett had certainly been correct when he had described Mr and Mrs Burton's home. If anything, he had actually undersold it. The house was an imposing, three-storey Georgian building, located towards the top of the hill, in one of the most sought-after, and therefore expensive, parts of the town. The high walls and impressive wooden gate gave it an air of seclusion. From this location, in addition to the river, there were also stunningly clear views of the town, immediately below, and the Great Pagoda, sited at the western edge of Kew Gardens. Towards the west, he could also make out the expanse of Richmond Park. As DC Bennett had said, the type of location where they could only ever dream of living.

The room was quite spacious and, alongside the stunning views of the river, was tastefully decorated. On the walls were a number of professional photographs of Mrs Burton and her husband, together with a series of photographs of them with their children at various stages of their lives. There was also a clearly quite old and slightly battered cabinet on which rested an elaborately framed photograph featuring a girl, aged about twelve.

'Thank you for seeing us, Mrs Burton,' said Tom. 'I know this must be a very distressing time for you, but my colleague DS Milner and I would like to ask you a few questions. If you feel that you are not able to answer them, we can always come back at a more convenient time.'

Mrs Burton was also seated. She was probably in her early

forties, quite tall and slim, with long dark hair. She was dressed in a way which reflected her environment: elegant and expensive. All in all, she gave the impression of a woman who spent considerable time and money on her appearance. As Tom looked at her he could, however, see just a hint of darkness under her eyes, suggesting a degree of anxiety and tension, probably the result of lack of sleep, crying or a combination of both.

'No, that's all right,' she answered in a voice which surprised Tom. Given her immaculate appearance he had expected her to have a more upmarket accent. In fact, he thought that he could detect more than a hint of East London in her voice, even with just those few words. 'Although I did answer all of the questions that other policeman asked me.'

'Yes, he did say that. It's normal procedure, though, for these follow-up visits, especially given the unusual circumstances.'

'What do you mean, *unusual circumstances?*' she replied, clearly alarmed. 'My husband left the house just over a week ago and is still missing. Surely it's very straightforward?' Those last few words seemed to trigger an outbreak of emotion as they were said with a slight quiver in her voice. 'Have you found him?'

'I'm sorry, Mrs Burton,' replied Tom. 'I didn't mean to upset you. Perhaps I used the wrong words. What I meant to say was that, given what we know about your husband, especially his wide circle of friends and acquaintances, he doesn't seem to be the type of person who would simply disappear without contacting someone.' He paused briefly before continuing. 'I'm afraid to say we have not made any real progress so far, but I can assure you that we are doing everything possible. And it's my experience that, in this type of situation, things can suddenly develop. As I said earlier, if you don't feel you can talk right now, we can always come back at a later date.'

'No. Let's do it now,' she quickly answered. 'I know you are only doing your job, but I just find it very difficult to even mention his name.'

'I understand,' said Tom, as sympathetically as he could. Once again, he allowed himself a brief pause before continuing, having already decided that he would ask the most difficult question first. 'Mrs Burton, I'm afraid this is something which I have to ask you.' He paused again. 'Were you and your husband experiencing any difficulties in your marriage? It's a fact, I'm afraid, that many sudden disappearances relate to marital troubles.'

Mrs Burton was surprisingly calm when she replied. 'I assume you mean that Glyn might have left me for another woman?'

'Well, yes, it is a possible explanation,' answered Tom. 'It's something we do have to ask you, if only to discount the possibility. As I said, it is something which happens quite a lot.'

'Like most marriages we've had our ups and downs,' she answered, reflectively. 'Well, who doesn't?'

It was Milner who next spoke. 'And were there any downs recently?'

Even Tom was slightly taken aback by Milner's directness, but it clearly had the desired effect as Mrs Burton quickly answered. 'Yes, it's true there had been a few problems lately. You see, Glyn's job meant he tended to stay away regularly during the week. He met with a lot of his clients in the evenings and so it was just more convenient for him to stay in town rather than keep having to come backwards and forwards. I know it's not that far, but the nature of his business means there is quite a lot of entertaining which doesn't end until late into the night. As I said, it's just more convenient.'

Of course Tom and Milner already knew about the existence of the flat. What they didn't know was whether or not Mrs Burton knew about her husband's extramarital entertaining. Tom resisted the temptation to mention that all the convenience seemed to be one-way.

'You mentioned recent problems,' said Milner. 'If you don't mind me asking, what specific problems have there been?'

She hesitated briefly and then took a deep breath. 'We had a big row the night before he disappeared. To be honest, we've had a lot of arguments recently. But this one was really awful.' She paused and then added, almost talking to herself, 'Fortunately, the children were staying with my mum.' Another pause. 'I can't even remember what started it, but, before I knew it, I was accusing him of all sorts of things. Caring more about his business than his family. Leaving me by myself more and more. Not loving me. Finally, I asked him outright if he was having an affair. By then I didn't even know what I was saying. It all just came out.'

'And how did he respond?' asked Tom.

'As he usually did of late. He just told me I was being paranoid and that he would speak to me when I was less hysterical. He then went to bed.' She hesitated slightly before continuing. 'He has been sleeping in the back room for a few months now. In fact, I can't even remember the last time we slept together. Looking back, it's obvious that, over the past few years, we have been drifting further apart. There were times when I suspected he was seeing other women. But I think I must have just tried to block them out of my mind. Often I did think it would be best if we split up, but I suppose I never had the courage to carry it out. And anyway, I didn't want to do anything which would affect the children.'

'Do you think your husband felt the same?' asked Tom.

'I really don't know. Sometimes, especially lately, it seemed as though he couldn't care less about me. All he seemed interested in was his business. At other times, though, everything seemed to be good,' she said, almost wistfully. 'He wasn't the sort of person who tended to show that type of emotion.'

'Did you have your discussion with him?' asked Milner.

'No, because, as usual on a Sunday, he left early for golf. I was hoping that, when he got back, we could have a reasonable conversation but ...' At this point she suddenly began to cry.

'Please take your time, Mrs Burton,' said Tom.

Eventually she stopped crying and was able to continue. 'But we never did.'

'Is there anyone who could stay with you whilst we continue our investigation?' asked Tom, concerned about Mrs Burton's welfare.

'There's Mum, but the children are staying with her for the time being. I just don't want them here right now, while all of this is going on. The police liaison officer has been here a couple of times, but there's no one else.'

'You told my officer that, when your husband got back from golf, he immediately went into his office, and when he later came out he appeared to be very angry,' Tom said. 'Would it be possible to take a look in his office?'

'Why do you need to do that? I've told you what happened,' she said, a little brusquely.

'I know,' replied Tom, 'but it would help if we could. It's standard procedure to try to put ourselves in the environment where the person had been immediately prior to going missing.'

'Okay, if you think it will help,' she answered, seemingly reassured by his explanation.

She led them into a surprisingly small room, located just before the kitchen. In fact, the room was so small there was barely enough space for all three of them.

On one side of the room was the window, under which were a large table and accompanying chair. On the table were a keyboard and large computer monitor, together with a stapler and hole punch. In one corner of the table there was a printer. On the other side of the table was a framed photograph featuring four golfers. A solitary filing cabinet stood in one corner of the office. On the wall opposite the window were various photographs of Mr Burton, attending what looked like social functions. In the centre of the wall, however, was a framed but faded newspaper article, with the headline *Local man making his mark*.

Tom examined the photograph of the golfers. 'Which one is your husband?'

'It's him,' she answered, pointing towards a tall, well-built, good-looking man, with dark, swept-back hair, standing in the middle part of the group. To his left was an older man – probably in his early fifties – whilst on his right stood the other two, both slightly younger-looking than Mr Burton, one of them quite muscular and as tall as Mr Burton himself.

'Was he keen on golf?' Tom asked, his eyes remaining on the four men.

'Very keen. He used to say that it helped him relax and take his mind off his business. Although sometimes I did wonder if it actually made him more uptight, especially when he came back quite upset with the way he had played.'

'Who are the other men?' asked Tom.

'Just some of the regular people he played with. This photo was taken a year or so ago when a few of the men from his club went on a golfing holiday to Portugal.'

'Would you mind if I borrowed the photograph for a short while? I'll make sure I return it as soon as possible.'

Mrs Burton looked slightly puzzled. 'Why?'

'It's just that it's quite a recent photograph of your husband. Sometimes these things do help us with our inquiry.'

Mrs Burton simply shrugged her shoulders and said, 'I suppose that will be okay, but I would like it back.'

'Of course. Thank you,' answered Tom, picking up the photograph. Changing the subject, he then asked, 'Do you know if your husband spoke with anyone when he was in his office?'

Mrs Burton hesitated briefly before answering. 'I've got no idea. All I know, as I've already told you, is that when he came out he seemed very angry.'

'So you didn't hear him speaking with anyone on the phone?'

'How many more times do I need to tell you?' she answered, angrily. 'I didn't hear anything.'

'Thank you, Mrs Burton, for letting us take a look in his office.'

They made their way back into the main room.

'I understand you received a text from him later that day. What did it say?' asked Tom.

Mrs Burton reached for her mobile phone, which was on the small coffee table immediately in front of them. She found what she was looking for and handed the phone to Tom. He read out the text: '*Have to meet someone later. I might not be able to get back tonight.* And this was the last communication you had with your husband?'

'Yes, it was the last time I heard from him. There has been nothing since. Not a text, not a phone call or even an email.'

'Did he regularly text you when he was staying away?'

'Sometimes. Usually to ask about the kids, though. It seems a long time since he asked how I was.'

Tom read the text once again. As he read it, he could see that this was indeed the last one in the text stream she had received from her husband.

He could also see that she was, once again, becoming distressed.

'Are you happy to carry on?' he asked, as he handed Mrs Burton's phone back to her. 'There are just a few more questions we'd like to ask.'

'You might as well, now that you are here,' she replied, in a slightly resigned voice.

It was Milner who now took up the questioning, notebook and pencil in hand. 'You mentioned your husband had left to play golf but came back early. Did he say why?'

'He didn't at the time, but I later found out, from someone who he usually plays with, that they couldn't play because of the fog. Apparently, there was quite a long wait until the fog cleared. My husband was not the most patient of men. He never liked to hang around anywhere if he could possibly avoid it. He hated queueing. He considered it a waste of time.'

'So, what time did he arrive home?' Milner asked.

'Some time just before twelve o'clock. I can't remember the exact time.'

Milner wrote down the time in his notebook. 'And then when he left the house again, you have no idea where he might have gone?'

Milner's question appeared to upset Mrs Burton because, not for the first time, she began to cry. Eventually her crying subsided and she was able to speak, albeit between intermittent sobs. 'I've got no idea. I've told you that already. Maybe it was to do with his business, or maybe it was because ...' Her sobs had now intensified to the extent she was finding it difficult to speak. 'Maybe ... maybe he was seeing another woman. I don't know.'

Both Tom and Milner waited until Mrs Burton had stopped crying before Milner spoke. 'I know you have already spoken to my colleague DC Bennett, but would you mind confirming what your husband was wearing when he left the house?'

It was with some obvious weariness that she answered. 'Beige trousers. A white polo shirt and a dark blue sweater. He hadn't changed out of his golf clothes.'

'Was he wearing a jacket or coat?' asked Milner, writing the details in his notebook.

Mrs Burton paused, briefly, before replying. 'He was wearing a dark blue fleece.'

When Milner had finished writing he spoke again. 'Did your husband mention any problems, for example, related to his work, in the days prior to his disappearance?'

'Even if he had problems he would not have discussed them with me. He kept all of those business things to himself.'

'What exactly was your husband's business?' asked Tom.

'It was something to do with finance. Investments – that sort of thing. Although, as I said, he never really spoke to me about exactly what he did.'

'He had a business partner, I understand. A Craig Blackwell,' interjected Milner, reading the name from his notebook.

'Yes, that's right,' she replied. 'They set up the company together a number of years ago.'

'*Investment and Wealth Management*,' continued Milner. 'Isn't that the name of the company?'

'Yes,' she simply replied.

'If you don't mind me saying, you live in a very exclusive and expensive part of London,' said Milner. 'His business must have been very successful.'

Mrs Burton's earlier anger resurfaced. 'There is nothing wrong with being successful. Or don't you think people like us are entitled to make their lives better?' Before Milner could reply, she carried straight on. 'Both of us came from the same East End council estate. Glyn might have had a few rough edges, and maybe he didn't speak with the right accent, maybe he wasn't always grammatically correct, but everything he achieved was due to his efforts. He had no wealthy parents who could afford a private education. He – in fact both of us – went to the local comprehensive school. Like his two brothers, he was a bit of a tearaway in his teens and got himself into trouble with the police a few times. But he grew out of that. Even then he was always good with numbers. He even managed to get himself into university – the first person in his family to do that. Everyone could see he was exceptional at maths. He finished with a first-class degree and when he graduated he was offered a job with a big London finance company. He worked there for a few years, was headhunted by a bigger company and then decided to set up his own business. So, yes, we do live in an exclusive and expensive area, but that's because we worked hard to achieve all of this.' She gestured at her surroundings.

It was Tom who next spoke. 'Please don't think we were being critical. If anything,' he added, in an attempt to lighten the atmosphere, 'I'm a bit envious of what both of you have obviously achieved. You should be very proud of that.'

Tom's comments clearly had the desired effect because, when Mrs Burton next spoke, her earlier anger had disappeared. 'I'm sorry, but sometimes, even after all of these years, I feel as though we are still outsiders.'

Tom, picking up on this, said, 'What do you mean? Do you have any examples of that?'

'Nothing specific,' she replied. 'The neighbours are quite friendly – or at least the ones we know; everyone tends to keep themselves to themselves around here – but it's more a feeling that we still aren't quite accepted. Although I know Glyn has, in the past, had a few run-ins with some of the people at his golf club. It's the West London golf club, just a few miles from here. He's some sort of shareholder and part of the management committee there, but, from what he told me, I don't think they really took to an East Ender hobnobbing with them. He took me there once for their Christmas ball, but I hated it.'

'Why?' asked Tom.

'Maybe it was me, but I just felt that I was on show all the time and that people were judging me. I couldn't wait to leave.'

Both Tom and Milner remained silent, hoping Mrs Burton would carry on in the same vein. When it was obvious that this wasn't about to happen, Tom spoke. 'Would it be possible for us to have a look at his business files and computer?'

'Why would you want to do that?' she answered, her voice rising. 'What has his business got to do with the fact he's missing?'

'I really don't know,' replied Tom. 'But what I have found, over the years, is that it's always best to keep all options open until we know for certain. Our priority, right now, is to try to find out the most likely reason for your husband's sudden disappearance. And to achieve that we need to look closely at every aspect of his life, however seemingly trivial or irrelevant. It might give us a lead as to who he was meeting.'

After a brief pause Mrs Burton simply said, 'I suppose so.'

'Thank you,' answered Tom. 'DS Milner will contact you to arrange a convenient time.' He paused. 'Were there any other unusual things that happened prior to his disappearance?'

'What do you mean?' she asked.

'Well, did your husband, for example, have any health

issues? Had he recently met any new people? Had he been staying away longer than usual? Anything, really, which was new or different from his normal behaviour.'

Mrs Burton was briefly silent, clearly trying to remember. Finally, she said, 'Nothing that I can remember. He stayed away on business sometimes, but, as I've already explained, that was quite usual, at least during the week.' Once again, she became quiet before adding, 'Well, at least that's what he told me he was doing. Maybe it was a lie and he was with a woman.' She shook her head. 'I'm sorry; it's just that I don't seem to be able to think straight any more. I've hardly slept over the past week or so.'

'That's quite all right,' answered Tom. 'Please take your time.' He waited for her to say something else, but, when she didn't, he spoke again. 'Do you have CCTV fitted around the house?'

Mrs Burton seemed to be slightly taken aback by Tom's question, although, when she spoke, she simply said, 'No, we don't.'

Tom decided that now was probably a good time to finish. He stood up and offered his hand to Mrs Burton, who, without any great enthusiasm, simply went through the motions of shaking it.

'We really appreciate you spending time with us,' Tom said, handing her his card. 'If there is anything you remember, however seemingly trivial, please call me on the number.'

As they made their way towards the door Mrs Burton said, 'Oh my God, I can't believe all this has happened. It's a nightmare.'

As they went out of the front door they could hear Mrs Burton sobbing uncontrollably.

*

'What do you think?' asked Tom, as he and Milner were driving back to the station.

'It's amazing, isn't it?' replied Milner. 'Despite all that wealth, they had obvious problems just like everyone else.'

'Why would wealth guarantee happiness?' asked Tom. 'It's my experience that the more money a person has, the more problems there usually are.'

Chapter 6

Back at the station, and despite what he had said earlier, Tom was trying to reduce the number of emails that had accumulated whilst he had been away. Over the years he had developed the knack of being able to open an email, quickly scan it and then decide if it needed any action or response from him. This allowed him to press the delete button on a significant proportion of them. The remaining ones he left on his computer for further follow-up. Nonetheless it still took him the best part of an hour to get up to date. As he leaned back in his chair and stretched his back, DC Bennett appeared carrying a cup of coffee.

'I thought you might like this, sir,' said DC Bennett, handing Tom the cup.

Although Tom was always careful to use full titles in front of other colleagues, he was happy to adopt a more informal tone when it was just the two of them, given their history. 'Thanks, Gary,' he answered, 'although I wouldn't go so far as to say that I will like it. I suppose it's too much to think that the quality of the machine drinks might have improved whilst I've been away.' He took a sip and with an affected grimace said, 'Thought so,' before continuing. 'Have you been able to make any progress whilst we were with Mrs Burton?'

'I've started the ball rolling with regard to getting access to Mr Burton's bank details. I should have them in the next day or so. From the information we have been able to get hold of I've also started putting together a list of all of his business clients. I understand from DS Milner that Mrs Burton has agreed for the techie boys to start looking at her husband's computer. Hopefully that might throw a bit of light on possible reasons for his disappearance.'

'Let's hope so,' answered Tom. 'We need something to work on.' He fell silent for a moment. 'Get hold of his recent telephone records. It would be interesting to see who he has been in contact with, particularly on the day he disappeared. In the meantime, I'd also like you to go back to his flat and conduct a thorough search. Speak again to the other people who live near him to see if you can get a description of some of the women who he brought back – particularly the last one. I also suggest you speak with some of Mr and Mrs Burton's neighbours in Richmond and see if any of them have CCTV. You never know; something might have been caught on camera. Then check with the airports and ferries to see if there is any record of a Glyn Burton leaving the country. If he's moving about then he will be spending money. So keep looking out for any cash withdrawals or credit card payments. It's a bit ominous that, so far, there is no record of any payments. He doesn't strike me as being the type of person who skimps on things.' He paused. 'But you never know. One other thing: I think we should go and pay a visit to his golf club, especially as he was there on the day he disappeared.'

He suddenly became silent, mentally ticking boxes on his own investigation checklist. Finally, he simply said, 'You've met Mrs Burton. What do you think? What are your instincts telling you?'

'Well, knowing what I did about Mr Burton's lifestyle, despite their obvious affluence, I felt sorry for her. She seemed a very lonely woman. He can't have been an easy man to live with.'

'I agree,' replied Tom. 'She didn't give the impression of someone enjoying life. If it turns out he has gone off with another woman, maybe that will be a relief to her.'

*

It wasn't long after DC Bennett had left that Tom's phone rang. It was Jenny, Superintendent Birch's PA. Jenny had originally started at the station as a temporary cover for the previous PA, who had been arrested for her involvement in a crime. It had coincided with the time Tom had been asked to temporarily run the station, until a permanent replacement could be appointed. It wasn't a role which Tom was naturally comfortable with and it had merely confirmed that he was temperamentally unsuited to this type of office-based job. Nonetheless, one of the good things which had come out of his time in that role was his working relationship with Jenny. In addition, during that time, and to his great delight, Jenny's relationship with Milner had, coincidentally, developed into something more than merely professional.

'Jenny. How are you?' he asked, genuinely pleased to hear her voice again.

'Very well, thank you,' she answered. 'David ... sorry, DS Milner told me last night that you were due back. How was your holiday?'

'Very enjoyable. Thank you. Although it's always nice to get back to something you are more familiar with,' he answered.

'That's good. At least you've been able to get a bit of sunshine. It's not been very nice here. Anyway, the reason for my call is that Superintendent Birch would like to meet up with you. He said that you were bound to be busy catching up on things, but if you had some time later today that would work for him.'

'How about in half an hour?' suggested Tom. 'But only if you let me share in that superior coffee you all enjoy on the fifth floor. We plebs down here on the second floor have to make do with that stuff which comes out of the machine. And pay for it, as well.'

Jenny laughed. 'I'm sure that will be possible. I'll let Superintendent Birch know.'

After they had ended their conversation, Tom suddenly found himself smiling. He still couldn't quite believe, after the depths of despondency of a year or so ago, that he was now engaging in this type of conversation with the station superintendent's PA.

Thirty minutes later Tom was seated in Superintendent Birch's office. It felt quite strange for him to be there as it wasn't too long ago that it had been his own office, albeit temporarily.

'Good to have you back, Tom,' said Superintendent Birch, in a way which suggested he meant what he said. A smile appeared on his face. 'I've been told that you are not someone who likes to spend time talking about their holiday, so I won't waste your time.'

Tom was momentarily taken aback but resisted the temptation to ask who had mentioned this to Superintendent Birch. He quickly concluded that it was probably Jenny, although, he suspected, the original source might have been Milner. He made a mental note to speak with him about this later.

As Tom did not reply, Superintendent Birch carried on, now in a less flippant tone. 'I expect you would like to be brought up to speed with the situation regarding Commander Jenkins and Charles Cope?'

'Well, I already know they were almost immediately released without, as far as I can make out, any formal charges being brought against them, and that DS Milner and DC Bennett have both been forced to sign a document preventing them from discussing what they know. I assume I will now have to do the same?' Tom said in a resigned tone.

'I'm afraid you will, yes,' replied Superintendent Birch, placing a single typed page in front of Tom.

Nothing was said for a moment, but, eventually, Superintendent Birch must have felt as though he had to offer some sort of justification.

'I'm sorry, Tom. Frankly, I'm as disappointed and frustrated as you are, but it really is out of my hands.'

'I doubt that very much, sir,' answered Tom, irritably. He quickly scanned the page and then added his signature at the bottom, before handing it back. 'Frankly, you can't begin to understand just how disappointed I am. But,' he quickly added, 'I know there's nothing you can do about it.'

Superintendent Birch, quite wisely, did not immediately respond and, after a while, it was Tom who finally broke the silence. 'I'm sorry, sir. I shouldn't have been so sharp with you. As I said, I know it's not your decision and that you had no choice. It's just that ... well, I'm sure you know how I feel.'

'To be honest, I'm sure I can't possibly understand how you feel,' Superintendent Birch replied, 'but it is what it is. The powers that be have deemed this to be an issue of national security and, as such, have decided on this course of action. There's nothing you or I can do which will change that.' He paused. 'I don't have to remind you just how serious it is to sign these things and the likely consequences of non-compliance.'

Recalling his earlier conversation with DS Milner and DC Bennett, he simply answered, 'I understand, sir.'

Chapter 7

As Tom had found it difficult to concentrate after his conversation with Superintendent Birch, he'd had a brief discussion with Milner and then decided to leave early for the day. In fact, unusually, he was home before Mary and so made himself a cup of coffee and sat down at the kitchen table and tried to make sense of the day's developments.

What now was becoming clear to him was that a total information shutdown regarding the arrests had been implemented whilst he'd been away. That, given the people involved, was not really surprising. What was ominous, however, was the fact that they had both been released, and without any bail being sought or granted. As far as he was concerned, this now had all the hallmarks of a cover-up.

He was under no illusions. Even if he decided to personally continue progressing the case, the establishment would use all their considerable resources to prevent it from becoming public knowledge. If that meant undermining the evidence he had accumulated, then he didn't doubt they would do just that. And, in truth, there were many opportunities to do so. His recent accusation regarding how he had been briefed against by Commander Jenkins during the Aphron case was a prime example. Although he was certain that it had happened, there was no definitive evidence. It would be his word against the word of Commander Jenkins, and he knew who was most likely to be believed. Then there was the unapproved use of the wiretap during his conversation with Commander Jenkins. As Sir Peter had pointed out, this, more than anything else, was a potential legal game changer. Worse still, he realised that what he decided to do next could also be a personal career changer.

Despite his earlier burst of anger directed at Superintendent Birch, his recent holiday had given him time to consider what was important to him. He'd arrived back at work as relaxed as he was personally capable of, but the news that both DS Milner and DC Bennett had effectively been gagged had quickly reduced that relaxation. His subsequent conversation with Superintendent Birch had then removed it completely.

He also knew, however, that a key part of his current state of mind was entirely of his own making. It had been his choice to short-circuit the whole process when he arrested both men. He also now realised that perhaps he hadn't been thinking as clearly as he could, or should, have. His actions had been driven by emotion, bordering on outright anger – always a dangerous motivator.

As he sat there, he couldn't help asking himself, if he could turn back the clock, would he have done anything differently? He quickly, though, put this thought out of his mind. He might have acted out of anger and emotion, but that was how he felt at the time. Anyway, he couldn't turn back the clock and so he had to now manage the situation as best he could.

Suddenly he was shaken from all these thoughts when he heard the front door open. A short while later Mary appeared in the kitchen.

'Your car was on the drive,' she said. 'I couldn't believe you'd got home first.' She then became more serious. 'Is everything okay?'

They hadn't been living together for long, but she was perceptive enough to know that when he arrived home early it often meant bad news. She seated herself alongside him.

'Everything is fine,' he answered as positively as possible. 'There wasn't much going on and so I thought I'd come home early.'

He could see that Mary was not entirely convinced, and his suspicions were confirmed when she spoke. 'What is it? I would have thought that there'd been more than enough going on whilst you've been away. And anyway, I can tell when you're holding something back from me. Is it related to the arrests of that politician and senior policeman?'

A thin smile appeared on Tom's face, and this was followed by a short laugh. 'I can't keep anything from you, can I? And we're not even married.'

'What is it?' Mary repeated, with a greater degree of assertiveness.

'Yes, you're right,' he replied, 'it does relate to the arrests.'

He went on to tell her about Milner and DC Bennett and then his own conversation with Superintendent Birch.

'Mary,' he then added, in a tone which was serious but not too alarming, 'I've no doubt already told you more than I'm allowed to, but it is what it is. It's important, though, that this is as far as it goes, and I think it's best for the time being that we don't discuss it again. It's not that I don't want to; it's that I'm legally not allowed to.'

He waited for a response, but, when none was forthcoming, he said, 'Why don't we go out for a meal? It would be a shame to waste the time we have.'

'Okay,' she answered, although without any great enthusiasm.

Chapter 8

'Anything happened that you think I should know about?' asked Tom. It was the following morning and he, along with DS Milner and DC Bennett, was seated in his office.

His evening with Mary had been a strange one. Whilst they had both tried hard to forget about their earlier conversation it had proved to be very difficult. In fact, they had talked about things which they normally wouldn't have just to ensure that they didn't stray anywhere near the subject.

The closest they did get was when Mary asked him if he had thought any more about retirement. He would soon be at the age when he could take retirement with his maximum pension entitlement and so, in that sense, it was a natural question. In truth, although he had said to DCS Small and Sir Peter that he wasn't ready to retire yet, the thought of retirement had suddenly become more appealing. But he knew it wouldn't be possible until the situation regarding Commander Jenkins and Charles Cope had finally been resolved, one way or the other. That assumed, of course, that the decision was his. So he had simply said that financially it would make sense to at least wait until his next birthday. That much was certainly true, but they both knew what had been unsaid was just as important, if not more.

'A quiet night, actually,' answered DC Bennett, in a way which suggested a degree of disappointment. 'The usual stuff, but nothing which would make the headlines.'

'That's good, then,' replied Tom, his mind turning back to yesterday's visit to Mrs Burton. 'Any update on our missing person?'

'Nothing yet, although I have asked for details of his company's finances as soon as possible. Also, I've arranged with Mrs Burton for the techie boys to go around and copy the data on his computer. I'm planning to go and visit their neighbours just to see if they saw anything unusual. It will also give me the opportunity to see if any of them have CCTV. Nothing regarding any credit or debit card payments since he went missing, though.'

'Not even on petrol?'

'Nothing at all, sir,'

'Isn't that a bit ominous?' asked Milner. 'You would have thought, given his lifestyle, he would have used the cards by now.'

'That's exactly what I was thinking,' answered Tom. 'On the other hand, if he wanted to disappear then he would be smart enough not to use them. Perhaps he's using cash.' He turned to face DC Bennett. 'When you get his financial details, check to see if there were any large cash withdrawals in the days leading up to his disappearance.'

Tom fell silent, and Milner and DC Bennett, recognising that this was DCI Stone's thinking time, joined in with the silence. Eventually, when Tom did speak, it was not something that either of them had expected. 'Milner, what do you know about golf?'

Milner, although momentarily surprised, quickly realised where this might be going. 'Not a lot. Other than that it's usually played by older men who probably have too much spare time on their hands.'

Tom could emphasise with Milner's disparaging comment. He had tried golf once and had found it a complete waste of his time. Whoever had said that golf was *a good walk spoiled* had his vote.

'Well,' he said, 'I wouldn't say Mr Burton was old, and, by all accounts, he certainly didn't have too much spare time. It helped him to relax. According to his wife, it was, after his business, his favourite pastime.'

'Apart from his womanising, of course,' said DC Bennett, with a slight laugh.

'Was there just a hint of jealousy there?' asked Tom.

'I think I'll stick with Julie,' DC Bennett answered. 'And, anyway, I'd struggle to look after the kids without her.'

'I don't blame you,' said Tom. 'I've met your wife. You would have to be either brave or foolish to try and deceive her.'

Milner, keen to get the conversation back to the matter in

hand, interrupted their discussion. 'I assume, sir, you'd like to go and visit his golf club?'

'Well, it might be helpful. You never know. Why don't you arrange it? We don't want to turn up unannounced. That might put them off their swing – or whatever they do.'

Chapter 9

Less than an hour later, Tom and Milner were seated in a small office at West London Golf Club.

It was only because they had trusted their sat nav that they had arrived on time. Without it they would probably still be driving around. There had been a solitary, small, faded wooden sign, midway along a short B road, indicating a left turn. But even this was partly obscured by an overhanging tree branch. They then had to drive along a narrow, and heavily tree-lined, private road, which had several very impressive houses set back on either side. At the very end of the road were some solid-looking automatic gates, controlled by a security code panel, with a small sign asking visitors to either enter the daily code or press a separate button for assistance. It was almost as though the club were trying to keep people away from it.

The clubhouse itself was an imposing building, constructed mainly from bricks but with alternating light and dark wood on the front facia of the building. This type of building was unlikely to be built in the modern age and, even though it had clearly seen better days, its architectural grandeur remained its defining characteristic. As they had approached the main entrance they had been met by a woman who, clearly expecting them, introduced herself as the office secretary, and then led them down a long corridor panelled in dark wood, along which were lots of head-and-shoulder photographs of various men.

The office was very much in keeping with the rest of the décor, dominated by dark wooden wall panels. Numerous scratch marks and indentations on the table and four chairs suggested many years of use. There was no evidence of any effort to repair them. The overall impression all of this gave was of something from a completely different age.

Seated opposite Tom and Milner were two men.

'I'm Detective Chief Inspector Stone and this is Detective Sergeant Milner,' Tom said, presenting his identification. 'Thank you very much for seeing us at such short notice. I'm sure you have lots of other things which you could be doing,' he added, although he himself wasn't sure what these could possibly be.

'Well, I wasn't surprised when I took your call,' said the younger of the two men. 'Glyn's disappearance has been the talk of the club all week.' He hesitated. 'I assume that's the reason why you are here. Has anything happened?'

Tony Cook was the general manager and the person who had taken the call from DS Milner. As a result of this, Tony Cook had thought it prudent to immediately contact the club's chairman, Roger White.

'No, there has been no change. Mr Burton is still missing,' Tom simply replied. He carried straight on. 'I understand that Mr Burton didn't actually play the last time he was here. Do you know why that was?'

It was Roger White who answered. 'We were due to tee off at around nine o'clock, but there was quite a bit of fog – we tend to get fog at this time of year – and so everything was on hold until it was safe enough to play. Glyn hung around for a while but then decided he couldn't wait any longer.'

'Did he explain why?'

'Nothing specific. Just that he could be doing other things.'

'And what time was that?' asked Milner.

'I can't give you the exact time, but I think that it was around ten o'clock,' Mr White replied.

Tom suddenly recognised him from the photograph which had been on Mr Burton's desk in his office. He had brought it with him and, as he showed it to Mr White, he said, 'So, you regularly play with Mr Burton.'

'Yes, that's right. We try to play together every week.'

'By *we*, do you mean just yourself and Mr Burton or the others?' he asked.

'The weekends are busy times for all golf clubs and so they try to ensure that all four spots are filled. In our group, apart from myself and Glyn, there was Gus Thomas and Greg Wallington.'

'Are they these men?' Tom asked, pointing at the other two men in the photograph.

'No. That's Mike Preston and Jim Mason. They aren't members here any more.'

'Any reason for that?' asked Tom, still looking at the photograph.

'I think it was something to do with their family commitments. Mike has young children, whilst Jim had work commitments which meant that he was finding it hard to commit the time. Unlike the majority of members, they both still work.'

'Does that mean most of your members are retired?' asked Milner.

'Yes, I'm afraid it does. The profile of our members tends to fall into the older age group.'

'Is that a problem?'

'Well, it doesn't augur well for the future. Like most golf clubs, we are struggling to attract younger members.' A hint of disapproval entered his voice. 'The younger generation just don't seem to want to spend a few hours playing golf any more. They'd rather do something which doesn't take quite so long.'

Suddenly, for probably the first time in a while, Tom could sympathise with this younger generation.

'Would it be possible to get a contact number for these two?' he asked, tapping the photograph.

Roger White turned his gaze towards Tony Cook. 'That shouldn't be a problem, should it?'

'No. We still have all of their contact details.'

'Thank you,' replied Tom. 'If you could let Detective Sergeant Milner have them after we have finished, that would be much appreciated. And do you know what they do? You said they both still worked.'

'Why do you need to know that?' Mr White asked.

'It's standard procedure. You can't have too much information,' Tom replied.

Despite neither man looking totally convinced by Tom's answer, Mr White provided the information. 'Mike works in sales. Something to do with business software, I think. Not my strong point, I'm afraid. Jim is a PE teacher. Works at a comprehensive school, somewhere in Twickenham.'

'Thank you,' Tom replied. 'Incidentally, did you play after the fog had lifted?'

Mr White shook his head. 'No, I personally didn't. You can never be sure when the fog will clear, so I decided not to play. Instead, I spent the time in here working on finalising the annual management report.'

'So did you stay at the club for the rest of the day?' asked Tom.

'Not all of the day. I had something to eat and then left, I suppose, just after noon.'

'And you then went home?' asked Tom.

Roger White looked at Tom suspiciously. 'Why are you asking me these questions? Do you think I had something to do with Glyn's disappearance?' he asked, a hint of anger in his voice.

'Not at all,' answered Tom. 'I'm just trying to get a clear picture of everyone's movements. It's simply standard practice.'

Despite Tom's explanation there remained an uncomfortable atmosphere, which wasn't helped when Tom then added, 'So, *did* you then go home?'

'Yes, I did,' he answered, in a slightly curt tone.

Milner now joined in the conversation. 'I understand Mr Burton was a member of the club's management committee. Is that correct?'

'Yes, he was finance secretary. Given his background it seemed a logical choice,' answered Tony Cook.

'When we last spoke with Mrs Burton, she said that her husband thought that ...' At this point Milner referred to his notebook. '*They didn't take to an East Ender hobnobbing with them.* Why do you think he would feel that way?'

'I've got absolutely no idea,' Mr Cook replied. 'As far as I was concerned Glyn was an important part of the club. I personally always got on very well with him.'

Tom now spoke. 'That's as may be, but a person can be important but still disliked.'

There was a brief silence before Roger White spoke. 'Perhaps I can answer that. We are a private members' club and, even though quite a few of our members are wealthy people, it doesn't mean that we don't occasionally have financial difficulties. Glyn joined a few years ago, before Tony, at a time when we were having a few problems. He was able to inject a considerable amount of money into the club, which

42

helped to get us back on our feet. Perhaps some people – maybe some of the longer-standing members – resented that. I personally was not aware of any animosity, but I suppose it's possible there might have been one or two of the longer-standing members who took a dislike to him.'

'Why do you think that might have been?' asked Tom, determined to press the point.

'Glyn was a . . . how can I put this?' Mr White said, before finding the words. 'He was quite a loud man, with a big personality. Perhaps some of the older members felt uncomfortable with a man with that sort of personality.'

'So, how long have you been a member, Mr White?'

'I've been a full member here for over thirty years now,' he answered, with obvious pride.

'What exactly did Mr Burton do to help out the club?' asked Tom. 'He must have done something significant, given everything you've just said about him.'

'The club had had a long-running dispute with the tax authorities, going back over a number of years, which finally was resolved – unfortunately, not in our favour – and it was then that Glyn stepped in and offered to help.'

'Was it money?'

'It was, yes.'

'And what was the scale of that help?' Tom asked.

'About half a million pounds,' Mr White simply replied.

Tom was now far more engaged. 'Half a million pounds?' he asked, in genuine amazement. 'That's a huge amount of money in anyone's language. It must have been a big tax bill.'

'As I said, the dispute had been going on for a number of years and the amount involved, what with accumulated interest and our legal costs, built up. It was always thought that the decision would come down in our favour and so, unwisely as it turned out, we had not prepared for any potential financial liabilities.'

'You said that Mr Burton stepped in to help. Was it a loan or a simply a gift?'

'It was a loan, albeit a long-term loan, secured against the assets of the club.'

It was Milner who next spoke. 'Did Mr Burton receive anything else in return for loaning the money to the club?'

'He was allocated new shares in the club and it was then he was elected to the management committee.'

'And how many shares were allocated?' asked Milner.

'I can't remember the exact amount. New shares were allocated as part of the financial restructuring. I think it meant Glyn had approximately twenty percent of the new total.'

'Would that make him the biggest shareholder?' asked Tom.

'Yes, it did.'

'It seems a lot of shares to give to a newcomer, especially for a club with such an obvious heritage as this one,' said Tom.

'I suppose it was, but, as I say, we owed a lot of money in tax, and it was increasing all the time due to the additional interest being charged on the debt. At that time, we were finding it difficult to raise the money. It wasn't too long after the financial crash, and a lot of our members had seen their own personal wealth and pension pots significantly reduced during that time. Perhaps if we'd had more time we could have raised the money via the members, but, at the time, it was felt the priority was to settle it as quickly as possible in order to protect the club's reputation.'

Tom looked as though he were about to ask a follow-up question but, instead, stood up and offered his hand, first to Mr White and then to Mr Cook. 'Thank you very much for your time.' He handed each of them a card. 'If you remember anything else that might have a bearing on Mr Burton's disappearance, please call me.'

Milner looked towards Mr Cook. 'Are you able to let me have the contact details of those two former members now? It might save me another visit.'

'I'll let you have them right now. It shouldn't take too long.'

Mr Cook left the office, leaving the three of them there, and an uneasy silence developed, until Tom broke it. 'Would you mind telling me, Mr White, if you are also a shareholder?'

'Yes, I am. In fact, in varying degrees, every member is a shareholder.'

'And what is your particular degree?' asked Tom.

Once again, Roger White looked at him with suspicion before replying. 'I have about ten percent of the total.'

'What do you actually get for that?' asked Milner, with genuine interest.

'The main benefit is that I get a lifetime's membership of the club.'

'Is that all?' asked Milner, with obvious disappointment in his voice.

'I assume you don't play golf, Detective Sergeant Milner,' Mr White replied, with undisguised brusqueness.

'I'm afraid I don't.'

'Well, if you did you would, I'm sure, appreciate the value of being able to play at one of the top golf clubs, not just in the region, but in the whole of the country. Our course is regularly featured in the top hundred UK golf courses. It is something we are very proud of.' He then added, with undisguised passion, 'Given its history, it is an honour and a privilege to be a member of this golf club.'

Milner nodded, seemingly satisfied with his answer. 'Do you, as a shareholder, receive some sort of dividend or other financial bonus?'

His earlier sharpness now seemed to have disappeared. 'Although we are essentially a non-profit-making club, occasionally, in unusual circumstances, there might be a one-off payment to all members. But it doesn't happen very often as money is always needed to maintain or make improvements to the club. Usually, the opposite happens. If, for example, funds were needed for anything outside the normal, day-to-day operation of the club, then members would be expected to contribute.'

'Like what, for example?' asked Tom.

'Well, just last year we had to spend almost £200,000 on replacement greenkeeping equipment and building a brand-new greenkeeping shed.'

'That's a lot of money just to run a golf club,' said Milner.

'I agree. It is,' replied Roger White. 'No doubt you have seen for yourself that this clubhouse, due to its age, regularly needs a lot of money spent on it. Whilst we will never change the basic structure of it, there are things – expensive things – which need doing. We also had a problem with the location of the old shed. It was in one of the more isolated parts of the club, alongside a few other old huts. In fact, they originally were built during the early stages of World War II, when the army took over the course. They sited a few anti-aircraft guns there and erected the huts for the support troops. As you can imagine, they are now mostly derelict and falling down.' He shook his head. 'Like a lot of golf clubs in this area, we were regularly broken into and had expensive equipment stolen. In the end we decided to relocate the shed to an area closer to the clubhouse. That way we could make better use of the security measures.'

'And has it worked?' asked Tom.

'Well, we haven't had a break-in since the new shed was built, but, if you want my honest opinion, it's just a question of time until we do. All we can do is make it as difficult as possible for the criminals to break in.'

Just then Tony Cook returned. 'Here are the details,' he said, handing an A4 sheet to Milner.

Milner looked at the details on the sheet and, satisfied that everything he needed was there, folded it up to put it in his pocket. 'Thank you very much.'

'Yes, thank you very much for seeing us,' added Tom. 'It has been very useful and educational. I didn't realise just how much is involved in running a golf club. All that, just to be able to knock a little white ball into a hole.'

No one there could tell if he was joking.

Chapter 10

On their way back to the station, Tom glanced over at Milner. 'What do you make of that?'

'Well, it certainly adds a new dimension to Mr Burton's disappearance. Money and envy can be a toxic mix. Mrs Burton's comment about her husband not being too popular at the club has certainly got a ring of truth about it. I got the impression Roger White was trying hard to downplay Mr Burton's popularity or, more accurately, his unpopularity.'

'Very perceptive of you, Milner. We'll make a copper of you yet,' Tom said, with a slight laugh. 'The club is 110 years old and, during that time, has clearly had some very privileged and famous members. I agree with you that they were trying very hard to make it seem that Mr Burton's membership, and, more importantly, his shareholding, was entirely normal. However they spin it, the appearance of an East Ender with seemingly bags of new money to buy his way into such an exclusive club, and the history and tradition which goes with it, cannot have been well received by everyone.'

'How do you know it's 110 years old?' asked Milner.

'It says so on this,' he answered, producing one of the club's scorecards. '*The West London Golf Club. Founded in 1909.* Not only that, but the whole ambience and décor of the club smacked of tradition. I don't know about you, but I felt as though I was almost stepping back into another time.'

'And how do you know that they have had some very famous members?' asked Milner. He was keen to know, but he also suspected this would allow DCI Stone an opportunity to, once again, provide him with the benefit of his extensive policing experience and observational skills. He wasn't disappointed.

'Didn't you look at the photographs on the wall as we walked down the corridor?' replied Tom, in a way which suggested that they were almost impossible to miss. 'There were lots and lots of them, and they were all former club captains. I could only see a few, but even I could recognise some of the names and faces. Businessmen, military officers, as well as a few famous politicians. The West London Golf Club is clearly not your local municipal pitch and putt course.'

Milner didn't know whether or not he was supposed to comment. Tom made the decision for him. 'You see, with policing, it's important to use all of your senses. But especially your eyes.'

'I'll try and remember that, sir,' said Milner, thinking that that was classic DCI Stone. A compliment quickly followed by a put-down.

When they arrived back at the station they were met by DC Bennett. 'How did it go at the golf club? Did you both join?'

'Somehow I don't think we could afford to join,' answered Milner.

'Or that they would want us,' added Tom quickly. 'Especially DS Milner. He's far too young.' He waved the two of them into his office. 'Anyway, what's been happening here whilst we've been away looking at how the other half live? Any news?'

'Yes. A few updates. Firstly, I received Mr Burton's latest bank statement. There doesn't seem to be anything out of the ordinary. Certainly no large cash withdrawal; just regular small amounts. If he was hoping to run away with a woman then he hasn't used this account to help pay for it. And he certainly wasn't planning to go anywhere too exotic.'

'I assume that was his personal bank statement,' said Tom. 'What about the business one? He must need some source of funds. We know he's not the type of person who lives a frugal lifestyle.'

'Still waiting for that, I'm afraid, but hopefully I'll have that soon as well.'

Milner spoke again. 'Let's assume, for the moment, that he has gone off with another woman. What if she is the one who is providing the funds?'

'Very good point,' said Tom, reflectively, and then, almost to himself, 'Why didn't I think of that?'

'As you always say, sir, no one has a monopoly on ideas,' answered Milner, inwardly smiling.

48

Before Tom could respond, DC Bennett said, 'Some good news, though, as far as CCTV is concerned. I've been making some local enquiries and, this morning, one of the Burtons' neighbours contacted me to say that not only do they have CCTV, but he also personally saw Mr Burton driving his car away from his house just before 2.30 pm. The techies are working on accessing the CCTV footage. I should have it sometime tomorrow.'

'Good,' said Tom, choosing to ignore Milner's earlier comment. 'That's something, I suppose. Let me know when you've set it up.'

Tom now turned to face Milner. 'I think you should go and visit those other two golfers he played with before they left. Also, see if you can get hold of a full list of club members, together with their shareholding.' He paused briefly. 'I'm still a bit puzzled, despite his cash injection, as to why Mr Burton was allocated so many shares.'

He then turned towards DC Bennett. 'And I think you and I should meet a friend of yours. Mr Burton's business partner. What's his name?'

'Craig Blackwell,' answered DC Bennett.

'Yes, that's right. Why don't you call him and set up the meeting?'

Both Milner and DC Bennett left the office, leaving Tom alone. As he sat there, by himself, he suddenly realised that he had not thought about Commander Jenkins and Charles Cope at all during the previous few hours. Whilst a man's disappearance was probably not the biggest investigation he had ever worked on, it had provided the relief and distraction he had needed. But now everything came flooding back and, however many times he thought through all of the possible outcomes, he always kept coming back to the inescapable conclusion that whatever happened was unlikely to be beneficial for him personally.

Chapter 11

'I've got something to tell you,' said Mary, with more than a hint of both excitement and nervousness in her voice.

Tom had, once again, left the station early, or at least earlier than he normally would. The distraction of Mr Burton's disappearance had proved to be short-lived and he just couldn't clear his mind of what the future would bring. In a way, remaining at the station simply reinforced this apprehension, and so he had decided to leave for home.

He had arrived back before Mary and had started to prepare dinner. It wasn't something he would normally do. In fact, the number of times he had cooked dinner he could almost count on the fingers of one hand. And, in truth, he had a very limited repertoire when it came to meal options. Something involving chicken and rice was always a safe choice, and that was what he was currently preparing.

'At least take your coat off first,' replied Tom, suddenly intrigued by what she had to tell him. At the same time, though, he was slightly disappointed that she had made no comment about him cooking dinner.

Mary took off her coat and kissed him on the cheek. 'Yummy. That smells nice. Is it chicken?'

'Well, I thought I would surprise you,' he replied, not knowing if she was being sarcastic or not. 'What is it you want to tell me?'

Mary seemed to take a deep breath before saying, 'I had a phone call earlier today.' She hesitated, almost as though she couldn't carry on.

Tom decided to help her out. 'Well, that's not so unusual, unless it was from, say, the Queen.'

'It wasn't the Queen. It was from Paul,' she answered in a breathless voice.

Tom and Anne had married when they had both been fairly young, and quite early in Tom's career, and their marriage had quickly been followed by the birth of their son, Paul. As his police career had developed, Tom had found himself prioritising this more and more over his new family. Inevitably he and Anne had started to drift apart until, finally, they had decided to split. In truth, it had been Anne who had made the decision, unable to continue in such a one-sided marriage.

After the initial pain of their split, Tom had realised that it had probably been for the best. It wasn't that he didn't care for Anne and his son; it was more that he didn't truly love her and, despite Paul, didn't want to spend the rest of his life with her.

He continued to see his son, but it was nonetheless made clear to him, by Anne, that Paul's future upbringing was down to her alone. This was dramatically brought home to Tom when, a couple of years later, she informed him that she would be emigrating to Australia. She had a sister who lived there, and it was this sister who had suggested Anne might want to start a new life there for herself and Paul.

This was, without a doubt, the most traumatic time in Tom's life, and it was only then that the true consequences of his actions really hit home. After Anne and Paul's departure, Tom had thrown himself fully into his career and, although he'd had the occasional relationship, it was his work which had provided the distraction and relief he needed.

As the years had gone by, he had thought less and less about them, almost as though he was deliberately trying to blot them completely out of his memory. Occasionally he received news about them, and it was on such an occasion he'd heard that Anne had remarried.

Recently, though, he had found himself thinking more and more about them both, but especially Paul. He'd also come to realise that Anne had been right all along. It had been selfish and inconsiderate of him to have put his career before his family.

As he approached the end of his career, these thoughts became stronger and stronger. Just a couple of years ago, when he was, both personally and professionally, at one of the lowest points of his life, he had suddenly realised just what he had given up by prioritising his career over his marriage. At that particular point he had nothing to show for the previous almost thirty years of his life. He lived alone, had no close family, and his career was just about to end in ignominy with colleagues feeling sorry for him. But then he met Mary, and everything changed.

Well, almost everything. He still didn't have any immediate family.

Just for a moment Tom couldn't speak. Finally, though, he simply said, 'Paul? Do you mean Paul, my son?'

'Yes, Paul, your son,' answered Mary, with a slight laugh, relieved that Tom's initial response had not been one of anger.

'But why?' he asked, still clearly shocked. 'Why did he call you?'

'Why don't you sit down?' she suggested.

Tom dutifully sat at the kitchen table and then Mary sat next to him.

'I know you must have lots of questions,' she said, 'but, please, just hear me out first. There will be time for those questions afterwards.'

Once again, she took a deep breath before continuing. She now knew Tom well enough to know how he hated surprises. She had thought carefully about how she would explain this to him but, even so, was still aware that it could all backfire.

'Recently you've started to talk more and more about Paul. If you remember, it wasn't that long ago you wondered what he was doing, was he married and even if he had any children himself. So I decided I would try and contact him.' She looked at him and then took his hand. 'I knew you wouldn't do it, so I thought I'd do it for you.'

This was probably the moment of truth for Mary. Either he would become angry with her for taking such a huge step on his behalf or he would accept what she had done.

She waited for him to respond. Time seemed to stand still while she waited for a reply. Just as she was about to continue, he said, 'I'm sorry. I'm a bit stunned by what you are saying.'

Mary was relieved that the tone of his voice suggested he was surprised in a pleasant way, rather than shocked and angry, and this tone continued when he asked, almost with a hint of trepidation in his voice, 'And did you contact him?'

'I did, yes,' she replied. 'It wasn't easy, and it took a couple of weeks, but, today, he called me when I was in the shop.'

'But how did you find him?' Tom asked.

'I found him via Facebook. I know you think Facebook is just so that people can talk about how wonderful they are or engage in mindless gossip, but sometimes being on Facebook does have its benefits. Anyway, eventually I found him. When I first entered his name, I think about fifty people came up. But one profile stood out, from what you had told me about him. Born in 1988, in London, but moved to Melbourne when he was still very young. So all I had to do then was message him and ask if he was the person I was trying to find. Fortunately, he responded and gave me his email address.' She hesitated. 'I say *all I had to do*, but it wasn't really quite as simple as that. I thought long and hard about whether it was the right thing to do.' She paused, allowing a space for him to say something. When he didn't, she carried on. 'We exchanged a few emails. I told him a bit more about you and me, and—'

Before Mary could finish, Tom interrupted her. 'What did you say about us?'

'I told him how we were living together, how long we had been together, where we were living and that we were planning to get married,' she answered. 'He was genuinely interested to hear what I was saying.' Without giving him the opportunity to comment she continued. 'By the way, I think you should know that you are a grandad. Paul is married, and they have two young children. A boy aged eight, Sam, and a seven-year-old girl, Emily.'

This time she did allow time for what she had just told him to fully sink in.

'I'm a grandad? I can't believe it,' Tom said. He had suddenly become quite emotional – something Mary had rarely seen in him before – and so, once again, she gave him some more time.

'What did you say about me?' Tom asked at last, in a slightly hesitant voice.

Mary smiled. 'Well, you might be surprised to know that he actually knew quite a lot about you already. It seems that the investigation you were involved in a couple of years ago – the one where Philip King murdered all of those people – not only made the UK media but also reached Australia.'

'So he realised who I was?' asked Tom.

'Actually, he didn't. It was his mum who recognised you

and then told him. It seems he then couldn't get enough information about you.'

'Anne?' he asked, with surprise and interest. 'Do you know how she is?'

Mary's demeanour suddenly changed. 'I'm afraid she died last year from breast cancer. I'm sorry.'

'Dead?' Tom was visibly shocked. 'She was younger than me.'

'Apparently she had been diagnosed a few years previously. After treatment she was considered to be in remission but, unfortunately, the cancer reappeared, in a more aggressive way. I'm sorry,' she said again.

'You've nothing to be sorry for,' he quickly said.

'I know, but I'm still sorry that it was me who had to tell you. I know it's been a long time, but Anne was, at one point, your wife and mother to your son.'

Mary was right and Tom, genuinely shocked by what she had just told him, could not speak. Although he hadn't seen Anne for a very long time and when they had split it had been quite messy, she had still been his wife who, at least during the early stages of their marriage, he had loved. There were suddenly lots of questions buzzing around in his head, but he just couldn't get them out.

Mary, once again recognising Tom's mental turmoil, took the lead. 'And there's another thing.'

Tom looked directly at her. 'There can't be anything more surprising than this. Finding out that you have two grandchildren, after all of this time, would be difficult to beat.'

'What about if I told you that you will soon get the chance to meet them?' she said, a huge smile appearing on her face.

Not for the first time over the past few minutes, Tom was genuinely stunned, and all he could say in response was, 'Meet them?'

'That's correct,' Mary said. 'That was one of the reasons why he called me today. To let me know that they – all the family – will be here, in the UK, the week after next. Apparently, they had always planned to visit the UK at some stage, when their children were old enough. I think our recent contact just accelerated that process.'

'Where will they be staying?' asked Tom.

'Tom, I think you're now getting ahead of yourself. We

didn't get into that level of detail. I'm sure he will let us know once he's finalised the travel details.'

'Yes. Sorry, you're right. To be honest, my head is still buzzing.' He paused before adding, almost to himself, 'I can't believe that this has happened.'

Mary took hold of his hand again. 'I'm so relieved that you seem to be happy about it. I honestly thought that you would be angry that I'd done all of this without telling you.'

'Really?' he asked, with slight indignation. 'Why would I get angry?'

Mary smiled. 'Well, let's just say that, in the past, you haven't always been appreciative when someone has done something for you without your knowledge.' She didn't allow him time to comment. Instead she said, in a more serious tone, 'Just enjoy the time you will have with Paul and his family. Given what you've been through lately, I think you deserve it.'

Tom simply said, 'As ever, you are probably right.'

Inside, though, he couldn't help thinking that life wasn't always fair and, anyway, he had always subscribed to the law of unintended consequences.

Chapter 12

The following morning Tom and DC Bennett were both in Tom's office. After the events of the previous night it was almost a relief to be back discussing more mundane things.

Once the shock of what Mary had told him had dissipated, Tom and Mary had spent most of the rest of the evening discussing the various practicalities and implications of his son's visit. As the evening had gone on, though, Tom had found himself becoming more and more apprehensive. Mary had been right. He didn't like surprises. He liked to be in control of events rather than letting events control him. It was his emotional safety net. All of that was true, but he had to admit, at least to himself, that he was also excited. How could he not be? After all, he was about to see his grandchildren for the very first time and his son for the first time in almost thirty years.

'I've set up the footage from the CCTV, sir,' DC Bennett said. 'It starts at the time Mr Burton has just left his house to go to golf. It's not crystal clear but still good enough to pick him out.'

'Let's take a look, then,' replied Tom.

DC Bennett pressed the play button on the machine and immediately a quite grainy picture appeared on the screen. At the bottom of the screen was the date, together with a time counter.

'Here he comes,' said DC Bennett. The time was apparently 8.01 am. As the car reached the middle of the screen, DC Bennett pressed the pause button and a head-and-shoulders image of Mr Burton could be seen in the driver's seat. He allowed Tom time to study the image before cancelling the pause mode.

'This is him returning,' said DC Bennett, fast-forwarding until Mr Burton's car was once again on screen. The time showed 11.52 am. Once again, an upper-body shot of Mr Burton could be made out.

Tom looked at the image for a while before DC Bennett interrupted him with another fast-forward. 'And this is him leaving the house again.'

The time at the bottom of the screen showed 2.25 pm. Tom spent some considerable time studying the image closely.

'And finally, there's this other one. The one which includes his neighbour.' DC Bennett carefully moved the images forward, frame by frame, until he found the one he was looking for. 'That's the neighbour – a Mr Perry. He just happened to be walking down the street, in view of the CCTV camera, when Mr Burton's car went past.' Once again DC Bennett nudged the frames forward. 'This is where Mr Perry waves to Mr Burton, who, as you can just make out, waves back.'

'And there's nothing else of him after this time?' asked Tom.

'Nothing, sir. I spent most of last night looking at the footage, from the moment he left the house until after 5 pm. Those three shots we just saw are the only ones.'

'Hmm,' said Tom. 'Not much to go on there. I was hoping there might be something a bit more revealing.'

'Like what, sir?' asked DC Bennett.

'I've got no idea,' he answered. 'With CCTV it's often the case that you won't know until you've actually seen it. Why don't you also look a bit further afield? See if you can find his car on any other CCTV footage. Concentrate on the major routes out of Richmond from 2.25 pm onwards. If we can pick him up travelling in a certain direction, that would be a great help, as the key to this is knowing where he went after he left his house. You never know; we might get lucky.' He turned away from the screen. 'Anyway, good job, Gary. Now, have you been able to set up a meeting with his business partner yet? You know, your new best friend.'

'Very funny, sir,' DC Bennett answered with a laugh. 'I just didn't take to him, that's all. But, to answer your question, yes, I spoke with him late yesterday afternoon and arranged to meet at two thirty this afternoon, at their offices in the City. He did suggest meeting here, but I thought you'd like to see where they were based.'

'And, no doubt,' Tom said, 'you wanted him to experience the embarrassment of a visit from two police detectives.'

'Never crossed my mind,' DC Bennett replied, a big smile suddenly appearing.

Just then Milner reappeared. 'Well, it certainly all goes on at a golf club,' he said.

Both Tom and DC Bennett could sense that Milner had some news he was keen to impart – which he then duly did.

'I just received a call from Tony Cook, the general manager of the golf club, who informed me that perhaps Roger White wasn't being entirely honest with us when we asked him why the other two golfers in the photograph were no longer members of the club. It may be true that they had family and work commitments, but what Mr White chose not to tell us was that, a few months ago, there had been a big argument between Glyn Burton and Mike Preston. In fact, it got so heated that, at one point, they had to be pulled apart. Apparently, for a while, it was the talk of the golf club.'

'I bet it was,' replied Tom. 'And do we know the reason for the argument?'

'Yes, we do,' said Milner. 'It seems that Mike Preston had found out that our missing man had been having an affair with his wife.'

'Really?' asked Tom, surprised. 'And do we know that as fact?'

'The way Mr Cook told me suggested that it was,' Milner said. 'Although I got the distinct impression he was trying hard to downplay it.'

'Something they seem to do all of the time at that particular golf club,' Tom said, more to himself than to anyone else. 'Anyway, didn't he phone you? It's difficult to downplay something if you are the person who initiated the conversation.'

'Exactly. That's what I thought as well. He said that later, after we had left, he had remembered the fight and thought that, even though he claims it had nothing to do with Mr Burton's disappearance, we should at least be aware of it.'

'Mm,' replied Tom, clearly not totally convinced. 'That was very good of him, although I doubt very much he would have forgotten about something which, in his own words, was the talk of the club. The real question is why didn't he tell us at the time? And, also, of course, why Roger White, who seems to have known Mr Burton quite well, did not mention it either.' He paused. 'Anyway, I think we now know which of his golfing buddies we should go and visit next. Why don't you call him and fix up a time?'

Just as Milner was leaving, Tom suddenly said, 'Oh, and there's one other thing. Check to see if anyone we're interested in, including Mr Burton himself, has their own Facebook page. There might be something there which could be of interest to us. Even though I think Facebook is a *wonderful* development, sometimes people can give away all sorts of information on there which, under normal circumstances, they just wouldn't do.'

Milner smiled a little. DCI Stone's dislike of Facebook was almost legendary. 'Of course, sir.'

Chapter 13

'Thank you very much for seeing us, Mr Blackwell,' said Tom, displaying his ID card. 'I'm Detective Chief Inspector Stone, from West London police. I think you have already met my colleague, Detective Constable Bennett.'

Mr Blackwell hardly even acknowledged DC Bennett, instead focussing his attention on Tom.

The offices of Investment and Wealth Management were in one corner of the ground floor of a converted warehouse, on the northern side of the River Thames, and in an upwardly mobile part of East London. The office was modest in size, with just enough room for two desks and chairs, together with a small circular table around which they were now seated. As far as Tom could see, apart from Mr Blackwell, there was just one other person in the office.

'Sarah is our PA,' Mr Blackwell explained. 'I'm sure if I asked her nicely, she would rustle up a cup of coffee or tea for you both. Which do you prefer?'

'That's very good of you,' replied Tom. 'White coffee with no sugar would be fine for me.'

'I'll have my usual, please, Sarah,' Mr Blackwell said, and then, directly facing DC Bennett for the first time, he asked, 'And what about you?'

Tom could see DC Bennett almost flinch at this and wasn't entirely surprised when he replied, 'Nothing for me.' DC Bennett seemed determined not to be beholden to Craig Blackwell in any way at all.

Sarah quickly returned with their drinks and then left the room, closing the door behind her.

'Is there any news yet on Glyn?' Mr Blackwell asked, with some obvious concern in his voice.

'I'm afraid not. That's why we wanted to meet with you, in order to see if there's anything else you could tell us which might help us find Mr Burton. It's now almost two weeks since he disappeared, and as each day passes we are becoming increasingly concerned about his wellbeing.'

'Well, of course, if there's anything I can do to help then I will, but I've already told your constable everything I know.'

'*Detective* constable,' DC Bennett put in.

Tom didn't know whether or not Mr Blackwell was deliberately trying to provoke Gary, but, sensing that Gary might do or say something untoward, he quickly intervened. 'That's right, DC Bennett did say you have been very helpful and already provided him with lots of information, but I asked him to set up this meeting between us so that I could get a full picture myself. So, if you could tell me a little about your business, that would be a good start.'

'Glyn and I started the business about ten years ago. We got to know each other when we both worked on the same desk at a company in the City. We handled smaller clients. Those with investments of less than half a million. When the credit crash took hold, in 2008, we were both offered redundancy. The company had decided that, in future, they just wanted to concentrate on their bigger clients.'

'So half a million pounds is considered to be small beer?' asked Tom.

'In the world of finance, it is, yes,' answered Mr Blackwell. 'Some of the other desks were handling individual accounts in the tens of millions.'

Tom could see that Gary was about to say something in response, so he gave him an almost imperceptible shake of the head, making it clear that he should remain silent.

Mr Blackwell continued. 'It was at this time that we decided to set up ourselves and focus our business on these smaller clients. Fortunately, the company allowed us to bring some of our clients with us.'

'And I'm assuming it has been successful,' said Tom.

'Well, yes,' he answered. 'In the first few years things were a bit dodgy, but we managed to get through that. Since then, especially over the past five or six years, things have gone pretty well. Glyn now tends to handle existing clients whilst I try to get new ones.'

'And what is the size of your business now? Are you able to tell me?'

'That's not a problem,' he answered. 'Last year our client book was worth over £50 million.'

DC Bennett let out a quiet whistle whilst Tom, also impressed, made do with simply raising his eyebrows. '£50 million?'

'That's not what we turn over,' Mr Blackwell explained quickly. 'The fifty million is the total value of the funds we manage on behalf of our clients. We take a commission, as well as charging an annual fee, for doing that.'

'So, what is the value of that commission?' asked Tom, keen to get an idea of the company's actual income.

'I'd rather not divulge that, if you don't mind. It is confidential information and not something we would want our competitors to find out.'

If the implication was that Tom and DC Bennett could not be trusted with this information, Tom decided not to challenge it. Instead he said, 'Do you mind me asking you where you live?'

'I live in Hampstead,' Mr Blackwell answered.

DC Bennett was unable to resist making a comment. 'Nice.'

Mr Blackwell looked directly at him. 'Do you have a problem with that?'

'Not at all,' DC Bennett answered quickly. 'I just wish I could afford to live there.'

Fearing that the conversation could take an unfortunate turn, Tom tried to bring it back onto a more professional level. 'Is there any reason you can think of why Mr Burton would want to disappear?'

'None at all. We have been friends for a long time. We work together. We socialise together. Susie and I would often go out with Glyn and Jane. Sometimes we would even go away on holiday together. We have a place in Spain, near Marbella, and occasionally they would come down with the kids to stay with us for a couple of weeks. If Glyn was planning to do a runner, I can assure you that I would know about it,' he answered with real conviction.

'What if, though, he was about to do a runner with another woman? Would you know about that as well?' asked Tom.

'Another woman? Why would Glyn do that? He was happily married,' Mr Blackwell said, although Tom couldn't help but detect that, this time, his answer carried far less conviction.

'Well, from what we now know about Mr Burton he was known to be ... how can I put this? Well, let's just say he liked the company of women.'

Mr Blackwell didn't immediately respond, as though he was considering what to say. 'Glyn liked the company of women,' he finally admitted. 'That's for sure. And maybe he'd had a few flings in the past, but that was when he was much younger.'

'That's what he may have told you, but we have spoken to some of his neighbours where he has his flat. They have told us that Mr Burton quite regularly brought back different women, late at night, when he was staying there. They say that recently, however, it has been one woman in particular who has stayed there overnight.' Tom watched carefully for a reaction as he spoke. 'There is also some speculation that he had been having an affair with someone linked to the golf club where he played.' He paused briefly. 'I think that all adds up to more than the occasional fling in the past. Don't you?'

'Okay, I accept that there have been a few, but, as far as I know, it's not against the law, is it? Well, not yet, anyway.'

'No, it's not yet against the law,' said Tom. 'And, incidentally, it's not our job to be judgemental. But, I come back to my previous question. Is there a chance that Mr Burton has gone somewhere with another woman?'

'Not as far as I'm aware. No,' he answered in a matter-of-fact tone.

'Thank you,' said Tom. 'In many ways I was hoping you would have said yes; then we could spend our time on more serious matters. Incidentally, would you have any idea who the woman might be who Mr Burton has been seeing recently? The one who his neighbours say has been a regular visitor.'

There was a momentary hesitation as Mr Blackwell considered how to respond. Tom, sensing this, added, 'It would be extremely helpful to our inquiry if you could give us some idea of who she might be. I can assure you we will treat whatever you tell us in the strictest confidence.'

This seemed to, at least partly, reassure Mr Blackwell. 'As I told you earlier, Susie and I have known Glyn and Jane for many years. The last thing I want is to see Jane hurt.'

'I understand that,' answered Tom. 'But I think you will

find that Mrs Burton is feeling quite a lot of hurt right now anyway. The police are not in the habit of deliberately and unnecessarily causing marital problems. We have far more important things to be doing.'

'Well, there was one woman who Glyn seemed especially keen on. I could sense that she was somehow different from the others.'

'How could you tell that?' asked Tom.

'Nothing specific, but he just seemed a bit different. As though he had something on his mind. Plus, there were a few times when she left messages with Sarah asking him to call her back urgently.'

'And who is that woman?' asked DC Bennett, notebook in hand, and speaking for the first time in quite a while.

'It's actually the wife of one of his clients. Caroline Mercer.'

'And the name of her husband?' asked Tom.

'Jonathan Mercer,' he replied.

'Thank you,' replied Tom. 'Are you able to provide us with a contact address and telephone number?'

Once again he hesitated before responding. 'Do you really need those? As I said, there was nothing specific, just a feeling that I had. If they find out that it was us who gave you their details then, as I'm sure you can imagine, it wouldn't look too good for us. Mr Mercer is one of our biggest clients and I wouldn't like to lose him because of some speculation about Glyn and his wife.'

'I totally understand that,' said Tom in his most reassuring voice. 'But I wouldn't ask you for her details unless I felt it was important to the investigation. And, anyway, we could get the details ourselves. It's just that this way would save a lot of time.'

Mr Blackwell didn't immediately answer. Finally, though, he simply said, 'Give me a minute and I'll get them,' before standing up and leaving the office.

Whilst he was out of the office Tom looked at DC Bennett. 'Are you okay, Gary?'

'Fine, sir,' he replied, in a manner which suggested the exact opposite.

Just then Mr Blackwell reappeared and handed a piece of paper to Tom. Tom glanced at the contact details on it and stood up. 'Thank you very much, Mr Blackwell. As I said earlier, please be assured that we will be discreet.' He paused. 'Incidentally, how did you feel about Mr Burton having an affair with the wife of one of your clients? Surely that was an even bigger risk, especially as he was one of your biggest clients? Exactly how big was his investment?'

'I'm not able to divulge the value of the investment portfolio we are handling on Mr Mercer's behalf. That would compromise client confidentiality. What I can say, though, is that Mr Mercer is actually our largest client.'

Tom was momentarily taken aback by this information and, whilst he was still considering what he'd just been told, DC Bennett cut in. 'I would have thought that client confidentiality was the least of your problems.'

'What do you mean?' Mr Blackwell asked.

'It wouldn't have looked good for your business if your other clients found out that one of the partners was sleeping with the wife of your biggest client. How do you think they would have reacted? If you were looking after my money, and I found that out, I'd withdraw it pretty sharpish.'

Mr Blackwell hesitated. He was clearly struggling or reluctant to answer DC Bennett's question, and so Tom decided to help. 'My original question to you was how you felt about what Mr Burton was doing with Mrs Mercer.'

This time he did answer Tom's question. 'Well, as you can imagine, it wasn't something which I was particularly happy about. Having an affair is one thing. Having this type of affair is something completely different. Believe it or not, Detective Chief Inspector, there are a few lines in our line of work which you just don't cross.'

'Really?' replied DC Bennett, with a slight laugh. 'Maybe you could tell me what they are?'

Mr Blackwell looked directly at him, and said, his voice dripping with sarcasm, 'Well, of course, the police are well known for their high moral standards. If only the rest of us could be as righteous as you obviously are.'

There followed a brief silence, but fortunately DC Bennett did not respond, and it was Tom who next spoke. 'Just another couple of final questions, if you don't mind. When was the last time you saw Mr Burton?'

Mr Blackwell's immediate response suggested he had been expecting this question. 'The Friday night before Glyn

65

disappeared. We went for a quick drink together after work. I left at about seven thirty.'

'Did he leave with you?'

'No. He said he'd finish his drink first.'

'Was it just the two of you or were you with someone else?

'It was just the two of us.'

Whilst Tom was mulling this over, DC Bennett rejoined the conversation. 'Did he contact you on the following Sunday? The day he disappeared.'

'No. As I said, Friday was the last time I saw him.'

'I understand that, but I asked if Mr Burton had contacted you, not if you'd seen him,' DC Bennett replied, the brusqueness of his tone clearly indicating his rising annoyance.

For the first time it seemed that Mr Blackwell was about to lose his temper, but, with almost supreme willpower, he simply said, 'He did not try to contact me. I did not see him, and I did not speak with him. Does that answer your question?'

'Perfectly. Thank you,' answered DC Bennett.

*

Tom and DC Bennett were in their car, heading back to the station, when Tom spoke. 'I know that the *good cop, bad cop* approach works on television but, in my experience, it's not always as successful in our world. You really don't like him, do you?'

'Whatever gave you that impression?' DC Bennett replied, unsmiling.

Chapter 14

'How was your meeting with the business partner?' asked Milner, back at the station later that same day. 'Any leads?'

'Well, he was, albeit reluctantly, able to confirm that Mr Burton was a bit of a ladies' man and that he had latterly been paying attention to one particular lady. The wife of their biggest client, apparently. He even gave us her contact details. So, yes, I think we did get a new lead. Whether or not it's important is, of course, another matter entirely. Anyway, we should go and meet her.' Tom turned towards DC Bennett. 'Can you set it up? I'd like to meet this particular lady, especially as she was apparently so special to him.'

'Why was it special with this one?' asked Milner.

'I don't know, but there seems to be more between them than with some of his other women. We'll need to meet her to find out. Anyway, what have you been up to whilst we've been away?'

'I've also been to see someone about one of his ladies. I contacted Mike Preston. As you can imagine, he was a bit surprised to hear from me, although, of course, he did know about Mr Burton's disappearance. He is some sort of salesman but was working from home today. His wife works for the local council and she was at work. I suggested to him that now might be a good time to meet, whilst she was out.'

'And he obviously agreed, then,' said Tom.

'Well, he could certainly see the advantage.'

'What happened? What did he have to say?' asked Tom.

So Milner told them. He told them how Mr Preston had readily confirmed that he and Mr Burton had had a public altercation in the car park of the golf club. In fact, he also readily volunteered that he regretted the fact that they had been pulled apart. It appeared that he had found out about Mr Burton's affair with his wife, Amy, and had then challenged him, in the car park, one Sunday morning after Mr

67

Burton had finished playing golf. At first Mr Burton had denied it, but eventually he had admitted to it. The fact that he had played it down, almost as though it were just one of those things, had simply inflamed the situation, provoking Mr Preston to try to hit him.

'And is that the reason why he left the golf club?' asked Tom.

'Yes, that was the main reason, although he also mentioned how the club had placed all of the blame for the fight on him.'

'I'm assuming, then, that Mr and Mrs Preston are still together,' said Tom.

'Yes, that's right, although he gave me the impression that things are still a bit strained between them.'

'I bet they are,' Tom said. 'Do you know if Mr Preston still has his membership shares in the golf club?'

'I do, actually,' replied Milner, clearly quite pleased with himself for anticipating the question. 'He only ever had a small number of shares, but he was able to sell them back to the club.'

'And what about the other man who left at the same time?'

'That's Jim Mason. I haven't actually spoken with him personally, but I did ask Mr Preston if he knew why Mr Mason had left the club at the same time as he did. Apparently, they have been close friends since their school days, and Mr Mason wanted to support him. It looks as though, like Mr Preston, he also sold his few shares back to the club.'

'Hmmm,' replied Tom, in his characteristically conspiratorial tone, before asking, 'and do you think that Mr Preston might have had anything to do with Mr Burton's disappearance? After all, he would have had a valid motive. Revenge, especially where marital affairs are concerned, can make a normally rational person do some strange things.'

'It's possible, of course,' answered Milner, 'but my personal judgement is that it's highly unlikely he had anything to do with it. He didn't seem concerned about deflecting suspicion, at least. In fact, I got the impression he wouldn't be too upset if something untoward has happened to Mr Burton.'

'Anything else?' asked Tom, his tone suggesting he wasn't really expecting anything.

'Actually, there is, sir,' answered Milner. 'Remember you

asked me to get hold of the list of shareholders at the golf club? Well, I received it this morning. It's not right up to date but still very interesting.' When DCI Stone did not respond, Milner took this as his cue to carry straight on. 'When we spoke with Mr White, he told us that he had about ten percent of the total shares. In fact, now he only has about one percent. He also mentioned that Mr Burton was the biggest share-holder with twenty percent. Well, Mr Burton is now not only the biggest shareholder but is the majority shareholder with just over fifty percent. I checked back, and it seems that he has regularly been buying shares over the past couple of years. Not large numbers individually, but enough, in total, to signif-icantly increase his total holding. And here's the interesting thing. Earlier this year he purchased most of Mr White's shares, and it was this final purchase which took him over the fifty percent mark.'

'Now, that is interesting,' said Tom, as much to himself as in response to Milner. 'I wonder why he considered it so important to get control of the club.' He paused. 'And why Roger White, an obvious and passionate stalwart of the golf club, decided to sell him his shares. I think you and I, Milner, should go back and ask him those very questions.'

But, before they could do that, and as so often happens in a police investigation, other events suddenly got in the way.

Chapter 15

'And you are sure it's Mr Burton?' asked Tom.

The following morning Milner had arrived at the station to find a report of a dead body. It had been found in a long-abandoned gravel quarry, quite close to the northern section of the M3, which had filled with water over the years and was currently being used as a water activity centre. Just recently, a diving company had also started to use it to teach new divers. It was during one of their dives that they had spotted a car which had settled at a depth of about twenty feet. The car itself was resting, upside down, on a narrow ledge, which had stopped it from falling much deeper to the very bottom of the quarry. Despite this, and due to the murky colour of the water and the thick weeds, it was impossible to spot from the surface. The divers had started to explore the car, and it hadn't been long, despite the darkness of the water, before they had made out the outline of what looked like a body, still in the car.

'It looks very likely that it's him,' replied Milner. 'The car's registration number belonged to Mr Burton. Also, when they recovered the body, they found a wallet which contained all his personal details – credit cards, driving licence, that type of thing.'

'How did the car get into the quarry?' asked Tom. 'Is there access?'

'It's in quite an isolated place, although there is a narrow lane which runs parallel to that part of the quarry. Alongside it is a wooden fence. It looks as though the car was deliberately driven through the fence into the quarry. According to the report, the fence at that part is almost falling down, anyway, and so it wouldn't have taken much to break through it.'

'It's possible, then, that whoever did this had some knowledge of that part of the quarry. It was isolated and they knew the fence wasn't very secure.'

'That's what I thought as well, sir,' Milner said. 'Forensics are checking for footprints near the scene, and along the lane itself. They are not confident, though, that they will be able to find anything specific.'

'Why not?' asked Tom.

'Apparently the lane that runs parallel to the quarry is popular with horse riders and so, because it's been raining recently, has been churned up. So they have been concentrating on the area just in front of the quarry itself.'

'Okay, but keep chasing them to see if they've found anything,' Tom said. 'What about his phone? Did they find that?'

'Not as far as I know,' replied Milner. 'It's certainly not on the list of things they recovered. It's possible, of course, that it's at the bottom of the quarry. Apparently most of the doors were open and so it, along presumably with other items, could have fallen out.'

'Hmm, that's a shame,' Tom said. 'I'm assuming Mrs Burton hasn't been informed yet.'

'I doubt it,' answered Milner. 'It's probably still too early. The body has only just been recovered. And, anyway, as we are the lead officers in this investigation, that should be our job. I'll speak with the pathologist's office and establish when the body will be ready for formal identification.'

Tom remained silent as he considered what to do next, but it was Milner who made the obvious suggestion. 'I'll also find out the earliest date when the post-mortem can be carried out. At the moment we don't know the circumstances of Mr Burton's death. It could be suicide, or it could be murder. We won't know until we get the pathologist's report.'

Tom now spoke. 'What we do know, though, is that it's unlikely to be accidental. I can't think of many people who would unintentionally drive through a fence and over the edge of a steep quarry in a fairly remote location.'

There was not much more Tom could do until Milner had got back with the information. In truth, Tom suddenly felt quite deflated. He had always felt there was a strong likelihood that Mr Burton was, unfortunately, dead. Although this was still to be confirmed, his instincts were telling him it was the case. In fact, right from the start of this inquiry, he had felt that was the most likely outcome. But, nonetheless, putting his instincts aside, he had continued to hold out hope that Mr Burton's sudden disappearance was due to a marital infidelity.

While he waited for Milner to return, he spent his time clearing his emails and generally catching up on all the admin issues which somehow needed his input. This time, at least, although he generally detested spending any time on these tasks, it proved to be quite cathartic. Not only had he managed to clear everything, something which always gave him a sense of satisfaction, but he had also managed to pass a couple of hours. This temporary sense of serenity was, however, broken when Milner, this time accompanied by DC Bennett, suddenly appeared in his office.

'I've brought you a cup of coffee, sir,' said DC Bennett, placing the plastic cup on the table in front of him.

'Thanks,' Tom said. 'You see, DS Milner, that's the way to look after your superior officer.' He picked up the cup, took a quick sip, grimaced and then put it back on the table. 'I don't ask for much in life. The odd cup of coffee is often enough.'

Milner was tempted to remind DCI Stone that he himself had regularly spent his own money providing him with drinks and food. Instead, he simply made do with, 'I'll put it to the top of my priority list, sir.'

Tom looked up, inwardly smiled, and then said, 'Okay. Why don't you both sit down? You look as though you have got something interesting to say.'

Milner, now having returned to his usual professional and methodical manner, provided him with the latest update. 'It does look almost certain the body is that of Mr Burton. More documentation was found in the glove compartment with his name on it. Insurance details, car service history *et cetera*.' He paused briefly. When it became obvious that no questions were forthcoming, he continued. 'I also spoke with the pathologist, who said he would not be carrying out the full PM until later in the week. Although there has, inevitably, been some deterioration, he did confirm that he would prepare the body for identification for tomorrow morning. I just need to let him know what time and he will make sure he's prepared everything.'

Anticipating what DCI Stone's next question was likely to be, he carried straight on. 'I did push him as to the likely cause of death, but, of course, he wouldn't be drawn on this until he'd completed his PM. Nonetheless, he did say that a very superficial examination – and he emphasised the word *very* – had revealed a few marks, on the head, which could be consistent with receiving blows. As far as when he died, he was a bit more forthcoming. Submersion in water can complicate matters, but it was his estimate that this person had died between seven and fourteen days ago. There were also a few bruise marks on both of his shoulders, suggesting, possibly, that someone had been gripping him there tightly, or perhaps trying to push him away.'

'You said *receiving blows*. Plural?'

'Yes, that's right. Apparently, there were at least three and possibly four.'

'That suggests quite a concerted attack,' suggested Tom.

'If that was what killed him, sir. We won't know for sure until we get the full PM report.'

'Yes, thanks for pointing that out to me, Milner. I wouldn't have thought of that myself,' he answered. Before either Milner or DC Bennett could work out if DCI Stone was genuinely annoyed or simply being ironic, he continued. 'But, just hypothetically, let's for the moment assume that Mr Burton died as a result of someone, or, of course, more than one person, repeatedly striking him on the head with something. After that, quite considerable effort then went into trying to hide the car with his body in it. If that was the case, then we are now talking about murder, and so it's more important than ever to find out where Mr Burton went after he left home on that particular Sunday. If I understood you correctly, Milner, that Sunday would fall into the timeframe suggested by the pathologist. That was the last time he was seen. There has been no contact with anyone since then. No record of any recent credit card transactions. And no phone calls or texts apart from the one received by Mrs Burton. So I think we should start to prepare ourselves. I want you both to go back over all your notes and double-check everything. Look for any inconsistencies in timings or statements. And, also, I would like to see the full inventory of the items found in Mr Burton's car.' Tom paused. 'I think we are all agreed that he was a larger-than-life character. He didn't get to be as successful as he was, especially given his background and upbringing, without upsetting a few people along the way. Perhaps one of those people, male or female, has taken it upon themselves to seek revenge.'

By now, Tom was in full thinking-out-loud flow, and clearly relishing the opportunity to, once again, fully immerse himself in a murder inquiry. Both Milner and DC Bennett had been around him long enough to know not to interrupt him when he was like this. His earlier sombre demeanour had disappeared.

Chapter 16

Tom and Milner, together with a uniformed female police officer, had arrived early at Mrs Burton's home and stood outside her front door. The main gate, fortunately, was already open.

The pathologist had contacted Milner, the previous evening, to inform him that the body had been prepared for identification. For Tom, this was the worst part of his job, but experience told him that it was better if it was done as quickly, albeit still as compassionately, as possible.

They had, however, decided not to contact Mrs Burton in order to arrange the meeting. This, they felt, would run the risk of unnecessarily alarming her; there was no need to keep her in suspense. So they had taken the chance that Mrs Burton would be at home and were, therefore, relieved that, when they rang the bell, it was she who opened the door, still wearing her dressing gown.

'Oh my God,' she said, as soon as she saw them, but especially the female officer. 'It's bad news, isn't it?' She immediately began to sob uncontrollably.

'Can we come in?' asked Tom. He didn't wait for her to reply, eager to move her away from the front door, and then almost leading her into the front room. 'Why don't you sit down?'

She sat, a little shakily.

Having earlier thought carefully about what his approach would be, but now taking his lead from her first question, Tom simply said, 'I'm afraid we have found a body and we believe it's your husband.' He paused and then added, 'I'm so sorry.'

For a while, nothing more was said, and the silence was only broken by the sound of Mrs Burton's continuing sobbing.

Tom finally continued. 'Although we do believe it is your husband, it's important that we make formal identification as soon as possible. Do you think that you are able to do this? I totally understand if you don't think you can. We could ask someone else who knew your husband to make the formal identification. Perhaps his business partner, Mr Blackwell?'

Finally, Mrs Burton spoke. 'How am I going to tell the children?'

It was Milner who answered. 'We have trained officers who can help with that.'

This did not seem to reassure Mrs Burton, who, once again, burst into tears.

'Is there anyone you could call to support you?' asked Tom. 'Didn't you say, last time we met, that your mum lives not too far away? Would you like us to contact her?'

Mrs Burton, still clearly finding it difficult to speak, simply nodded in agreement.

'Do you have her number?' asked Tom. 'Is it in your phone?'

'It's under *Mum*,' she somehow managed to say, handing over her mobile to Tom.

He took the phone from her. 'Thank you. I'll go and call her now, if that's okay?'

Once again she just nodded, and Tom headed towards the kitchen in order to make the call.

It was a while before he returned, during which nothing was said by anyone. At last he knocked on the open door and came back into the room. 'I have spoken with your mum. She should be here in about thirty minutes.'

By this time Mrs Burton, her composure sufficiently restored, was able to speak without the previous intermittent sobs. 'Where was he found?' she asked.

'The body was found by a group of divers in an old quarry, alongside the M3, that had filled with water. It looks as though his car had driven over the edge into the water.'

Mrs Burton suddenly looked up. 'What? Do you mean deliberately?'

'That we don't know. We'll have to wait for the results of the post-mortem. Then we will have a better idea.'

'Post-mortem?' she repeated. 'Why?'

'It's standard practice in these types of circumstances,' answered Tom, as vaguely as possible.

'And where is his body now?' she asked.

76

'It's at the mortuary.'

The mention of the word *mortuary* immediately prompted a further outburst of grief. This time, though, it was bordering on hysteria and Tom decided that, at the moment, there was little he could do to help Mrs Burton other than waiting for the grief to eventually subside. When he felt that had occurred he said, 'You told us last time that you have two children. Are they currently at school?'

'Yes. They are both now back at boarding school,' she answered, quietly, before the mention of her children caused her, once again, to cry.

'Whilst we are waiting for your mum to arrive, why don't you get dressed? My officer can help if you want,' Tom said, looking in the direction of the female officer.

'I can manage to dress myself,' Mrs Burton answered, quite sharply. She stood and walked towards the stairs, and then up to her bedroom.

Tom also stood and went towards a cabinet at the side of the room, on which were two photographs, both sitting in identical and expensive frames. One showed a teenage boy and the other one a slightly younger girl, whom he assumed to be Mrs Burton's children. After a while he moved towards the window, which overlooked the river, and stayed there for a while, just staring down at the water, before the silence was broken by the sound of the doorbell ringing.

'I'll get it,' said Milner.

A short while later Milner reappeared, followed by a woman, whom Tom estimated to be in her early sixties. Despite this, the resemblance made it obvious that this was Mrs Burton's mum.

'Where's Jane?' she asked, dispensing with any formalities.

'She's upstairs, getting dressed,' answered Tom.

The woman, without saying anything else, immediately left the room and headed upstairs.

'Should I go with her?' asked Milner.

'No. Let them have some time to themselves first,' Tom answered.

Despite it being such a large house, Mrs Burton could clearly be heard crying. After a while her crying began to lessen, and then, a little later, she and her mum reappeared in the lounge.

'Does Jane really have to do this?' asked her mum in a very distinct London accent. Her tone was quite aggressive.

Tom replied. 'No, she doesn't. I totally understand that this is not easy for Mrs Burton. If there is anyone else who could do it – someone who knew Mr Burton very well – then that would be fine.' He turned to face Mrs Burton. 'We really don't want to make you do something which you don't want to do.' Looking back at her mum, he added, 'Perhaps you could do it?'

Tom's suggestion suddenly prompted Mrs Burton into a burst of anger. 'He's my husband. I will do it. I have to.'

Tom faced her mum, who simply shrugged her shoulders before saying, 'I want to come with her, though.'

'Of course. That's not a problem.'

Chapter 17

Later that same day, and having returned to the station, Tom, Milner and DC Bennett were once again all together in Tom's office.

Not surprisingly, the process of identifying the body had been highly emotional. Despite the fact they had tried to prepare Mrs Burton by suggesting that they strongly believed the body to be that of her husband, nonetheless it still proved to be a traumatic experience for her when she confirmed that to be the case. It was almost as though she had still been desperately clinging on to some faint hope that it might be some other person, but the confirmation had then finally shattered that hope.

After the identification a police officer had driven Mrs Burton, and her mum, back home. It had been agreed that Mrs Burton's mother would be staying with her for the foreseeable future.

Tom was now standing, marker pen in hand, in front of a flip chart, in the centre of which was the name *Glyn Burton*. Immediately below were the names of various other people, all of whom had been identified as having a close connection to the victim. This was a technique which Tom had often used successfully in the past and, whilst there were more technologically up-to-date alternatives available, it was something which seemed to suit his eye and his brain. He had always preferred to write things down. This form of visualisation helped him to organise all his thoughts and find possible, not necessarily obvious connections associated with an ongoing investigation.

He stood back so that he could get a good view of his work. 'So, let's see who we have got. First of all, there's his wife, Jane. What few words could we add under her name? I think *strained relationship* would be a fair summary of their relationship,' he added, without giving the other two the opportunity to answer, as he wrote those two words under *Jane Burton*. 'Then we have Craig Blackwell.'

It was DC Bennett who immediately made a suggestion. 'How about *slimy*?'

This prompted Milner to shoot him a quizzical look.

'I think, for the time being, we'll make do with *business partner*,' said Tom.

'But he was more than a business partner, sir,' said DC Bennett. 'Due to Mr Burton's affair with Mrs Mercer, I would say that he was a very worried business partner.'

'Okay,' answered Tom. 'Let's add *very worried*, then.'

As neither Milner nor DC Bennett responded, Tom carried on, pointing his marker towards the name of *Roger White*. 'There's no connection, other than that they seemed to be close golfing friends.'

'But Mr White was, at one time, a major shareholder at the golf club,' said Milner, 'and he did, fairly recently, sell most of his shares to Mr Burton. I think that is quite a strong connection.'

'Very true,' answered Tom, before writing *sold shares to Mr Burton* under the name. 'Which then brings us on to Mike Preston. He, out of all of them, had the most obvious motive. I'm sure that when one of your golfing buddies has an affair with your wife it can make you do very strange things. With the way you described him, Milner, it was almost as though he was hoping something bad had happened to Mr Burton. Not the behaviour of someone who might be trying to cover their tracks. However, we should put him on the chart.' He wrote *revenge?* under Mike Preston's name.

'Shouldn't we add his wife Amy as well?' suggested Milner.

Before Tom could respond, however, DC Bennett said, 'And, on that basis, I think we should add *possible revenge* alongside Mrs Burton. She is the one who seems to have suffered most by her husband's behaviour.'

'Okay,' said Tom, although his tone suggested that he wasn't entirely convinced. Nonetheless he added both suggestions to the chart. 'Then, finally, there is Mr and Mrs Mercer, Jonathan and Caroline. It's difficult to form a view yet, as we have still to speak to them. But they should both go on the chart, for the very same reasons that Mike and Amy Preston are on it. So I think we should pay the Mercers a visit next, although let's see them separately as we don't know if Mr Mercer knows what's been going on.' He turned to face DC Bennett. 'Let me know when you've done that. I suggest we start with Mrs Mercer.'

'Aren't we getting ahead of ourselves, sir?' asked Milner. 'We still haven't had the full PM report. You always tell us how it's best not to make important decisions until you have all of the information. Isn't there a danger we are trying to fit the available evidence to our theory rather than the other way around?'

Tom suddenly smiled. 'At last, you have finally listened to what I've taught you.' He looked to DC Bennett again. 'But set up the meetings anyway.'

Chapter 18

According to DC Bennett, Mrs Mercer didn't seem to be too surprised to be contacted by the police and readily agreed to meet with him and DCI Stone. It was as if she had been expecting the call. Unsurprisingly, however, she was reluctant to hold the meeting at her own home, making it clear that she would prefer to come to the station, so the meeting had been arranged for early the following morning.

Before she had arrived, however, Milner appeared with a copy of the full post-mortem relating to Mr Burton's death.

'Mr Burton was dead before he went into the water. So it does look as though he was definitely murdered, sir,' he said. 'The cause of death was three blows to the head, one of which was just below the right temple, and it was this which was most likely to have been the fatal blow. There was also bruising near the top of the head. The report suggests that this was almost certainly the result of him hitting the ground. Then there was the bruising on his shoulders suggesting a close struggle, possibly before the fatal blows were made.'

'He was hit repeatedly on the head, then,' said Tom, 'with one of the blows of sufficient force to kill him. He then fell and hit his head on the ground. Just before that the killer appears to have been holding him, quite tightly, by the shoulders.'

'Or trying to push him away,' added Milner.

'That's always possible,' replied Tom. 'Does the report say what it was that was used to hit him?'

'Nothing very precise, I'm afraid, other than that it was probably something fairly small. The bruising would have been much more significant, and the wounds much bigger, if it had been a large weapon. There was a small laceration, under his temple, which suggested something relatively sharp.'

'Any DNA, other than his, on the body?' Tom asked hopefully.

'None, sir,' answered Milner, clearly disappointed. 'Anyway, as the pathologist keeps telling me, any DNA evidence would almost certainly be compromised by the presence of water.'

'And what about the car and all the things inside it? Anything which might give us a clue there?'

'The car, and its contents, are still being examined. I've asked for the report as soon as that's finished. Hopefully, it should be within the next day or two. We should be receiving an inventory of everything that was found in the car later today.'

'Good work,' replied Tom. 'It looks like you've got everything in hand.'

Milner waited for the usual put-down. When none came, he spoke again. 'Do you want me in on the meeting with Mrs Mercer?'

'I know you are starting to become a good judge of character, and it's always best to have more than one perspective – even I don't have a monopoly on that – but I think DC Bennett and I can handle it. And, anyway, I'm sure you have lots of other things you could be doing.'

As Milner was still trying to take in the fact that he had just received two compliments from DCI Stone within the space of a minute, his thoughts were interrupted by DC Bennett's arrival.

'What do we know about her?' asked Tom.

DC Bennett held up a single sheet of A4 paper and began to read from it. 'Mrs Caroline Mercer. Thirty-six years old. Married to Jonathan Mercer. No children, although Mr Mercer has three grown-up children from his first marriage. He's quite a bit older then her – he's fifty-eight – and they married about seven years ago after his first wife died. Apparently, she had been his secretary.'

'Well, if she and Mr Burton had been having an affair then it looks like the curse of the seven-year itch has struck again.'

'That's definitely a possibility, sir,' DC Bennett said. 'It's possible, of course, that their age difference might have been another reason.' He looked back at the paper. 'Looks like they are quite wealthy. They live in one of those very expensive areas in North London. Mr Mercer is the owner of an import–export company which specialises in fine art, jewellery, gold, diamonds. That type of thing.'

'That would explain, then, why he was Mr Burton's biggest client. I suppose you have to do something with all of that money,' Tom replied. 'And what about Mrs Mercer? Does she still work at her husband's company?'

'Not as far as I can see,' answered DC Bennett. 'She's certainly not on the list of company directors. They seem to be Mr Mercer's own children.'

Just then another officer stuck his head around the door to say that Mrs Mercer had just arrived.

DC Bennett went to get her whilst Tom walked the short distance to the room they had chosen to conduct the interview. A couple of minutes later, DC Bennett returned along with Mrs Mercer.

'This is Detective Chief Inspector Stone,' DC Bennett said. 'Please take a seat. Can I get you anything to drink?'

'Nothing for me, thank you,' she answered, before sitting down.

Mrs Mercer was of above-average height and wore a black knee-length coat and matching boots. These, together with her long blonde hair, sparkling blue eyes and almost perfect complexion and make-up, suggested someone who paid a lot of attention to appearance. If that was the case then she was very successful. Although Tom knew, from DC Bennett's briefing notes, that she was thirty-six years old, she could quite easily pass for someone ten years younger from where he sat.

'Thank you for coming in, Mrs Mercer. We do appreciate it.' Without any further preamble or pleasantries, he got straight to the point. 'As you know, a friend of yours, Mr Glyn Burton, disappeared some time ago. I'm afraid to say that his body has recently been found.'

Tom had suddenly realised he didn't actually know if she was aware that his body had been found, but now it was too late. The sudden expression of shock on her face immediately provided the answer. Whatever little colour was in her face instantly disappeared.

'Oh my God,' she cried, tears suddenly mixing with her mascara to roll down her cheeks, leaving some black streaks on her face. 'Are you saying Glyn is dead?'

'I'm afraid so,' he answered. 'I'm really sorry to have to break the news to you like this.'

For a while, nothing more was said until Tom judged that he could continue.

'As I said, I apologise that you had to hear it like that. I thought you might have known. Please take your time.' He handed her a box of tissues.

'Thank you,' she said, taking one of the tissues from the box and wiping her eyes with it. 'I knew he was missing, but I ... I never expected this. How did he die?'

'We are still trying to determine that,' replied Tom, making the decision that it was probably best to limit how much they told her. 'His body was found in his car in a lake.'

'Was it an accident?' she asked, between fresh sobs.

'As I said, that's something we are still trying to find out. Is there any reason why you might think that it might have been an accident?'

'Well, it certainly wasn't suicide. Glyn wasn't that type of person. He was so full of life,' she said, before starting to cry again. 'Or are you saying that he was murdered?' she asked, incredulity clear in the tone of her voice.

'That's what we are still trying to determine,' he answered. 'I'm afraid, at this stage, we are not ruling out anything.' Once again, he waited patiently before continuing. 'I understand you and Mr Burton were close friends. When was the last time you saw him and how did he seem to you?'

She wiped her eyes, looked directly at Tom. 'We were more than just friends. We had been in a relationship for a few months. I loved him. I'm not ashamed of that,' she said, before the shock of realising he was dead once again took hold of her emotions.

During the pause DC Bennett stood up, walked towards the water cooler, filled a plastic cup and then placed it in front of her.

'Thank you,' she said, before taking a small sip. This seemed to revive her as she was then able to continue. 'The last time was on the Sunday he disappeared. He called me to say he wanted to meet up. It was a surprise, as I knew he played golf every Sunday morning, but apparently for some reason he had decided not to play that particular morning.'

'Can you remember what time that was?' asked DC Bennett.

'He called me at about ten o'clock and we met about thirty minutes later.'

'So, at about ten thirty,' he said, whilst writing the time in his notebook. 'Where was that?'

'Probably a few minutes after that. Say, ten thirty-five. I arrived just before Glyn. We met in a coffee place just off the North Circular Road. We'd met there before. It's about halfway between where he lived and my home. When I got there I ordered us a couple of coffees and by the time I'd got them he'd arrived.'

'And what did you discuss?'

Mrs Mercer seemed to take a deep breath before answering. 'Glyn had decided to leave his wife. Apparently, they'd had a big row the night before and that was what finally decided it for him. I knew he was unhappy, and it was then he told me how he just couldn't go on like that. We were discussing when it would happen and, of course, what we would do.'

'So you had also decided to leave your husband. Is that right?' asked Tom.

'I had, yes. I told you. I loved Glyn and he loved me.'

'So, when was all this going to happen?' asked DC Bennett, his tone suggesting he somehow doubted it would have happened at all.

Now she focussed her gaze on him. 'We had still to decide when I would tell Jonathan and Glyn would tell his wife. But,' she added, with a degree of forcefulness which surprised them, 'we were going to do it. We had discussed it before, but ... well, there were complications.'

'What type of complications?' asked Tom.

'I'm not sure if you are married,' she answered, looking directly at Tom. 'But, when there are children involved, it does tend to create complications. Although Glyn's children are not small, they are both at a difficult age and Glyn was concerned about the effect it would have on them.'

Tom almost wished he had not asked that particular question, especially given the latest news regarding his own son. It immediately brought back the feelings of guilt he had been recently experiencing.

Fortunately for him, DC Bennett suddenly said, 'Have you ever visited Mr Burton's flat in London?'

'If you mean "have I ever stayed there with him overnight", then the answer is yes. I've been there quite a few times in the past few months. In fact, I was there on that Sunday evening waiting for him, but ...'

'Please take your time,' said Tom.

Mrs Mercer paused for a moment before she continued. 'We'd agreed to discuss exactly what we would do when we were back together at his flat. He did mention, though, that he had to be back at his office the following day for some sort of meeting. Anyway, after we'd met at the coffee place, I went home and packed a few things and then drove to the flat. I arrived at about six o'clock that evening and I was expecting him a bit later. When he hadn't arrived by seven o'clock, I called him a few times, but I couldn't get through.'

'So, what did you do then? Did you go home or stay there?'

'I left it until ten o'clock and then decided to go home. I just couldn't stand the thought of being there by myself.'

'You must have been very worried,' suggested Tom.

'I was, yes. It wasn't like him not to return my calls. I kept trying again all the next day but, again, still couldn't get through. Then I began to really get worried and wondered if ...' She wiped a few tears from her eyes. 'I wondered if he'd changed his mind about us.'

'Was that likely? I thought everything had been agreed?'

'So did I,' she answered. 'When he arrived at the coffee shop, he seemed quite excited.'

'When he arrived?' asked Milner. 'Did he say why that was?'

'I did ask him, but he just said it was something to do with business and that he had to meet someone later that day to finalise a deal.'

'Do you have any idea who that might have been?'

'No. He just said he had to meet someone. I didn't ask him who it was, as it concerned his business. And anyway, to be honest, I was more concerned about what we were going to do.'

She suddenly started to cry again as the memory of what they had planned together took over her emotions.

Tom handed her a tissue and, after a moment, said, 'I assume your husband didn't know about all of this.'

She shook her head. 'I don't think so. We had been very careful whenever we met. Jonathan spends quite a bit of time out of the country on business, which made it easier, and that's where he was on that particular Sunday. He'd left on the previous Friday morning and wasn't due back until the following Monday evening.'

DC Bennett continued with the questioning. 'I understand your husband is a client of Mr Burton's. Is that correct?'

'Yes, he is. That's how Glyn and I met. He had invited both of us to a social function, but Jonathan had to unexpectedly leave early. I stayed, and we just seemed to get on so well together. A few days later he came to the house to drop off some papers for Jonathan to sign. Jonathan had just left on one of his trips. As I said, we seemed to get on so well together.' She paused momentarily. 'We didn't mean it to happen.'

DC Bennett didn't respond.

'Have you ever fallen in love?' she asked, looking directly at him.

Tom was suddenly also genuinely interested in DC Bennett's answer. Unfortunately for him, Mrs Mercer continued without waiting for a response. 'If you have, then you will know that it's something you can't really control, and you do things without even thinking about the likely consequences.'

'But you did think about Mr Burton's children,' suggested DC Bennett.

'We did, yes. But only once we both realised it was more than just a brief fling.' Suddenly, it was as though she were completely opening her heart. 'You might not believe this, Detective Constable Bennett, but, up to this point, I had never been unfaithful to Jonathan. In fact, I never even looked at a man in that ... well, in that way. Don't you think I kept asking myself if this was truly different? And every time I did, I came back with the same answer.' She shook her head. 'I loved Glyn and wanted to be with him.'

Tom decided to intervene and bring the discussion back to more mundane matters. 'What time did Mr Burton leave on the Sunday?'

'Around eleven fifteen. We didn't stay together long because, as I've said, we'd already agreed to meet up later that day at the flat.'

'And you didn't hear from Mr Burton again? Not even a text or phone call?'

'I've told you already,' she answered, for the first time showing signs of anger. 'I tried to call him, but he wasn't answering.'

'One final question,' said Tom. 'Did he ever mention his business whilst you were together?'

'What do you mean?'

'Well, for example, any problems, any other clients. That type of thing.'

'Nothing,' she quickly replied. 'Not even about his dealings with Jonathan.'

'Were you aware that your husband was Mr Burton's biggest client?'

'No, I wasn't,' she replied. 'But, even if I had been, it would not have made any difference. I don't know how many times I have to say this, but I loved Glyn and I think he loved me.'

'Thank you very much, Mrs Mercer. We appreciate you coming to the station. I know this can't have been easy. Is there anything we can do for you?'

'Nothing,' she replied, once again wiping away her tears. 'Unless you can bring him back.'

Everyone stood.

'What happens next?' she asked. 'You won't have to speak with my husband, will you?'

'What happens next is that we will continue with our inquiries until we have determined just how Mr Burton died,' replied Tom, choosing not to answer her last question.

*

'What do you think?' asked Tom, after Mrs Mercer had left.

DC Bennett frowned. 'She clearly loved Mr Burton. That came across loud and clear. What we don't know, of course, is if he felt the same. I know he told her that he had decided to leave his wife, but it's one thing to say it and quite another, when it comes to it, to actually carry it out. I have to say, though, that she did give the impression she'd thought through all of the possible implications of what they were going to do.'

'Apart, of course, from the one where Mr Burton is murdered,' added Tom, quite cryptically. 'Try and get hold of any CCTV footage that might be available from the coffee shop. It would be interesting to see them both together as well as being useful for checking the timelines.' There then followed one of his characteristic pauses. 'She also mentioned how, when he arrived, he seemed to be in an excited mood. Later in the day, though, something seems to have happened which changed his mood. I wonder what that was.'

Chapter 19

Later that same evening Tom and Mary were having dinner together at her house.

Previously they had spoken about Tom selling his own home in Staines and, in fact, he'd even placed his house on the market, but nothing had happened, and, in truth, he had not really pushed it any further. There had been a few discussions regarding marriage as well, but the idea of this had also seemed to cool of late. It was almost as though they were both content with the current arrangements and so couldn't bring themselves to make the final jump.

In the past, it seemed to Tom, it had been the crises in his life – both personal and professional – which had provided the motivation to take their relationship further. He suspected that perhaps Mary had recognised this in his behaviour, and for that reason was reluctant to initiate any discussion about making their relationship more formal. So now they found themselves at a sort of relationship impasse with neither of them, for their own different reasons, willing to raise the issue. Fortunately for both, the impending visit of Tom's son Paul and his family was a convenient distraction, even though it brought its own anxieties.

'Now we know the dates, have you thought about taking some time off work when they are here?' she asked.

The truth was that Tom hadn't considered that, other than, perhaps, the odd day.

She immediately continued. 'Because I think you should. They are only planning to stay in the London area for about a week before they travel up to the Midlands to visit your ex-wife's brother. So I think you should try and spend as much time as possible with them before they go back home. It might be a long time before you get the chance to see them all again.'

Mary had now received confirmation from Paul regarding

their itinerary. They had booked their first week's accommodation in a hotel on the Cromwell Road, using it as a base to sightsee in London. So far, however, there had been no discussions regarding when or where they would all meet. As Mary had made the initial contact Tom accepted that all communication had been between her and Paul. Notwithstanding this, he still found it strange that this should be the case.

As he heard what Mary was suggesting he suddenly felt a sense of apprehension. He was not, by any stretch of the imagination, a romanticist, where everything ended happily ever after. In his experience, he had found it was usually best to expect disappointment and so prepare accordingly. Mary's first inclination, however, was always to believe that things would work out well.

'That's a good idea,' he answered, as positively as he could. 'I'll try and make sure that I plan for the time off.' He hesitated. 'As I've just had some time away, it might be a bit difficult, but hopefully it will still be possible.'

Mary, recognising exactly what Tom was trying to do, immediately responded. 'I thought you said you still had a few weeks' holiday to take. I'm sure they can do without you for another few days.' There was rising annoyance in her voice. 'You are not indispensable, you know. That's why you have other people working for you. I'm sure David is perfectly capable of doing whatever is required whilst you are away. And anyway,' she added, her annoyance turning to borderline anger, 'this is your family we are talking about. If you can't find the time for them, after all these years, then ...' Her voice suddenly tailed off, before quickly resuming. 'Well, what chance is there for us?'

She hadn't meant to reopen this tricky subject, but it was clear her anger had got the better of her. It was a recurring issue between the two of them and the source of most of their problems that he always seemed to put his career before any personal relationships.

There followed a tense silence, with neither of them quite trusting themselves to respond without making the situation worse. Finally, though, it was Tom who spoke. 'You are right. I'm sorry, especially after everything you've done to arrange this. To be honest I'm a bit nervous about seeing Paul again and how things will turn out. You are very fortunate that you still see your own children and grandchildren regularly. You have a normal relationship with them. Mine is anything but normal. I haven't seen my own son – in fact, my only son – for about thirty years. And that was because of my own actions. I didn't even know I had grandchildren. How do you think that makes me feel about myself? So I'm not expecting him to greet me as if everything is normal. In fact, if I were Paul, I would certainly want some answers, especially to why I hadn't tried to contact him for all of those years.'

Tom's honesty seemed to take Mary by surprise and she suddenly reached across and kissed him on the cheek. 'Don't you think he will be just as nervous as you? Probably more so, given that Detective Chief Inspector Stone's successes have travelled as far as Australia.' She hesitated. 'I think, for the very first time, you have let your guard down. That's the most honest thing I've ever heard you say. I know it's not easy, but I do like you much more when you show your true feelings, rather than always putting up some sort of barrier.'

She took his hand. 'Don't you realise that I'm here to help? Please don't think you have to do all of this by yourself. Why don't you just try and enjoy the time you have together? If things work out well, then great. If they don't go as everyone hopes, then at least you will have the memory of seeing him and his family, two of whom, let's not forget, are your own grandchildren.'

For the second time in about a minute Tom simply said, 'You're right.' He leant forward and kissed her. 'What would I do without you?'

Chapter 20

'So, this is everything that was found in Mr Burton's car, is it?' asked Tom, a sheet of paper in his hand. It was early the next morning and he was once again with Milner and DC Bennett in his office.

After his heart-to heart with Mary the previous evening, Tom had woken feeling much more enthusiastic about meeting Paul and his family. He knew what Mary had said was right. Perhaps he had just needed her to say it to him as she seemed to be the only who could break through his natural emotional barrier, or possibly the only one who he would allow to do it. Either way, whilst, at his age, he was unlikely to change his personality, he recognised he could no longer just pay lip service to what she had to say when it came to their relationship. He also knew that he did want to spend the rest of his time with her, but it was now up to him to take the final step.

'That's everything, sir,' replied Milner. 'In fact, you'll see there are three lists. The first one shows everything found on Mr Burton's body and the second one lists everything that was still in the car. The car itself has now been fished out of the quarry and is currently being examined by a specialist forensics team. There have also been divers searching for anything which might have fallen out of, or off, the car and sunk lower. Their findings are shown on list three. Nothing of any significance there, I'm afraid, just the sort of things you would expect to find when there has been an impact. The odd piece of bumper and metal which must have broken off, together with some pieces of glass. The boot had apparently sprung open when it hit the water, and so a few things probably also fell out then. Anyway, the divers say they've found as much as they are ever likely to find.'

Tom spent some time looking at the list again, before handing it back to Milner. 'And they didn't find Mr Burton's phone?'

'That's everything which was retrieved,' confirmed Milner.

'Okay, anyway, let's hope forensics find something, then,' Tom said, disappointment clearly apparent in his tone.

DC Bennett, sensing this, asked, 'Do you think Mr Burton's phone is important, sir?'

'I think so, yes,' he answered. 'I suspect that someone like Mr Burton spent a lot of time on his phone, and so it's likely to be a real goldmine of information. It would help if we knew who he'd recently been speaking with. Mrs Mercer mentioned how Mr Burton seemed to be in a good mood when they met on the Sunday morning. It might have been the result of a phone call he'd either received or made. Later, though, according to his wife, his mood had changed. Anyway,' he added, looking at the flip chart in the corner of the office, 'I think we now need to have a little chat with Mr Mercer, as well as speaking again with Mr White. I don't think we should go in too mob-handed with Mr Mercer. We don't want to go charging in asking him about his wife's affair, especially if he had no idea what had been going on between his wife and Mr Burton. At this stage let's simply focus on their business relationship and find out when they last spoke. General stuff. I think this calls for someone with experience and tact. As I'm not available, I think you, DC Bennett, should go and see him. I know how much you like the world of high finance.'

DC Bennett didn't reply but, instead, let out a slight laugh, prompting Milner to look towards him with one of his slightly quizzical expressions.

It looked as though Milner was about to say something. Before he could, however, Tom carried on. 'I do think, though, you should push him to confirm where he was on the Sunday.'

Now Milner did say something. 'But didn't Mrs Mercer say that her husband was out of the country on business?'

'Well, that's what she certainly thought. But who knows? He might have been lying, of course. Anyway, let's confirm it one way or the other. In the meantime, you and I, Milner, are going back to the West London Golf Club. So why don't you give them a call to let them know? I'm sure they will be delighted to see us again.'

*

Whilst Milner and DC Bennett were following up on all of this, Tom decided that now might be a good time to speak with his boss, Superintendent Birch, about taking some time off for Paul's visit. It wasn't long before he was standing outside Superintendent Birch's office on the fifth floor.

As usual, Jenny, the superintendent's PA and Milner's 'friend', seemed genuinely delighted to see him. 'I've already got your coffee ready,' she said, after they had finished exchanging pleasantries. 'David – sorry, I mean Detective Sergeant Milner – mentioned how you are both working on a murder investigation. That must be exciting.'

'Well, first of all, Detective Sergeant Milner shouldn't really be discussing this type of thing with you. It's not very professional and I'll need to have a word with him about it.' Tom said this in as jovial a way as he could, but, even so, she seemed to be quite embarrassed about what she'd said. He decided to help her out. 'Don't worry; sometimes I speak to my partner about some of the cases I'm working on. It helps sometimes, although, of course, you do have to be very selective as to whom you discuss them with.' Before she could reply, he added, 'Speaking of partners, how is your relationship with DS Milner? As someone who is always concerned about the wellbeing of his team, it's usually useful to know at least a bit about their personal lives.'

Jenny started to laugh. 'That's not what I heard.'

Under normal circumstances Tom might start to get defensive about such a comment, but with Jenny he had found that was never the case. He always came away from seeing her in a much happier frame of mind.

'To answer your question, though,' she said, 'we seem to be getting on really well together. But, as I told you the last time you asked, it's still early days.' She paused before adding, with a bit more seriousness in her voice, 'Sometimes it's difficult for him to unwind, especially when there is a big investigation going on. I can almost see his mind still thinking about it.'

Tom resisted the temptation to say that it came with the territory and that, based on his own experience, it was only likely to get worse as his career progressed. Instead he simply said, 'That's why he's such a good copper. You never know, it might be him' – pointing towards Superintendent Birch's office – 'sitting in that office someday.'

Coincidentally, the very same door then opened, and Superintendent Birch appeared. 'Morning, Tom. Good to see you. Please come in.'

Tom followed him into the office, followed in turn by Jenny carrying the coffee tray. She placed it on the large table and then walked back out, although not before giving Tom a final friendly smile.

'I understand your missing person investigation has now turned into a murder investigation,' Superintendent Birch said.

'Yes, unfortunately, that's right,' Tom replied, before giving him a brief update.

'Any significant leads so far?'

'Not at the moment, although we do have a number of different things we are pursuing. It seems there are several people he has come into contact with recently who didn't especially like him, but that, of course, doesn't mean that they would murder him. One thing all this has done, however, is expose me to the world of golf. I always thought it was something elderly men did after they had retired, but it would seem that's not the case.'

'What do you mean?' asked Superintendent Birch.

Tom suddenly had a thought. 'You're not a golfer yourself, are you, sir?'

'Actually, I am,' he answered. 'I've been playing for over twenty years. It's something I really look forward to. It seems to help me relax. And as far as I know I haven't retired yet.'

'Well, according to Mrs Burton, his golf did exactly the opposite and he often came back more stressed than when he left.'

Superintendent Birch started to laugh. 'Actually, that's true as well. You have to understand that all golfers are masochists. Otherwise why would we return every week to put ourselves through the same stressful few hours? I have yet to meet any golfer, amateur or professional, who doesn't still, at least occasionally, beat themselves up after playing a round of golf. Sometimes the feeling lasts until you get the chance to play again. Even then you never fully know what's going to happen. In fact, with golf, you never quite know what's going to happen from one shot to the next.'

'So why do you still play?' Tom asked, genuinely interested.

'Because we like to. It's that simple. It's the thought that, one day – just one day – you will have the perfect round,' he answered, almost wistfully. 'But I accept it's difficult for non-golfers to understand that.'

'Strange,' replied Tom, still struggling to understand the logic. 'What I have found out, though, is that being a member of a golf club is much more than just playing the game. Infidelity, high finance, envy and jealousy all seem to be there. Well, at least at the West London Golf Club.'

'I suspect that they are far from being the exception,' answered Superintendent Birch.

For a moment, Tom thought about asking him to explain, but instead he said, 'Anyway, I'll keep you updated. Although, if I need to learn more about the goings-on at golf clubs, I now know who to speak with.'

Taking Tom's lead, Superintendent Birch then said, 'You asked to speak with me. Nothing serious, I hope. It seems, just lately, when you ask to speak, it's never about anything mundane.'

'Well, there's always a first time and I think today is that day,' replied Tom, in an equally light tone of voice. 'I just wanted to ask if it would be okay if I took some more time off. I wouldn't normally, especially after just returning from holiday, but something has cropped up at home which means I will need to be around.'

Although Superintendent Birch had not been in charge of the station for too long, he did know Tom's reputation for being a real workaholic. 'Is everything okay?' he asked, his earlier joviality now replaced with concern.

'Everything is fine,' Tom answered. 'It's just that my son Paul and his family will be visiting the UK soon and I would like to spend time with them before they return to Australia.'

'I'm sorry, Tom, but I didn't know you had a son. I knew you had been married but not that you had family.'

So Tom told him about his family. In fact, he found himself perhaps saying more than he had intended. He told him about the failed marriage. He told him about how his ex-wife had then taken their son to live in Australia and that he hadn't seen Paul since that time. He told him how it had been Mary who had established contact with his son. He even told him just how apprehensive he was feeling about seeing Paul, after so much time had gone by.

As he did this he suddenly realised that, even though he was now in his mid-fifties, he didn't have any real close friends. Yes, he had many acquaintances and colleagues, but no one who he felt comfortable confiding in. In fact, when he had finished, he felt much better, glad that he had found someone he could open up to.

This wasn't lost on Superintendent Birch. 'I appreciate you sharing this with me, Tom. You really didn't need to, though. I know you well enough to realise that if you ask for time off then there must be a good reason.' He paused. 'It's not for me to offer you any advice, but ... I will do anyway,' he said, a slight laugh in his voice. 'Just enjoy the experience and the time you have together. I'm sure your son will be feeling equally nervous.'

'That's exactly what Mary said.'

'She sounds like a wise woman,' replied Superintendent Birch.

'Yes, she is,' Tom said, more to himself than in reply.

'Tom, there's something I'd like to speak with you about,' said Superintendent Birch, this time in a far more serious tone. 'I was going to wait a while before I told you, but I think now might be as good a time as any.'

'You're not making me take retirement, are you?' he asked, still in the light-hearted manner of their previous conversation.

'Is that what you want?'

'No. Well, not yet anyway.'

'No, it's not about that. I wanted to update you on the situation regarding Commander Jenkins and Charles Cope.' He paused briefly before continuing. 'I suspect you are not going to like what I tell you, but I thought you should hear it from me rather than from someone else. Commander Jenkins will be retiring from the force at the end of this month. Charles Cope will resign from his role as an MP at the same time. The official explanation will be that he has some health problems. Confidentially, I understand that, like you, he has also recently established contact with his son and wants to try and spend time with him and his family. It's rather ironic, really, don't you think, that it was you who first told him he had a son?'

Superintendent Birch fell silent, allowing Tom to comment

on what he had just been told. Eventually Tom responded. 'It doesn't surprise me. I could see which way the wind was blowing some time ago. Does this mean that any charges will be dropped and that there will now not be a court case?'

'It looks that way, I'm afraid,' Superintendent Birch replied, surprised by Tom's calm response.

'And that they will retire with their index-linked, gold-plated pensions, I suppose?'

He chose not to reply specifically to Tom's question. 'What they won't have is any official recognition for their time in office. No knighthoods or other honours. I suspect, more importantly, though, they will not have the respect of their peers. At least, that is, from those who know the details.'

'It still sends a message, though, that, if you are in a certain position, then you can, literally, get away with murder. It seems that, actually, you *can* be above the law.'

'I'm sorry, Tom. I know it's easy for me to say, but I'll say it anyway. I don't agree with it, and, incidentally, for what it's worth, neither does DCS Small. My understanding is that even the Commissioner himself fought against this decision. Frankly it stinks. But the decision was a political one and so, ultimately, was taken out of our hands. They believed there might be a security risk, and that it was not, therefore, in the national interest for this to become public.'

'I suppose it also means that the confidentiality order I signed will remain valid.'

Superintendent Birch simply nodded in agreement. 'The same will have to apply to DS Milner and DC Bennett. It's likely you all will receive a visit from the security services to remind you of that point.'

For a few moments nothing else was said. At last Tom spoke again. 'It makes a mockery of everything I've stood for over the past nearly forty years. And, to be honest, it makes it difficult for me to continue as a police officer, knowing this.'

Chapter 21

It was a somewhat deflated DCI Stone who returned to his own office on the second floor. Waiting for him were Milner and DC Bennett, and his demeanour was not lost on either of them.

Typically, given their long association, it was the latter who raised this. 'Are you all right, sir?'

'Perfectly all right, thank you,' he lied.

Not quite believing him, DC Bennett spoke again. 'You don't seem to be your usual self.'

'And what is my usual self, DC Bennett?' Tom asked, immediately regretting his slightly tetchy reply.

'Well, for a start, by now you'd be asking us what we'd been up to over the past couple of hours and whether or not we'd followed up on what you had previously asked us to do.'

A thin smile appeared on Tom's face. 'You really do know me too well. Am I that predictable?' he asked, clearly not expecting any answer. 'It relates to the Jenkins–Cope case. All I can say is that you should not, under any circumstances, speak to anyone – friends, family, partners, colleagues, and I mean *anyone* – about this. Also, you should expect to receive a visit from the security authorities shortly, who will, no doubt, reinforce this point.'

'Does that mean they are not going to charge them both?' asked Milner, a hint of incredulity in his voice.

'It looks that way,' Tom simply replied. 'Anyway, my strong advice to you both is to now forget all about it.'

'But what about—' Milner began, before he was abruptly interrupted by Tom.

'Milner, please stop. I don't want to hear you even mention it ever again. Have I made myself clear?'

'Yes, sir,' he replied, taken aback by Tom's strength of feeling. 'Perfectly.'

Tom waited for a moment, until the full implications of what he had just said had sunk in, before continuing. 'Right, let's start applying ourselves and solve this murder. As you seem to have anticipated my questions, I hope you can now answer them.'

It was a still less than enthusiastic Milner who took up the conversation. 'DC Bennett is meeting with Mr Mercer this evening and I've arranged for us to see Roger White at three o'clock this afternoon. In the meantime, I've been chasing up forensics to see if they have, at least, a preliminary report.'

'And?' asked Tom, hopefully.

'So far they haven't found anything unusual. They made the point, yet again, that any DNA evidence would almost certainly have been affected by its contact with water. But, apparently, there are new techniques being developed all the time. So they haven't given up hope entirely of making some sort of breakthrough.'

Now DC Bennett spoke. 'We do, though, have some interesting news from the techies. You'll remember that they took away Mr Burton's computer. Well, they did whatever it is they do and sent me a report. As I said, there are a few interesting things which they found.'

'Such as?' asked Tom, now fully engaged.

'Well, for starters, there have been a number of unusual cash transactions, and most of them were outgoings.'

'Why would that be unusual?' asked Tom. 'Surely that's what you would expect anyway in their type of business.'

'It's the timing and scale of them.' DC Bennett referred to his notebook. 'Looking at the bank statement, it seems that £5,000 was withdrawn, each month, for the two months leading up to Mr Burton's disappearance. The last one was just a few days previously. At first I thought that they might be repayments, or some sort of dividend, paid to an investor, but, when I checked further, I found that they were all withdrawn in cash. If it had been an investor then I would have thought that the money would have been paid by electronic transfer. Also, there doesn't seem to be any paperwork confirming any such transfer.'

'Hmm,' said Tom. 'That is a bit unusual. Who withdrew the money?

'Craig Blackwell,' he simply answered.

'It might be that it is a coincidence and he just needed the cash for something,' suggested Tom.

'That's always possible,' said Milner. 'But haven't you always said that you don't believe in coincidences?' This was not the first time Milner had reminded DCI Stone about this and, no doubt, wouldn't be the last, but he still quite clearly enjoyed doing so.

'So that's now both of you who seem to know me a little too well for my liking,' Tom replied, taking the opportunity to lighten the mood after their earlier discussion. 'I think we should go and pay another visit to your favourite person, DC Bennett, and see what he has to say about it.'

'Is there something going on which I'm not privy to?' asked Milner.

'Mr Blackwell, for some reason, doesn't seem to be DC Bennett's cup of tea. Personally, I think DC Bennett is just jealous of his good looks. Plus, of course, he's also quite wealthy.'

Although Tom had said this, at least partly, in jest, DC Bennett clearly failed to see the funny side. 'He might be wealthy, but he suddenly had to find another £5,000 each month for something. You mark my words,' he said as he made his way out of the office, 'that man is up to something and I'm determined to find out what it is.'

Tom and Milner were now alone in the office. 'Why is DC Bennett so fixated on Craig Blackwell?' asked Milner. 'It's almost becoming personal. Do you think I should have a word with him?'

Tom looked directly at him. 'And what are you going to say? Just ignore what your instincts are telling you. My advice is to allow him his head – well, at least up to a certain point. I'm sure there will come a time when the evidence will answer DC Bennett's theory, one way or another.' He paused and then added, 'But, of course, it's your call. You are his boss.'

Milner, on his way out of the office, suddenly stopped and turned to face Tom. 'Sir,' he said, in a quiet but nonetheless clearly concerned tone, 'you are not going to do something silly with that copied file relating to Commander Jenkins and Charles Cope, are you?' This was a reference to the file which Tom had, at one stage, asked Milner to look after for him.

Tom was momentarily taken aback by Milner's obvious concern for his wellbeing. 'Just make sure you and DC Bennett do as I suggested,' he replied.

Chapter 22

This time, Tom and Milner were able to find the West London Golf Club much more easily than the last time they had been there. As they drove through the gates, they were also able to take in more of the features of the club.

'There's so much land here, sir,' said Milner. 'You wouldn't expect it, with it being so close to London.'

'That's just what I was thinking,' said Tom. 'It's like a large, hidden oasis. Unless you've been here before, you just wouldn't know it even existed.'

'Perhaps that's the intention,' replied Milner.

They parked the car and got out.

'So it must have been around here where Mr Burton and Mr Preston did their pushing and shoving. It would certainly have been in full view of everyone.' Tom said, pointing towards the nearby clubhouse, which directly overlooked the car park. 'I wonder what the other members made of that. Anyway, as we're a bit early, let's go for a little walk,' he suggested, before heading towards the eighteenth green, on which a group of golfers were still playing.

Tom and Milner stood watching them until they had all finished playing, shaken hands and then started to walk back towards the clubhouse.

'Very civilised. Good manners,' Tom whispered to Milner.

'Can we help you?' one of the golfers suddenly asked.

'We were just admiring the view,' replied Tom. 'It's a beautiful golf course.'

'You do know this is private land?' said one of the other golfers, quite threateningly. 'It's for members only.'

'Yes, we are aware of that,' answered Tom, in a matter-of-fact manner. He then took out his ID card and showed it to the man who had challenged him. 'I'm Detective Chief Inspector Stone, from West London police, and this is my colleague, Detective Sergeant Milner.' He glanced at Milner, who also showed his card. 'We are investigating the murder of one of your members. Mr Glyn Burton.'

Tom was certain they already knew Mr Burton's body had been found and that a missing person inquiry had now turned into a murder investigation. Nonetheless he paused, briefly, allowing what he had just said to fully register with all of them. It seemed to work as it was clear that he now had their full attention.

'Did any of you gentlemen consider yourself to be close friends with Mr Burton?' asked Milner.

It was the man who had spoken first who responded. 'Not really. To be quite frank with you, he wasn't the type of person who seemed to have many close friends. There were a few people who he played with regularly, but, other than that, he kept himself to himself.'

'But I understand Mr Burton held quite a senior position within the club?' asked Tom. 'Surely that meant he met lots of people?'

'Yes, he did, but that doesn't mean they were all friends. Mr Burton had only been a member for a few years. Many others have been members for considerably longer than that. Mr Burton provided financial help to the club at a time when it was in difficulties. But this club has been around for over a hundred years and, God willing, will be around for another hundred years.' He paused, before continuing. 'During that time, the club has experienced far worse. Do you know, Detective Chief Inspector, that a few German bombs were dropped here during the last war? If it could survive that then I'm certain it could survive anything.'

'Do I take it you didn't especially like Mr Burton?' asked Milner.

'Personally, I didn't dislike him, but that's not to say I would have gone out of my way to spend time in his company.'

'Why was that?'

'This is a very traditional golf club and that's the way we like it. Personally, I don't like change. As I said, we have survived for a very long time without having to make the changes which some of the other clubs felt they had to, just so they could claim to be modern. Mr Burton thought differently.'

'In what way did he think differently?' asked Milner.

'Well, for starters he wanted to completely refurbish the clubhouse.'

'Wouldn't that be a good thing?' asked Milner, clearly puzzled as to why there would be any objections.

'We like it this way. It's what gives the club its unique atmosphere. If I wanted to be a member of a more modern club, then I'd join ... well, I'd go elsewhere.'

'Surely any refurbishment would cost a considerable amount of money, especially given the age of the club,' suggested Tom. 'As it had only recently experienced financial problems, where would that money come from?'

'That's a very good question. I suppose we'll never know now.'

'Yes, I think that might be correct,' said Tom. He then moved on to another issue. 'Presumably you all knew about the altercation between Mr Burton and Mr Preston. How did you feel about that?'

This time it was one of the others, who so far hadn't said anything, who answered. He was a tall man, probably in his early sixties, with a full head of almost white hair. 'It was unseemly. Whatever their differences, they shouldn't be settling them in the car park. This is a golf club, not a boxing ring.'

'I'm sorry,' said Tom. 'I didn't catch your name.'

'I'm Nigel Robertson and I'm the club captain,' he answered in a way which suggested a degree of not just pride but also authority.

'I understand Mr Preston has now left the club,' said Tom.

'He most certainly has. Frankly, after such behaviour, the club had no choice but to ask him to leave.'

Tom couldn't suppress his surprise. 'I thought he left of his own volition.'

'He was asked to leave. We can't condone that sort of behaviour,' Mr Robertson replied.

'So why wasn't Mr Burton asked to leave?'

'The committee's view was that, in this particular instance, Mr Burton had been the victim. He might have had a relationship with Mr Preston's wife, but the physical attack on him, within the club grounds, was totally unjustified. We are not here to judge people's morals, just their behaviour,' Mr

Robertson said. 'Now, unless you have any more questions, we would like to get back into the warmth of the clubhouse.'

As neither Tom nor Milner had anything else to say to them, they all headed in the direction of the clubhouse, leaving the two of them alone alongside the eighteenth green.

'It was interesting how no one expressed any regret about Mr Burton's death,' said Tom. 'I thought you said Mr Preston had told you he left voluntarily?'

'He did. He certainly didn't mention to me, when I spoke with him, that he'd been asked to leave,' said Milner.

'It's becoming apparent he's not the only one who hasn't been telling us the full story. Let's go and hear what Mr White is willing to now tell us.'

Chapter 23

They were now back in the same small room where they had first met Tony Cook and Roger White.

Tom decided the time had long gone for any introductory niceties. 'Mr White, could you please tell us why you sold all of your shares to Mr Burton?'

'I thought I'd already told you,' Mr White immediately answered.

'You didn't so much as tell us you'd sold them. What you implied was that you had about ten percent. In fact, you now have less than one percent.'

'I'm sorry, then, if I misled you. It certainly wasn't intentional.'

Tom was unconvinced, but was willing, for the moment, at least, to let it go. 'But you haven't yet answered my question.'

Mr White looked in the direction of Mr Cook. 'Tony. Would you mind giving us a few moments?'

As Mr Cook was walking out of the room, Tom said, 'Please don't go too far, Mr Cook. I'd like to speak with you after we have finished with Mr White.'

Mr Cook didn't answer, but the level of tension in the room had suddenly increased significantly. When he had left, neither Tom nor Milner spoke, letting the silence do their work for them, and it soon had the desired effect as it was Mr White who finally broke the silence. 'I'm really not sure why this might be of any interest to you in your inquiries. It was purely a private transaction.'

By now, Tom was in no mood for all the continued ambiguity and obfuscation, and his tone clearly reflected this. 'The last time we met we were investigating a missing person. Since then it has turned into a murder inquiry. So I think I am the best judge of whether or not it's of interest. For the last time, I'm asking why you sold most of your shares to Mr Burton. If you don't answer this time, I can only assume you are not willing to tell me. And if that's the case then I will take it that you have something to hide. Do I make myself clear?'

Tom's change to a much harder tone had the desired effect. 'It's all a bit embarrassing, really,' Mr White replied, his earlier air of superiority now seemingly gone. 'That's why I would rather tell you in private.'

Tom was not about to help him and so remained silent.

'Earlier this year I suddenly found myself having to find a considerable amount of money in order to pay off a debt. I knew, of course, what Glyn did, and that he was quite a wealthy man, and so approached him to see if he would help me.'

'And that's why you sold your golf club shares to him, then?' asked Milner.

'Eventually, yes, but initially I simply asked if he could loan me the money.' He quickly added, 'I did, though, offer to pay interest on the loan. I might have made some bad decisions, but I'm not the sort of man who shirks his responsibilities.'

'How much were you asking for?' asked Tom.

'It was about £150,000,' he answered, a little uncomfortably.

'Was it a gambling debt?' Tom asked.

'It was, yes. But how did you know that?'

'I didn't,' he replied. 'Just a bit of an educated guess.'

'I'd got myself into difficulties at one of the London casinos. The debt gradually built up, and eventually they would no longer offer me any credit and asked for the debt to be settled in full. That had never happened before. I'd run up losses a few times previously, but had always managed to recover the situation and pay them off. So I was confident I could do it again. All I needed was access to funds and a little time.'

'And Mr Burton was willing to give you this?' asked Tom.

'Yes, well, not initially,' he answered. 'I was looking for a straightforward loan, but Glyn wasn't keen. Instead, he suggested buying my club shares.'

'And how did you feel about that?'

Mr White was now regaining his earlier confidence. 'I would have done everything possible not to have had to do it. This golf club means a lot to me, Detective Chief Inspector Stone. I've been a member here almost from the day I first started playing golf. My father had been a member before me, and many of the best moments in my life were spent playing with him here.' He paused. 'It might be difficult for you to imagine, but this golf club has been my life. So you can see just what a decision it was when I agreed.'

'Did anyone else know about your agreement?' asked Milner.

'No. No one. As you can appreciate, it was not something which I wanted the other members to know about. My plan was always to buy back the shares once I got my finances back in order.'

'And have you got them back in order?'

'Not yet, but things certainly look much better than they did. I had an agreement with him which basically allowed me to buy back at least some of the shares within six months of the date he bought them from me.'

'When was that date?' asked Tom.

'The six-month deadline is in two weeks' time,' he answered.

'So did you recently discuss it with Mr Burton?'

'We had a couple of brief conversations, that's all. I was hoping to finalise it shortly with him, but ...' His voice tailed off.

'But then he died,' said Tom, finishing his sentence for him. 'And what was his reaction to those brief conversations?'

Mr White seemed to hesitate momentarily. Finally, he answered. 'He said he couldn't discuss it at that moment, but should be in a position to do so shortly. I was hoping to have that discussion with him during our round of golf. But, as you know, we didn't play due to the fog.'

Tom remained silent for a while, before saying, 'Do you have a copy of your agreement?'

Roger White looked at Tom quizzically. 'Why would you want to see it? It was never a formal contract, just something we both put together and then signed.'

'I understand, but I'd still like to see it if you don't mind,' Tom said. 'Incidentally, have you spoken with Mr Burton's widow about it? Everything will now pass to her, including, presumably, this arrangement.'

Once again, Mr White looked at Tom with a sense of puzzlement, before simply saying, 'I didn't think the time was right. I assumed she had more important things on her mind than this.'

Tom didn't respond to his comment. 'Thank you, Mr White. If you could provide DS Milner with a copy of the agreement as soon as possible, that would be much appreciated.'

Mr White stood, and was about to walk from the room until Tom stopped him. 'Please remain here, Mr White. We'd now like to speak with you and Mr Cook about another matter.'

This clearly unnerved him. 'I thought you said I could leave.'

'No, I don't believe I did,' Tom answered, before adding, 'DS Milner, would you please ask Mr Cook to come in?'

Nothing more was said between them whilst Milner was out of the room.

'Thank you for waiting,' said Tom as soon as Milner returned with Mr Cook. He got straight to the point. 'When we last spoke, both of you implied that Mr Preston had left of his own accord, as he wanted to spend more time with his young family. That wasn't true, was it?'

For a moment, Tom thought Mr White was about to say something. When he didn't, Tom continued. 'Nonetheless, thank you, Mr Cook, for calling DS Milner to inform him about the fight. It would, though, have saved everyone's time if you had mentioned this when we all last met.'

Still, there was no immediate response from either Mr White or Mr Cook, so Tom continued. 'But we have just been informed by your club captain, a Mr ...'

'A Mr Robertson,' said Milner, referring to his notebook. 'Nigel Robertson.'

'Yes, thank you, DS Milner. In fact, according to Mr Robertson, he was *asked* to leave by the club, after his public disagreement with Mr Burton. Why didn't you mention that as well?'

'To be honest,' answered Mr Cook, 'at the time, I didn't think it was that important why he left. I suppose I was trying to spare him any embarrassment.'

'Frankly, honesty seems to be the one thing in short supply when it relates to this golf club,' answered Tom. Now he really had their attention.

'And also,' added Milner, 'having spoken with Mr Preston, I got the distinct impression that suffering a bit of embarrassment would not unduly worry him in the slightest.'

Tom was now in full flow. 'Just so you are fully aware of the seriousness of the situation, Mr Cook, I will repeat what I said to Mr White when you were out of the room. This is now a murder investigation. The time for playing games, or holding back relevant information, has now passed. If there is anything else either of you wishes to tell us, then now is a good time. Conversely, if we subsequently find out that you have still been withholding information, then you could be charged with perverting the course of justice. So I ask you both, once again: is there anything else which you would like to say to us?'

Tom continued to look at both men, but, when neither man answered, he continued. 'Mr Cook. Where were you between 11 am and 5 pm on the day Mr Burton disappeared?'

He seemed to be genuinely taken aback by this question. 'I'm not sure. It was a few weeks ago.'

'I understand that, but, nonetheless, it was quite a significant day. The day Mr Burton disappeared. You must have thought about it since then.'

'I wasn't working that particular day,' he answered.

'So you do remember. Where were you?'

'I was at home in the morning and then, in the afternoon, decided to go for a run. I'm training for the local half-marathon.'

'And what time was this?'

'I think I left at about two thirty and got back home just before it started to get dark. Just after four o'clock.'

'That's a long time,' said Tom.

'A half-marathon is a long way,' he replied.

'Did you go with someone else or by yourself?'

'By myself.'

'I would appreciate it if you could provide DS Milner with details of where you ran,' Tom said.

'Why?' Mr Cook asked. 'Don't you believe me?'

Tom looked directly at him. 'I'm not sure what to believe any more. Please provide DS Milner with details of your route. One other question. Do you own any shares in the club?'

He seemed to be taken aback by Tom's question but, nonetheless, quickly provided an answer. 'No, I don't. I'm an employee of the club, not a member. It's only members who have shares.'

Tom now faced Mr White. 'The last time we were here you mentioned that you left the club at about noon and went straight home. Is that correct?'

'It is,' he answered.

'And you stayed at home during the rest of the day?'

'Yes.'

'Is there anyone who can confirm that?'

'How dare you?' he asked, his voice level rising significantly. 'First you quiz me about my shareholding and now this.'

'We are police officers, Mr White. A key part of our job is to ask questions,' Tom answered, without any great emotion.

His matter-of-fact reply appeared to have the desired effect. 'I'm sorry,' Mr White said. 'I'm not used to having to deal with police officers. I think it's affected me more than I thought.' He shook his head. 'I was at home by myself. My wife was away that weekend, visiting her sister in Chiswick. She returned home later that evening, at about 7 pm.'

'Thank you,' said Tom. 'One final question. Did either of you contact, or try to contact, Mr Burton, after he had left the club at around 10 am?'

'No,' replied Mr Cook.

'And you, Mr White?'

Mr White's hesitation was not lost on everyone there. Eventually, he said, 'Yes. I called Glyn as I wanted to discuss buying back my shares. As I said, I'd intended to do this during our round of golf, but never got the chance.'

'When was that?' asked Milner, notebook in hand.

'It was not long after Glyn had left the clubhouse. So at about five past ten.'

'And what did he say?' asked Milner.

'He started mentioning complications and that he wasn't in a position to discuss it at the moment.'

'Did he give you any indication as to what the complications were?'

'Of course I asked him that, but he just said he couldn't tell me.'

'That must have made you quite angry,' said Milner.

He looked directly at Milner and said, 'Yes, it did. Very angry. But not so angry that I would want to murder him, if that's what you are suggesting.'

'I'm certainly not suggesting that, Mr White. We would need evidence first.'

The look in Mr White's eyes suggested real anger and so Tom intervened. 'We are simply trying to establish the facts. As I said earlier, it's what we do,' he said in a tone designed to reduce the tension. 'So, after that, you didn't speak to him at all?'

'No, I didn't,' Mr White answered, his voice now matching the calmness in Tom's. 'That is, I didn't speak with him. I did call him later, but his phone went to voicemail.'

'Why did you call him again?'

'I wanted to arrange to meet with him, later that day, so that we could sort it out. But, as I said, it just went to voicemail.'

'What time was that?'

'Somewhere around two forty-five.'

'Did you leave him a message then?'

'Yes. I said I would meet him at 5 pm that evening.'

'Where?'

'There's a lay-by not far from the entrance to the club. I said that I'd meet him there. I thought it might be more private than meeting at the club.'

'But he didn't arrive?'

'No, he didn't. I called again at five past five and again fifteen minutes later, but I couldn't even get through to his voicemail. So, eventually, I decided he wasn't coming and left for home at about five thirty.'

'And he didn't call you back later?' asked Milner.

'No. The last time I actually spoke to him was just after he'd left the club.'

'Thank you both, once again,' said Tom, offering his hand to each man. 'You both now have my card. If there's anything else you subsequently remember, please call me.'

'Will you need to speak with us both again?' asked Mr Cook.

'I would imagine that's a certainty,' replied Tom.

A short while later, Tom and Milner were in the car, heading back to the station.

'What do you make of all that?' Tom suddenly asked.

'It seems that each time we visit the golf club, we learn something new.'

'So what do you think we learnt this time?' asked Tom, interested to know Milner's thoughts.

'Well, firstly, as we suspected, Mr Burton was not universally popular amongst the members. That much was clear from the conversation we had with the club captain. It looks like there was, at best, a grudging acceptance of him being a member there.'

Tom interrupted him. 'And, incidentally, Mrs Burton thought the same thing.'

'Exactly,' he answered, before continuing. 'Then there is the situation regarding Roger White and his shares. What's obvious is how increasingly desperate he was to buy them back. I also got the feeling from what he told us that Mr Burton, for whatever reason, was stalling. Finally, of course, there's the issue of his so-called missed meeting with Mr Burton at 5 pm.'

'Why so-called?' asked Tom.

'Well, sir, we only have his word that Mr Burton never showed. He said he was hoping to meet at 5 pm, and that's not long after the last known contact with Mr Burton.'

When it became obvious Milner was not about to say anything else, Tom said, 'For the same reason, I don't think we should ignore Tony Cook. According to him he was out running at least part of the time after Mr Burton had left home. As with Roger White, there doesn't seem to be anyone who can confirm this.'

'Do you really think he's involved?' asked Milner.

'I really don't know. That's why you should contact him again and get the details of his route. Once you have that, check to see if any CCTV cameras picked him up along the way. We can, at least, then eliminate him from the list of potential murderers.'

'But what possible motive could he have?'

'Again, I've got no idea. But a common link right now is the golf club, and especially the shareholdings.' His antennae were now working overtime. 'There's just something about that place that doesn't quite add up.'

Chapter 24

It was 8 am on the following morning and, once again, Tom, Milner and Bennett were back in their usual place. This time, though, they were all focussed on the chart, on which were written all the names of the people who they felt featured strongly in the investigation. One additional name, at Tom's request, had just been added by Milner.

'Who is Tony Cook?' asked DC Bennett.

'He's the general manager of the West London Golf Club,' answered Milner. 'He knew Mr Burton but wasn't at the club on the day he disappeared.'

'That must apply to many people,' suggested DC Bennett. 'What's so different about him?'

Tom answered his question. 'I'm increasingly coming to the conclusion that the golf club is the key to this. As general manager Mr Cook, therefore, had the best insight into everything which went on there. And besides, he conveniently was out running during the crucial time period on that particular Sunday. Until we have a rock-solid alibi for him, he should stay on the chart as a potential suspect.' He walked towards the chart and added the word *alibi?* beneath Tony Cook's name. Before anyone could ask any follow-up questions, he said, looking at DC Bennett, 'I see you have copied the photo. Thanks.'

This was reference to the photograph Mrs Burton had loaned to Tom, featuring her husband and the three other men, a copy of which had now been stuck in the centre of the chart.

'So, how did it go with Mr Mercer?' Tom asked.

'Nothing revealing, I'm afraid,' DC Bennett answered, his voice tinged with disappointment. 'He knew, of course, about Mr Burton's death but, I have to say, still seemed genuinely shocked. He had last seen him about two weeks before his disappearance, when they had agreed a few changes to Mr

Mercer's investment portfolio. Other than that, he says, there hadn't been any other contact between the two of them.' As neither DCI Stone nor DS Milner made any comment, he carried on. 'I have checked his recent movements and he was, in fact, out of the country – in New York, actually – on the Sunday Mr Burton disappeared.'

'Did he mention his wife during your conversation?' Tom asked.

'No. He didn't mention her.'

'Hmm,' said Tom, in the way he sometimes did when he was considering what he'd just been told. 'I still think we should keep him on the chart, though.' He wrote the words *cuckolded husband* beneath Mr Mercer's name. 'Right, let's have a look at what we've got.' He took up a position at the side of the chart, still holding the marker pen.

'Here's our murder victim,' he said, pointing the pen at the photo. 'Apparently something happened, which made him angry, between the time he left Mrs Mercer and the time he left his house. What do we know about him?' He carried straight on. 'Not especially liked, particularly at the golf club. That much is obvious. Also a bit of a serial womaniser, but, of late, seems to have been focussing his attentions on this partic-ular one, Caroline Mercer. She was clearly besotted with him and was even planning to leave her husband so that they could be together permanently. Jonathan Mercer is her husband but, at least as far as we know, had no idea they were having an affair and, anyway, was out of the country on the day Glyn Burton was murdered. Next, there's Roger White.' He pointed once again at the photo. 'Played golf regularly with the victim. Sold most of his shares in the club to Mr Burton so that he could pay off a gambling debt.' He paused. 'And, I suspect, prevent it becoming common knowledge at his beloved golf club. Was hoping to buy most of them back, but this death has, so far at least, put paid to that. Tried to meet with Mr Burton on the evening of his disappearance but claims he never turned up, and I'm sure he's still not telling us every-thing he knows. Anyway, then there's this man, Tony Cook.' He pointed at the name. 'We've just discussed his involve-ment. We leave him on until his alibi is corroborated.'

He then moved his marker pen until it touched the image of Mike Preston on the photograph. 'Another of the victim's golfing buddies – well, that was until Mr Preston discovered that Glyn Burton had been seeing his wife. He, out of everyone, probably had the strongest motive to murder him, especially after their bust-up in the car park at the golf club. It also turns out that Mr Preston was, basically, thrown out of the golf club, due to the public fight with Mr Burton. So, looked at dispassionately, there's two strong motives. His wife, Amy, we still have to talk to, but all the indications are that she has been forgiven as their marriage seems to have survived the affair.' He went on. 'The third woman in all of this is, of course, the victim's wife Jane. She readily admitted that they were no longer living as man and wife and strongly suspected he was being unfaithful to her at the time of his death.'

Tom's flow was suddenly interrupted by Milner. 'Sir? Do we really think that one of the women might be the murderer? Mr Burton was quite a big man and it would need some sort of superwoman to be able to beat him to death, put him in the car and then push the car over the edge into the quarry.'

'That true. I had thought of that,' he answered, 'but that assumes the killer was one person. It could be that they had an accomplice.'

Milner looked far from convinced but decided not to respond, and so Tom continued. 'And that just leaves Craig Blackwell.'

'Leaving the best until last, then, sir?' said DC Bennett.

'What do we know about him?' Tom asked rhetorically. 'Understandably he was concerned about his business partner's affair with the wife of their biggest client, and recently he has been making regular cash withdrawals from the business. Why was he doing that?' The question was directed mainly at himself. He stepped back from the chart so that he could more easily see all the names on it. 'Anyone like to comment?'

'It's a difficult one,' said Milner.

'Murder usually is,' answered Tom.

Milner ignored this. 'You could make a case for any of them to be the murderer. They all, to a greater or lesser extent, had a motive, but I really do think we should focus on the men. I hear what you say, sir, about the possibility of more than one person being involved, but I just think that this is unlikely.'

'In my experience, Milner,' said Tom, 'when someone starts a sentence with *I hear what you say*, what they are really saying is that they absolutely don't agree. Is that what you are saying?'

'Yes,' answered Milner. 'I think that is what I'm saying.'

'Well, let's hope you are right. So you think we should just concentrate our efforts on the men?'

'I think we should, sir,' he replied.

A slight change in Tom's facial expression was enough to indicate that, whilst he didn't totally agree, he was, nonetheless, willing to go along with Milner's suggestion.

'DC Bennett? What do you think?' he asked.

'I think I've made my thoughts clear already, sir. Craig Blackwell is our man. I thought this from the very first time I met him and I haven't changed my mind. There's something not quite right about what he's been telling us. I'm sure he's been lying or trying to cover up something.'

'So, you, DS Milner, think it could be any one of the men – but not any of the women – whilst DC Bennett is sure it's his business partner.'

'And what about you, sir?' asked DC Bennett.

'At the moment, I've got no idea, but what I do think is that the golf club could be central to solving this. What we need, though, is just one more piece of information, or evidence, and then we'll have a much better idea as to which of us might be right.'

What he didn't know was that they would soon receive more than just one additional piece of information, although this wouldn't necessarily move the investigation much further forward.

Chapter 25

'Now, that is interesting,' said Tom, closely examining the piece of paper he was holding.

It was later that same morning and, after their meeting earlier in the day, DC Bennett had received an email. The attachment listed all the calls and texts that Glyn Burton had made or received on the day of his disappearance. Alongside each number was the name of the person who owned the phone. As soon as he'd received it DC Bennett had informed Tom and suggested the three of them get together again so he could share this new information with him and DS Milner.

'It looks like the last communication,' Tom said, 'was the one I've seen myself, when he texted his wife to say that he might not be home that night. After that, his phone just seemed to go offline, as there is no further record of any calls made or received.' He hesitated briefly. 'What's this here alongside the time?'

'It's the location of the telephone mast which picked up his signal. So he must have been somewhere relatively near that mast when he texted his wife,' answered DC Bennett.

'Isn't that also quite close to the quarry where his body was found?'

'Yes. It's only a few miles away.'

Tom was now deep in thought, as he considered what DC Bennett had just said. Eventually, he spoke again. 'That's really interesting. It increases the possibility he was murdered on the day he disappeared.'

'Given his track record it might also have been the place where he was seeing another woman,' suggested DC Bennett. 'I've checked on the map, and, although it's not that far away from the M3, it's still quite rural in that neck of the woods. The perfect spot if you wanted to be alone with someone else.'

'It's possible. Of course, it could be purely a coincidence;

perhaps he was murdered on another day and his body brought back and then dumped in the quarry. But ...'

Before he could finish what he was about to say, Milner did it for him. 'But you don't believe in coincidences, do you, sir?'

'No, I don't, DS Milner, especially when it comes to murder. Something, incidentally, you should think about during your career in the force.'

'Thank you for that advice, sir. I certainly will,' he replied.

Tom gave him one of his quizzical looks but decided to carry on. 'I think there is sufficient evidence, circumstantial or not, to check the location out. I know it's an isolated area, but there must be some CCTV coverage. Anyway, get on to it. To begin with, I suggest you concentrate on between, say, 4 pm and 7 pm on that Sunday evening. Hopefully, we'll at least pick up his car on its way there.'

He then continued reading from the sheet of paper DC Bennett had handed him. 'The first call listed is one he made at 10.02 am to Mrs Mercer and lasts two minutes. That stacks up with what she told us and must have been when he called her to arrange their meeting at the coffee place. The next one he received at 10.05 am from Roger White. That would have been when he tried to discuss buying back his shares. The next was at 10.29 am from a Brian Sharpe and lasted about three minutes. So that would have been after he'd left the golf club, but before he met with Mrs Mercer.' He paused and said, 'I wonder who Brian Sharpe is,' before immediately carrying on. 'Anyway, we urgently need to speak to Mr Sharpe. Milner, why don't you get on to that straight away?'

'Already on it, sir,' he answered, in a matter-of-fact tone. 'In fact, it was the first thing I did. DC Bennett showed me the list earlier and his name, being a new one to us, jumped out. I rang the number, but there was no answer, so I left a message. I'll keep trying.'

'Very impressive. You'll be telling me what I should be doing next.'

'I doubt that very much, sir,' he simply answered.

Tom returned to the sheet. 'He then received a call at 11.20 am – so presumably just after he'd left Mrs Mercer, and whilst he was on his way back home. It was from a Mr Jordan but lasted less than a minute. Almost immediately after he'd taken that call, at 11.22 he phoned Craig Blackwell, and that call lasted almost five minutes.' He looked up from the sheet he had been reading from. 'I wonder if the two calls are related. It would certainly make sense. Whatever he and Mr Jordan had briefly discussed would appear to have then prompted him to call Craig Blackwell straight away.'

Tom looked at DC Bennett, who couldn't resist making a comment.

'What did I tell you?' DC Bennett asked, an almost triumphant tone now in his voice. 'I knew Blackwell had lied to us. I specifically asked him if he'd had any contact from Mr Burton and he said no. Didn't he, sir?'

'He did, yes,' Tom replied. 'Looks like your instincts were right all along. But that doesn't mean he murdered Mr Burton.'

If Tom's comment was designed to dent DC Bennett's enthusiasm, it didn't appear to have been successful. 'He's definitely well in the frame now, though,' Mr Bennett said with obvious relish.

'I expect you've already contacted Mr Jordan as well?' asked Tom, looking towards Milner.

'Yes, sir,' he answered. 'I spoke with him just a few minutes ago. He does the accounts and tax returns for Mr Burton's company. He was a bit reluctant, at first, to tell me why he'd called Mr Burton, so I suggested we could always pay him a visit. That did the trick and he then told me.'

'And?' said Tom, impatient to find out.

'It seems Craig Blackwell has a bit of a history when it comes to sudden cash withdrawals. Apparently something similar happened a year or so ago, but the amounts then were less than the recent amounts. Mr Burton had asked Mr Jordan to let him know if they ever restarted. Mr Jordan had been doing some preparatory work on the accounts and spotted the two recent withdrawals on the bank statement. The last one was just three days before Mr Burton's disappearance. That's why he called Mr Burton.'

'Did they discuss it?' asked Tom.

'No. He simply passed the information on to Mr Burton, who just thanked him.'

'I wonder what Mr Burton said to Mr Blackwell,' Tom said. 'Anyway, it will be very interesting to hear what Craig Blackwell has to say about it. I wonder if he'll tell us the truth.'

'I wouldn't hold your breath,' said DC Bennett.

'Well, well. Now here's an interesting name,' said Tom, focussing again on the names on the sheet of paper, his enthusiasm level now almost matching that of DC Bennett. 'So, he called *my* friend, Tony Cook, at 11.35 am – just before he arrived home – and they spoke for about three minutes. Now, I wonder what all that was about. That should be an interesting conversation when we next pay him a visit. It's all suddenly getting very mysterious.' He went on down the list. 'The next one is from Roger White, at 2.45 pm, but it only lasted a few seconds. That, presumably, was when he called to suggest they meet later that evening, but it just went to voicemail.'

He placed the sheet of paper on the table. 'Excellent piece of work. Well done,' he said. 'It seems hardly anyone is telling us the truth. Or, at least, telling us the full story.' He turned to face DC Bennett. 'Could you set up another flip chart and write down the sequence of all these phone calls? I have a feeling that might help us find the answer as to who murdered Mr Burton.'

'How do you want to handle this, sir?' asked Milner.

'Well, let's wait until you've spoken with Brian Sharpe and found out who he is and why Mr Burton was calling him. After that I think we will be paying a visit to have a similar conversation with our friend Mr Cook.' He paused, remembering something. 'Before we do go and see Tony Cook, though, it would be useful if we could find out if he did actually go out for a run when and where he claimed.' He turned to face Milner. 'Are you making any progress with the CCTV coverage?'

'It's likely to be a long job, sir,' he answered. 'I've got details of his route but am still trying to set up the CCTV footage.'

'But that doesn't mean we can't have another go at Craig Blackwell,' suggested DC Bennett, with undisguised enthusiasm. 'Why don't I arrange another meeting?'

Tom fell silent for a moment. 'Okay, but I want to come with you. I'm not sure that I can trust you to be alone with him,' he said at last, only half-jokingly.

Just then Milner's phone rang. He looked at the number showing on the screen and immediately recognised it as belonging to Brian Sharpe. 'I think I should take this, sir,' and he walked out of the room.

Not long afterwards, he returned, the hint of a smile on his face. 'That was Brian Sharpe. I think he's just provided the answer as to why Mr Burton has been building up his shareholdings at the golf club. Mr Sharpe is a land procurement agent for a large construction company. It seems that he and Mr Burton had, for some time, been discussing the possibility of selling some of the land at the golf club for housing development. Well, luxury flats, to be exact. He'd called Mr Burton to let him know that his company had finally agreed a purchase price.'

'And what was that price?' asked Tom.

'Well, he wasn't too keen to tell me. Said that it was confidential commercial information.'

'But, you persuaded him, no doubt?'

'Yes, sir, I did. You might be surprised to hear that they had agreed a figure of two and a half million pounds,' he answered.

'Wow,' said DC Bennett.

Tom simply made do with, 'Well, that would explain why he seemed to be in a good mood when he arrived to meet Mrs Mercer.'

Chapter 26

'Mr Blackwell? Why did you lie to us when we last spoke?'

Tom had deliberately declined Mr Blackwell's earlier offer of refreshments, and he and DC Bennett had remained standing. Experience told him this instantly made the point that their visit was not a social call. Just as when he and Milner had last visited the golf club, he'd also decided to adopt a more direct, unambiguous approach to his questioning.

'I don't understand,' Mr Blackwell replied, clearly shocked by Tom's directness. 'Lied about what?' He paused, and when he spoke again it was in an impressive, quietly confident tone. 'I'm sure I didn't lie, but, if I did, it must have been unintentional.'

'I asked you if you had been in contact with Mr Burton after you left him at the pub on the Friday night,' DC Bennett said. 'In fact, I believe I asked you more than once. Each time you said you hadn't. We've now got hold of Mr Burton's phone records for that day and, in fact, he called you on the day he disappeared, at 11.22 am, to be precise, and the call lasted for five minutes. Are you saying that wasn't you who he spoke with?'

Both Tom and DC Bennett were now looking intently at Craig Blackwell, waiting for him to reply. After what seemed an age, their patience was rewarded.

'Yes, I remember now. I'd forgotten that he'd called. Sorry.'

'Really?' murmured DC Bennett, just loud enough for both to hear.

'Why did he call you?' asked Tom.

Once again there was a prolonged silence. Finally, Mr Blackwell said, 'He wanted to discuss what progress I'd made with a potential new client.'

'Which potential client was that?' asked Tom.

'It's somebody I've been working on for some time.'

'And the name?'

'James Wilton,' he answered, without hesitation.

Tom continued to look directly at him. 'Thank you. I'd be grateful if you could please let me have Mr Wilton's contact details before we leave.' Without waiting for a response, he pressed on. 'What else did you speak about? I'm sure it wasn't all about Mr Wilton.'

If Mr Blackwell had, earlier, shown any sign of anxiety, it had now been replaced by his normal confidence. 'I can't remember exactly, but I think we discussed family. That type of thing. We hadn't all been out together for a while and so were discussing when would be a good time.'

'And did you agree something?' asked Tom.

Tom could immediately sense a sudden look of concern on Mr Blackwell's face as he considered the nature of Tom's question, wondering if it was some sort of trap.

'Yes. We agreed to go out for lunch on the following Sunday,' Mr Blackwell answered.

'And where was that lunch to be?' Tom asked, determined to keep the pressure on him.

'I don't know,' he immediately answered. 'We left it that he would book somewhere.'

'Where were you on that Sunday, say, between 3 pm and 8 pm?' asked DC Bennett.

'I've got no idea,' Mr Blackwell answered, a little brusquely. 'Can you remember what you were doing over two weeks ago at that specific time?'

'I probably could if it had been my friend and business partner who had disappeared,' said DC Bennett.

'Well, I can't,' he simply replied.

'Perhaps, then, you should *try* and remember, as I'm sure we will ask you that particular question again."

Tom offered his hand to Mr Blackwell, although, conspicuously, DC Bennett didn't follow suit. 'Thank you for your time. If you could just let me have Mr Wilton's details, we'll leave you in peace.'

'Of course,' Mr Blackwell answered, a look of relief on his face, before scrolling down the contacts list on his phone. He read out the number and DC Bennett made a note of it.

Just as Tom was about to leave the room, he suddenly stopped, turned back to face Mr Blackwell and said, 'There was one other thing. We've checked your company's bank statement and it appears that £5,000 was withdrawn by you, on the same day, for the past two months. The second withdrawal was, in fact, only a few days before Mr Burton disappeared. Is there a particular reason why you needed the money?'

For the first time, Tom could just make out something close to panic in Mr Blackwell's eyes, but there was nothing but anger in his voice when he answered. 'What right do you have to go snooping into our bank statements? That's none of your business.'

'We actually have every right, Mr Blackwell, especially when we are investigating a murder,' Tom answered, calmly.

'There are such things as privacy laws in this country, you know. Does this mean I can go digging around in your personal finances?'

'If you were a police officer investigating a murder, then yes, you could.' He waited for a moment and then said. 'My strong recommendation, Mr Blackwell, is that you answer; otherwise, I'm afraid things might get serious for you.'

'What do you mean?'

'There is such a thing as perverting the course of justice. More importantly, though, your refusal to answer would strongly suggest to me that you have something to hide.' He paused momentarily, before adding, 'It's entirely your choice.'

Both Tom and DC Bennett remained where they were, waiting for a reply.

'It was for my own personal use,' Mr Blackwell eventually replied.

'That's a lot of money for personal use,' suggested Tom.

'I was considering buying a new car but wanted to pay by cash. It's a bit cheaper that way.'

'I understand this isn't the first time you've withdrawn cash amounts. Were the past withdrawals for personal use as well?'

Once again, there was a brief look of anxiety on his face, although he quickly regained his composure. 'I'm sure they were, although I can't remember the specific details. If you are suggesting I was taking money out without Glyn's knowledge, then that is just not true. We trusted each other implicitly. We'd both worked incredibly hard to build up the business. I told you last time you were here that things were very tough for us when we first set up together. Both of us had to put up our houses as security and, for a while, it looked as though we might lose them. So, if I occasionally took out some money to fund various things, then, frankly, Detective Chief Inspector Stone, I think that I'd earned that right.'

It was impressive, full of genuine passion. Once again, though, Tom remained silent, continuing to look directly into his face.

'Thank you again,' Tom finally said, before walking towards the outer office, where Mr Blackwell's PA was seated. 'As DC Bennett said, we will want to speak with you again. So please don't go anywhere far,' he added, just loud enough to ensure the PA also heard what was said.

As soon as they were outside the office building, DC Bennett said, 'He's lying through his teeth.'

'Of course he is,' Tom answered. 'Impressive, nonetheless. The question, though, is why.'

Chapter 27

'I've just received an email from Paul,' said Mary, excitement clearly evident in her voice. It was later that evening and Tom had just arrived home.

Despite her very positive tone, all Tom could think of to say in response was, 'Is everything okay?'

He was finding the situation very peculiar. When he was at work, and in the middle of a complex investigation, he could usually think very clearly. When, however, it came to any personal matter, but especially that of his son's visit, that clarity of thought seemed to disappear. And it wasn't something he felt comfortable with. Above all else, he liked to be in control of his own emotions. All through his adult life he had seen this as a strength. Just lately, though, he had found himself becoming more emotional, in both his thoughts and, occasionally, his words. He didn't know if this was due to his age, meeting Mary or the impending visit of his son and unknown family. What was clear, however, was that the visit had heightened those feelings.

'Everything is fine,' she answered. 'Don't worry. He hasn't changed his mind.' She gave a slight laugh. 'He's just updating me. Apparently they have packed and are just waiting for a taxi to take them to the airport. Providing their plane is not delayed, they should be in the air in about five hours' time and are due to land at terminal 4 at about 10 pm, the day after tomorrow.' She fell silent, giving him the opportunity to respond. When he didn't immediately do so, she asked, 'Do you think we should meet them at the airport or wait until later in the day?'

He hadn't really given any serious thought to this, although, as Mary said it, he realised it was a sensible and practical question. 'I think we should meet them later. They will be tired, especially the children, after such a long trip, and by the time they've cleared passport control and retrieved their luggage it will be very late. I think we should arrange to meet them at their hotel after they've had some rest. Anyway, I'm not sure that Heathrow's terminal 4 is the best place to be reunited with a son who you haven't seen for almost thirty years, and grandchildren you never even knew you had, let alone met.'

Mary smiled at him. 'You're not trying to put this off, are you?'

In truth, he didn't really know. Certainly what he had said was true, but, deep down, perhaps there were other reasons. 'No,' he replied. 'I think it will be better for all of us if we meet later at their hotel.' He suddenly had a thought. 'Is that what Paul suggested? That we meet at the airport?'

'No,' she quickly answered. 'We left it open. He'll text me when they are in the UK, so we can then agree when to meet.' Suddenly she seemed to think of something else. 'Incidentally, have you given any thought to what you would like to do whilst they are here?'

'Not really,' he said. 'I thought we would ask Paul when we see him. It's really up to them what they want to do whilst they are in London. I suspect they will want to do some sight-seeing.' He hesitated briefly before saying, 'Anyway, I'm not sure whether or not they'll want us tagging along with them all the time. Didn't you say that they have arranged to travel up to the Midlands during their second week?'

'They have, yes.' Now it was her turn to hesitate. 'My suggestion, Tom, is for you to play it by ear. Let's just wait and see. One step at a time, as they say.' She touched him on the arm. 'How are you feeling?'

'Well, I am starting to get a bit nervous, for all the reasons I mentioned the other day. Before, it was more anxiety than anything else. Now, though, it is more of an excited nervousness.'

'That's good, isn't it?' she asked.

'I think so,' he answered, before adding, 'Well, I certainly hope so.'

The reality was that the Glyn Burton murder investigation had, at least for a period of time, taken his mind off both the Jenkins/Cope situation and Paul's impending visit. Now, though, Mary's information about flight arrivals had suddenly brought it all to life.

There was another reason for his nerves as well. He sensed the murder investigation was coming to a crucial stage. In his experience, there was always such a stage in any investigation: the stage when things started to happen very quickly and key decisions had to be made. Decisions which could only be made if you were right in the middle of events. He had deliberately not told either Milner or DC Bennett about his planned time off, as he'd been hoping that crucial breakthrough would have happened by now. If it was to happen whilst he was around, he had just twenty-four hours left.

Chapter 28

'You're taking some time off?' asked a clearly astonished Milner. 'In the middle of a murder investigation?'

'I'm sure you and DC Bennett can handle it,' Tom answered, trying as best he could to make it seem like a perfectly natural occurrence. 'While I'm away, you will be acting SIO.'

'How long will you be off?'

'I'm not sure. A few days. Maybe five at the most.'

'Am I allowed to ask why you will be off?' Milner asked, this time with concern apparent in his voice. 'It's not ... well, it's not anything sinister, is it, sir?'

Tom suddenly felt almost emotional that Milner was showing so much concern for his wellbeing. But, nonetheless, he wasn't about to show those emotions. 'If you are asking if I'm about to have a last-ditch, life-saving operation, then I'm sorry to disappoint you. It's more mundane than that, I'm afraid.'

'You're not planning to get married, are you, sir?' asked DC Bennett, a question which Milner would not have felt able to ask.

'No, I'm not,' he answered. 'But, if and when I am, rest assured you will both receive an invitation. Now, let's get on with this investigation. What have we got? Anything new?'

It was DC Bennett who answered. 'You can see there,' he said, pointing at a second flip chart, alongside the one showing the names of the people considered to be central to the investigation. 'As you asked, I've written down all of the participants and times of the calls Mr Burton either received or made on the day he disappeared. I think there's weight to your theory that the key is somewhere in these.'

Tom's attention was now focussed on the chart and it was some time before he actually responded. 'Yes, thanks,' he simply said. 'Anything else?'

It was Milner who next spoke. 'Forensics have now got back to me with the final report of their examination of Mr Burton's car. Unfortunately, as they feared, they were not able to find any DNA in the car, other than Mr Burton's. What they did find, however, was this.' Milner took out an A4 photograph from his folder and handed it to Tom. 'It's a piece of metal that was found in the boot. As you can see, it's quite small and rectangular in shape.'

'Is that all?' asked Tom, his disappointment obvious.

'Except it could be part of the murder weapon. Forensics say it's the right size and shape for the wound found on the side of Mr Burton's head. The clincher, though, was that they found some of Mr Burton's DNA on it.'

'And you say it was found in the boot of his car?'

'Yes, sir. It would suggest, therefore, at some stage his body had been in the boot.'

Tom studied the photograph more closely, before giving it back to Milner. 'Anything else?'

'Actually, there is, although you might be disappointed when I tell you.'

'Just tell me,' said Tom.

'I've now had the chance to look through the CCTV footage on the route that Tony Cook ran. There wasn't full coverage and so there are quite a few gaps, but, nonetheless, I was able to regularly identify him whilst he was running. The times would seem to stack up with what he told us. But, as I said, there are still a few gaps in the coverage.'

Tom, conscious that the clock was ticking towards the time when he would be away, said, 'Okay. Let's go and pay him another visit.'

'What? Right now, sir?' asked Milner.

'Why not?' he answered. 'I'm starting to miss my daily fix of golf.'

Chapter 29

Less than forty-five minutes later they were, for the third time, seated in the small room that served as the club's office. Unlike the previous two times they had been there, this time there was just Tom, Milner and Tony Cook.

'I know it was short notice, and I'm sure you have lots to do, so thank you again for making the time to see us,' said Tom.

'That's not a problem,' replied Tony Cook. 'I'm obviously keen to do everything I can to help you with your investigation.'

'Incidentally, how is your training progressing?'

Clearly taken aback by Tom's question, Mr Cook took a moment to answer. 'Not too bad. I've been slightly injured recently – a problem with my calf muscle – and so I've been taking it steadily.'

'When is the race?'

Still quite surprised by this sudden interest in his running, he said, 'Two weeks' time.'

'Well, good luck. I hope it goes well.'

'Was there anything specific you wanted to discuss?' asked Mr Cook, not quite knowing where this conversation was going. He soon found out, though.

'Yes, there is, actually. It concerns the telephone conversation you had with Mr Burton on the day he disappeared. An analysis of his phone records shows that he called you at 11.35 am. Previously, you have led us to believe you had not been in contact with him after he left the golf club. Why did you lie to us?'

If Tony Cook had hoped that this meeting would be nothing more than a recap of their previous conversations, he now knew it wasn't and, for that reason, was clearly struggling to answer the question. So Tom decided to help him out. 'It would be in your interest to tell us now rather than later at the station. But the decision is yours.' Just to emphasise the options, Tom then added, 'Here or the station?'

This appeared to make up his mind for him. 'Will whatever I say to you remain confidential?'

'I'm sorry, but I can't guarantee that, Mr Cook. This is, after all, a murder investigation.'

Tom's much-tried silence tactic once again did the trick.

'Glyn called to let me know about a business deal he was involved in,' Mr Cook finally said.

'And why would he think it important to speak to you about it? From what you told me previously I didn't get the impression that you were that close. Certainly not so close that he would discuss one of his business deals with you. According to his wife, he rarely even discussed business with her. So why with you?' Tom was almost certain he knew the reason but wanted to hear the answer from Mr Cook. That way, he would then know if he was still not telling the truth.

'It concerned the golf club,' Mr Cook answered.

'Yes, I suspected that, but could you please provide us with full details?'

Milner, recognising DCI Stone's increasing impatience, now spoke for the first time. 'The call lasted three minutes. It's quite surprising how much can be said in three minutes.'

Whether it was what Milner had said or just the calm tone in which he had said it, it had the desired effect.

'Glyn called to tell me a deal he had been negotiating with a large construction company had been agreed by them.'

'And this involved selling off some of the club's land, didn't it?' said Tom, wanting to make the point that they already knew.

'It did, yes. You'll remember Roger mentioned how we've resited the greenkeeper's shed nearer to the clubhouse. I don't know if you've seen the old shed, but it actually is much bigger than the name would imply. There are also the old World War II huts alongside it. Anyway, it's freed up quite a lot of land. It's that land which Glyn has been trying to sell.'

'Wouldn't they need planning permission before they could start building on it, especially in an area like this?' asked Milner.

'Yes, they would, but, as you've no doubt seen, the government are under pressure to build more houses. They, in turn, are then pressuring local councils to simplify their planning permission procedures, so that houses can be built quicker. Also, the fact that the new houses would be built on the existing footprint of the old shed and huts makes the process much less complicated. Glyn mentioned to me that the land agent had already spoken with someone from the council's planning committee to sound them out about the possibility of getting planning permission. Apparently, they didn't see any problem, providing they only built on the place where the old shed and huts are currently sited.'

'And what is your role in this?' asked Tom, genuinely unclear as to what this would be. 'I assume you had a role? Especially as Mr Burton called you immediately after he'd received the call from the land agent.'

'Glyn wanted me to provide him with a copy of the club's deeds and constitution. He wanted to know if there was anything in them which would prevent any land being sold. Or, at least, anything which might make it more difficult. As he didn't want anyone else at the club to know that he was taking an interest, he approached me to find out. As general manager I had access to the documents.'

'And was there anything?' asked Milner.

'There was something – well, at least originally – which would undoubtedly have made it virtually impossible for one member, irrespective of their position within the club and irrespective of how many shares they held, to arrange to sell off any land. But that particular clause was removed when Glyn first arrived at the club. When he agreed to help settle the tax bill, the club's constitution was amended so that, in future, the final decision rested with the major shareholder, providing that person had over fifty percent of the total shareholding.'

'Wasn't that recognised, at the time of the change, as something fundamental?' asked Tom.

'Not to the extent that, perhaps, you would imagine. You have to remember that this club has always been based upon a sort of gentlemen's trust and, frankly, no one at the time thought for one moment that it might happen.'

'I'm still a bit unclear, though, as to why you would help with this,' said Tom.

After Mr Cook's earlier willingness to discuss this, it was now obvious he was struggling to continue with his explanation. Tom, not for the first time, decided to make it easy for him.

'He offered you money, didn't he?'

'Yes,' Mr Cook replied quietly.

'How much?'

'Fifty thousand pounds.'

No one spoke for a while, until finally Mr Cook continued. 'When Glyn approached me about this, I said I didn't want to get involved. But later he came back and offered me the money, saying that he was going ahead with it anyway. Fifty thousand pounds is a lot of money, Detective Chief Inspector. It would have allowed me to pay off a chunk of my mortgage. He said no one would ever find out that I had been involved.' Again, he seemed to hesitate. 'Things are very tight, financially, for us at the moment. The more I thought about it, the more it seemed like an easy way to get some money and get us back on our feet.'

'You're right,' said Tom. 'Fifty thousand pounds is a lot of money. I'm surprised he was willing to pay you that much.'

'Well, he was. I don't know the full details, but I got the impression from him that it was a multi-million pound deal. Whatever the size of the deal, though, he obviously thought the help I could give him was worth the money he was willing to pay me.'

'What was the nature of your financial arrangement? Did he pay you any money up front?'

'No,' he quickly replied. 'I haven't received one penny.' He shook his head. 'He was going to pay half when the deal with the building company was signed and the remainder once the first brick had been laid.'

'You must have been very happy, then, when you received the call from Mr Burton,' suggested Milner.

'I was, yes, but, of course, that didn't last long, did it?' he answered, with regret in his voice.

'Yes, it was very unfortunate that Mr Burton went and got himself murdered,' said Milner, in a tone which even surprised Tom. An uncomfortable silence followed.

'I'm sorry,' said Mr Cook. 'I didn't mean it to sound like that.'

'I know you didn't,' replied Tom, as sympathetically as possible.

'To answer your question,' Mr Cook said, focussing on Milner, 'it's true, I was happy. In fact, very happy. Although I knew, once it all got out, there would be repercussions, there was nothing to link me to what Glyn was doing. It was when he went missing that I started to get worried, and then, of course, his body was found.'

'You mentioned repercussions. What sort of repercussions did you have in mind?' asked Milner, now sounding his normal businesslike self.

'The members would have been up in arms. You have seen for yourself what sort of club this is. People here don't like change. They want the golf club to stay the same as it's always been and they certainly wouldn't want a housing development on the course. The disruption would have been considerable, what with trucks coming and going all the time and lots of workers on the course. As I said, the members would have hated it.'

'Incidentally, how many houses were to be built?' asked Milner.

'I don't know for sure, because, as I told you earlier, my involvement was limited, but I did once hear Glyn mention a combined figure of about twenty-five houses and flats.'

'That doesn't seem to be that many,' said Milner. 'I thought we were talking about a housing estate.'

'I think anything above that number might have made things more difficult,' Mr Cook said. 'And anyway, as you can see, this is a very exclusive location. Each flat, let alone house, would be very expensive.'

'Would each member have received a share of any profits?' asked Tom.

'Yes, they would have. That is very clear in the club's constitution. It would have been paid as a special dividend and be based, *pro rata*, on the number of shares held by each member.'

'But wouldn't the members have liked that?' asked Milner.

Mr Cook looked at him. 'Most of our members are over fifty-five years old, and quite a lot well into their sixties. At their age they are not especially motivated by money. What they care about most is keeping the club as it has always been.'

'But they couldn't have stopped it, though, could they?'

'No. As long as Glyn was the majority shareholder he could, basically, do what he wanted. Glyn wasn't the type of person who would get upset just because he wasn't liked. In fact, I sometimes felt that he would have enjoyed it.'

'You mean any subsequent confrontations?' asked Tom.

'Exactly. He knew he held all of the aces. He was a man who liked to do deals. In my experience, it was what drove him the most. And anyway, I suspect he would have got enjoyment out of doing this as revenge, almost.'

'Revenge? That's a strong word, Mr Cook,' said Tom.

'I think you got a flavour of this when you were last here. Didn't you say that you'd spoken with some of our members who had been playing and they weren't especially complimentary about Glyn? He was aware of how people felt, and that they only admitted him to the club because of his money. In my opinion, it was partly his way of proving to them that an East End man was not to be underestimated.'

'Is there any possibility some of those members had found out what Mr Burton was doing?' asked Tom.

'If they did, I certainly didn't tell them,' Mr Cook said, defensively. He paused. 'It's unlikely but, I suppose, not impossible.'

'Mr Cook. If you had told us this earlier, it would have saved a lot of our time. Is there anything else you want to tell us? This is now definitely your last chance.'

There was a moment's hesitation, which Tom immediately noticed. 'If there is, then you should tell us now,' he added as further encouragement.

'I'm not sure if this is relevant or not, but, a couple of days after Glyn's disappearance, Greg – that's Greg Wallington, one of those who Glyn was due to play with – mentioned to me he'd heard Roger and Glyn having an argument, here in this office, on that Sunday morning. Apparently, it was immediately afterwards that Glyn then left.'

'Could he hear what it was about?'

'I did ask him that, but all he could hear was their raised voices.'

'Is that everything?' asked Tom.

'Yes. I've told you everything I know.'

'Thank you,' said Tom. 'Next time, though, I hope you will be forthcoming a bit sooner.'

He didn't respond directly to Tom's comment. Instead, he said, 'I suppose I will now have to resign. When all this gets out, no one will trust me anyway.'

Chapter 30

'Should we bring in Roger White?' asked Milner.

They had arrived back at the station and DC Bennett had joined them.

'On what basis?' replied Tom. 'We don't have any firm evidence to charge him. All we know is he sold most of his shares to Mr Burton and was angry when Mr Burton seemed reluctant to sell them back to him.'

'He also, though, tried repeatedly to contact him on that Sunday and even, later, by his own admission, went to a lay-by to meet him,' Milner said. 'We really only have his word that Mr Burton didn't turn up. What if he did and something happened which resulted in his death? Mr White could easily have then driven the victim's car to the quarry – it's only a few miles away, after all – pushed it over the edge and then returned to his own car and driven home, before his wife returned.' He paused. 'And he had a strong motive. It's possible he had found out about Mr Burton's plan to sell the land and had confronted him with it. Perhaps that's the reason they were heard arguing on the Sunday morning? He would definitely benefit from Mr Burton's death, as it would stop the deal going through. And let's remember he has not been especially truthful each time we've met him. Why would the last time be any different?'

Tom considered what Milner had just said, impressed by the compelling way he had summarised his concerns. 'All of that is possible,' he admitted. 'Put like that, I suppose, it is fairly persuasive. What we really need, though, is some evidence, perhaps through CCTV, which puts him close to the quarry on that Sunday evening.' He paused briefly and then continued. 'You say the quarry is not too far away from the lay-by. It would help if we knew exactly how far away it actually is. If he did murder Mr Burton then, presumably, he would have put his body in the boot of Mr Burton's car, driven it to, and then pushed it into, the quarry, and then somehow returned to his own car. If all of this did happen, a key question then is "how did he get back to his car?"'

'It's unlikely he walked,' said DC Bennett. 'Which only leaves the possibility of him getting a taxi, or bus, for at least part of the way. If he did, then, although it might take some time, those are things we can quickly check up on.'

'If he had an accomplice he could, of course, have been picked up somewhere along the route,' suggested Milner.

'Anyone in mind?' asked Tom.

'Well, what about his wife? We haven't actually spoken with her yet. Why don't I do that straight away?'

Tom, warming to Milner's theory, quickly agreed. 'Okay, go ahead and do that. Perhaps I was giving Roger White too much benefit of the doubt.'

'And should I bring him in?' asked Milner.

'Why not?' answered Tom, persuaded by Milner's arguments but also increasingly conscious that his own availability clock was quickly ticking down. 'I still don't think we've got enough to charge him, but there's definitely enough for us to legitimately ask him a few more questions.'

'And what about Craig Blackwell?' asked DC Bennett. 'I hope this doesn't mean we've taken him off our list of suspects.'

'I don't think we would dare,' answered Tom. 'But, for the moment, we concentrate on Roger White. All of our efforts should be on him, at least until we've either charged him or eliminated him. Is that clear?' he added, mainly for DC Bennett's benefit.

'Yes, sir,' DC Bennett answered, albeit without any enthusiasm.

'And Tony Cook?' said Milner. 'Have we now eliminated him from our list of suspects?'

'I think so,' answered Tom. 'Having spoken to him, and heard about his involvement in the land purchase deal, I can't think of any possible motive. Mr Burton's death has meant Mr Cook has lost the opportunity to earn £50,000 and now, most likely, his job and reputation. I can't see him getting a similar job with another golf club any time soon.'

'So, should I cross him off?' asked Milner, looking in the direction of the chart.

'Why not?' agreed Tom.

Milner, marker pen in hand, walked towards the chart and put a large cross over Tony Cook's name.

'Let's have a look at who we are left with,' suggested Tom. 'Let's focus on the men, for the time being. First, we have our prime suspect, Roger White. I think we can now add the word *motive* under his name. Next we have Craig Blackwell. I don't, for one minute, believe his explanation as to why Mr Burton called him on the Sunday morning. I also don't buy into his explanation as to why he needed the two lots of £5,000 which he withdrew from the business account. I think we can now add another word under his name. How about *lying*? DC Bennett? I'll let you do the honours.'

DC Bennett quickly wrote the word but, even then, couldn't resist the temptation to add an exclamation mark.

'Then there's Mike Preston.' This seemed to trigger something in Tom's memory. 'Has anyone actually spoken with his wife yet?'

It was Milner who answered. 'In actual fact, I'm seeing her later today, after she has finished work. I can't say she was particularly keen to meet but eventually she did agree, although she asked if we could not tell her husband.'

'Understandable,' replied Tom. 'Try and find out if she still has feelings for Mr Burton. Anyway, Mike Preston? What are your thoughts?'

Again, Milner was first to respond. 'I don't believe it was him, sir. I know it could be claimed he had a motive, but, frankly, it's almost too obvious a motive, and he must have known he would have been the prime suspect. Also, if he was going to murder Mr Burton, surely he would have done it not long after their altercation, not some considerable time later, when he and his wife had just got their marriage back on track.'

'Unless, of course, he had deliberately waited for time to elapse before making his move. It could all be a very clever plan on his part,' said Tom. 'Anyway, we've already eliminated one suspect today. I think another one might be one too many, at least for the time being.' He considered the chart. 'And that just leaves Mr Mercer. It's difficult to pin a crime on someone when they were not even on the same continent on the day the crime occurred. We are sure of that, are we?'

'Absolutely,' replied Milner. 'I got the immigration people to double-check. Not only that, but they provided me with a photograph, showing the date and time, of his arrival back at Heathrow on the Monday evening. It was definitely him.'

Tom examined the chart, in silence, for a short while longer. 'Right. We are all agreed, then. Roger White is our main suspect. We need to speak with his wife in order to test his alibi. In the meantime we will try and get CCTV footage of him close to the quarry. Failing that, we will check to see if he used a taxi or public transport to get back to his car. So the next step is to get him in and see what he has to say this time.'

'Sir?' asked Milner. 'What happens if we can't see him until tomorrow? You won't be around.'

'I'm sure you can handle it yourself. That's what a SIO does. The clue is in the name. Senior Investigation Officer.'

'Just so I'm absolutely clear, sir, are you saying you don't want to be kept informed of any developments whilst you are away?'

'Only the important ones. I'll leave it to you to decide which they are,' he answered, not particularly helpfully.

Chapter 31

Just as Tom was about to leave the station, Superintendent Birch knocked on his door. 'Have you got a minute, Tom?' he asked.

After his update with Milner and DC Bennett, Tom had spent most of the rest of the day catching up on his emails. Whilst this wasn't his main priority, it had allowed him to make good use of his time. It had also meant he could occasionally look up at the chart, hoping for some flash of inspiration. Unfortunately, nothing had struck, but somehow he suspected the answer was on that chart.

'Come in,' said Tom. 'I'm just making sure that there's nothing important I have to do before I leave.'

'And is there?'

'Not unless you include a couple of reports I have to complete,' he answered.

'I'm sure they can wait,' replied Superintendent Birch.

'That's good,' said Tom, with a slight laugh, 'because one of them is for you.'

'Unless it's a matter of life or death, I'm still sure it can wait,' he said, before sitting down opposite Tom. He then carried straight on. 'I just wanted to wish you all the best over the next few days. I hope it works out well for you.'

Tom, genuinely touched by Superintendent Birch's concern, said, 'Thank you, sir. I really appreciate that.'

'They are arriving tomorrow, aren't they?'

'Tonight, actually. Although, as it will be late, we are not meeting up until sometime tomorrow.'

'And how are you feeling?'

Normally, Tom would be the last person to discuss his private life, particularly with a work colleague, but, for some reason he couldn't quite pinpoint, he didn't seem to have that problem with his new boss. 'A bit apprehensive, if I'm being honest. Their arrival has suddenly crept up on me.'

'I would have thought that's perfectly normal,' Superintendent Birch answered sympathetically. 'Anyway, I'm not going to give you some speech about making the most of the opportunity or suchlike. All I wanted to do was to wish you luck.' He paused briefly and then said, 'If you need to take more time off, just do so.'

'Thanks. I appreciate it,' he replied.

Superintendent Birch stood up. 'I almost forgot to ask. Have you made any progress with the murder investigation?'

Tom quickly updated him as to where they were with it. After he had finished, he added, 'DS Milner will be SIO whilst I'm away. So, if you have any questions regarding the case, just ask him.'

'Will he be able to handle it? I trust your judgement, but wouldn't this be his first SIO role?'

'It will be, but we all had to start at some time. He's more than capable of running it. And, anyway, in DC Bennett, he has an experienced officer to assist him. I've told him that if things do start to warm up then he's to contact me immediately.'

'Do you remember your first time as SIO?' asked Superintendent Birch. 'I certainly remember mine as though it was yesterday. I was so excited it was me who was in charge. Of course, it was also quite scary, but, as you say, we all had to start at some time.' He smiled a little. 'I suppose in some ways it was a rite of passage in our career, which we all had to go through.'

After a brief, almost reflective pause, he added, 'Do you think it's likely the case will be resolved soon?'

'I really don't know. You know for yourself how these things work. It might be there's a breakthrough tomorrow. Alternatively, it's possible there are still a few wild goose chases ahead of us before we finally get to the truth.'

'Well, if there are, just make sure you don't get yourself involved in them over the next few days. Understood?' Superintendent Birch asked, in a sudden assertive tone.

'Understood,' replied Tom.

Chapter 32

'They should be landing in a few hours' time,' said Mary. They had both just finished dinner and were seated together in the lounge.

'Are you going to keep looking at your watch and then giving a running commentary on where they are?' asked Tom, the accompanying light laugh being his attempt to play down Mary's increasing excitement. Although Tom was excited himself, it seemed that Mary was, if anything, even more excited than him.

'I'm sorry, but I can't help it,' she replied, confirming Tom's perception. 'I'm sure I won't be able to sleep tonight.'

'Don't you think you are taking all of this just a little bit personally? After all, it's not even your family.' He instantly regretted his comment. 'I'm sorry. I didn't mean it to come out like that. What I meant to say was that it should be me who is feeling that way. Not you.'

'I know that,' she said, taking hold of his hand. 'It's just that I want things to work out well for you. If, for whatever reason, they don't, then please remember that I will always be here for you.'

Tom found himself, uncharacteristically, swallowing hard. It was, as far as he could remember, probably the nicest thing Mary had ever said to him during their time together. It also gave him the reassurance he surprisingly realised he needed, that, come what may, he wasn't alone any more. Nonetheless, he was slightly concerned Mary might be building herself up for a major disappointment. It was his natural tendency to assume something might go wrong, whilst he was aware that it was Mary's to always assume things could only go right.

'And the same applies to you as well,' said Tom. 'Neither of us really knows how things are likely to turn out. If they don't work out, then I will always be grateful to you for giving me the opportunity to see Paul and his family. I'm certain that, without you, I would never have done this.'

They spent the rest of the evening watching television, or at least Tom did. Mary, though, kept regularly looking at her phone. Despite Tom's earlier comment, keeping up a running commentary on his family's location was exactly what she did as she monitored their progress on the airline's flight tracker.

'They've landed,' she suddenly announced. By now it was approaching midnight and, although the flight had been delayed slightly, this had obviously failed to dampen her excitement.

'I think we should go to bed now, then,' suggested Tom. 'Let's try and get some sleep, as I imagine it will be a very busy day for us tomorrow.'

'I can't possibly sleep,' she answered. 'I'm wide awake. If I go to bed now, I'll just lie there. And, anyway, Paul said he'd text me when they landed. You go up, if you want. I'll stay down here for a bit longer.'

'Okay, but don't stay up all night, otherwise you'll be exhausted when we meet them.'

Tom went to bed, leaving Mary watching television. In truth, he knew he would also find it difficult to sleep. Apart from the excitement of meeting his family, he also had the investigation on his mind.

He knew, though, through experience, that it seemed to help him work through difficult cases if he actually went to bed. Perhaps it was the change in environment or simply because the quiet allowed him to think more clearly, without any of the daytime distractions. Whatever the reason, it had worked in the past. So, as he lay in bed, he played through, in his mind, all of the key events in the case since he had become involved.

His normal technique was to start at the very beginning and try to visualise everything which had happened since, in chronological order. This time, though, it must not have provided the inspiration he was looking for. In fact, he must have fallen asleep at some early point, as he suddenly woke up when Mary climbed into bed.

'Are you awake?' she whispered.

'Well, I am now,' he answered.

'Sorry, but I thought you'd like to know that I've just

received the text from Paul. Do you want me to read it to you?'

Before he could answer, she had started to read out loud from her phone. '*Just landed and waiting to collect luggage. Everyone is really looking forward to seeing you both. See you later at the hotel.* You see, they are as excited as we are.'

By now Tom was wide awake. 'Well,' he said, pulling her towards him, 'why don't we make use of all of that excitement?'

Chapter 33

'Why have you asked me here?' asked Mr White.

Milner, taking a leaf out of his boss's book, decided not to answer that particular question. Instead, determined to take, and keep, the initiative, he adopted his own direct approach. 'Mr White, each time we have met you, so far, you have either lied to us or deliberately withheld vital information. The last time, DCI Stone indicated that, if you continued to do this, then you would be charged.' This had the desired effect, and Milner immediately noticed Roger White sitting lower in his chair. He carried on. 'So, to answer your question, you are here because, once again, we have found out you have been lying to us.'

Clearly shocked, he simply said, 'I've told you everything that happened. There's nothing more I can tell you.'

'But, yet again, Mr White, that is not true, is it?'

'I don't understand,' he replied. 'When was it I was supposed to have lied to you?'

'You told DCI Stone, and myself, that you had first got angry with Mr Burton when you called him, just after he left the golf club.'

'Yes,' he answered, with hesitation.

'Whereas, in fact, you were both overheard having a heated conversation *before* he left the golf club.'

'Who told you that?' he asked, aggressively.

'It was Mr Wallington. You and Mr Burton were in the office and, although the door was closed, he could still clearly hear raised voices. Why was that, Mr White?'

This latest information, once again, clearly shook him, and it was a short while before he could answer. When he did, all of his initial aggression had disappeared. 'I told you previously I had intended to speak with him about my shares during our round of golf, but the fog put paid to that. It was when he told me he wasn't planning to hang around that I asked him into the office.'

'So, why did you end up arguing?' asked Milner. 'I assume it was still about the shares?'

'It was, yes,' he answered.

'But what was so different this time?'

He seemed to take a deep breath before he answered. 'It was something about what he intended to do with *my* shares.'

'Mr White,' said Milner, irritation now in his voice, 'we already know what that intention was, so there's no point in you trying to be evasive. You either tell me or I charge you, here and now, with obstruction.'

Roger White didn't, of course, know for sure exactly how much Milner knew but evidently decided he couldn't take the chance. 'He was planning to use his majority shareholding to force through the sale of some of the club's land so that flats could be built on it.' He carried straight on, with increased anger. 'These were *my* shares he was intending to use to do something I would never, ever do.'

'I would, though, point out that, in fact, they were *not* your shares. You sold them to Mr Burton because you needed to urgently raise some money. In fact to pay off your latest gambling debt,' Milner said. 'Surely, therefore, he could do what he wanted?'

'I do know that, Detective Sergeant Milner,' he replied, with just a hint of sarcasm which was not lost on Milner. 'But he had agreed I could buy them back. That was still my understanding until I raised the issue of the sale of the land with him.'

'How did you find out about that?' asked Milner. He was tempted to ask if Tony Cook had told him, but resisted. That was a fortunate decision because, when Mr White answered, it became clear that he had no idea about Mr Cook's involvement.

'I have a friend who works in the planning section at the council. I bumped into him at a restaurant on Saturday night. He mentioned the discussions which had been going on between the building company and the council and that preliminary permission had just been granted. He assumed, of course, that I knew, so I just had to pretend I did.'

'And you had no idea, before then, that Mr Burton had been in discussions with a development company?'

'None at all. If I had I would have raised it with him much

sooner. In the event, the earliest I could speak to him was the following day, when we were due to play golf. But, as I keep saying, the fog prevented me from doing that.'

'Did you tell anyone else about what Mr Burton was planning to do?'

'No. No one. I was still hoping I could persuade him to change his mind.'

'Change his mind about what?' asked Milner. 'Selling the shares back to you or selling the land?'

'Well, both, really. It would have caused absolute uproar amongst the members if they had found out about the land sale.'

'I'm sure it would, although, as majority shareholder, he was perfectly entitled to do it.'

'How do you know that?' Mr White asked, in a puzzled tone.

'Mr Cook told us. Once we had found out what Mr Burton was proposing, we asked him if he could legally do that.' Although what Milner said was true, it was, nonetheless, sufficiently ambiguous not to reveal Tony Cook's true role in all of this. Milner couldn't see any benefit, at this stage anyway, of revealing his involvement.

'So, how did you find out about the plans?' Mr White asked.

'I'm afraid *that* I can't tell you. We are in the middle of a murder investigation and cannot reveal any information relating to that investigation.'

He seemed to readily accept Milner's explanation. 'So, am I now allowed to leave?'

'Not quite,' Milner quickly replied. 'You still haven't told me exactly what you said to Mr Burton. Did you threaten him?'

'How dare you?' he answered, angrily. 'You have no right to make that sort of accusation.'

'I have every right, Mr White. It seems to me you still do not fully comprehend the seriousness of this investigation.' He carried straight on. 'Let's examine the facts. Firstly, Mr Burton, from your own words, was reluctant to even discuss the sale of your shares back to you. Secondly, you found out he was now not willing to let you have them back, as he needed them to finalise the land sale. Third, you were heard arguing with him on the day he disappeared. Fourth, you argued with him again when you called him just after he'd left the club. Next, you even tried to arrange a meeting with him later that evening, not, incidentally, in a public place but, again by your own admission, in a place where you would not be noticed. Finally, we only have your word that Mr Burton didn't attend that meeting.'

If Milner's summary was intended to ensure that Mr White had finally grasped the seriousness of the situation, it appeared to have been successful. 'You are making it sound as though I was involved in his death,' he replied, with real anxiety.

'Were you?' asked Milner. 'Because, if you were, then I suggest now might be a good time to admit it. If you don't, then it can only make things more difficult for you if it's subsequently proven that you were.'

'I can't believe we are having this discussion,' Mr White said, as much to himself as to Milner. 'I have told you already Glyn did not turn up for our meeting. I waited for about half an hour and, when he didn't show up, went straight home.'

'The problem we have, though, Mr White, is we only have your word that's what you did. Tell me why I should now believe what you say when, on our previous encounters, you have not been entirely truthful or open with us.'

'This is ridiculous,' he answered. 'You have given me no choice but to refuse to answer any more of your questions until I have a lawyer present. This is clearly harassment.'

Milner was tempted to mention that he had still not refuted his point about Mr White's previous lack of honesty, but felt, if he were to now do so, it would only inflame the situation further. 'This is not a formal interview, Mr White. It's an informal discussion and you did agree to come here voluntarily. It could be, however, that we will be asking you back for a more formal interview. In that instance, you have every right to have a legal representative present.'

'Is that it, then?' he asked.

'Almost,' replied Milner. 'I need to make you aware that my colleague, DC Bennett, is currently speaking with your wife.'

'What?' he almost shouted. 'What possible reason do you have to involve her?'

'We need to check with her what time she arrived home

from her sister's on the Sunday evening. You will remember you have already told us how you were already back at home when she did return.'

'I've told you again and again that I was. How many more times are you going to ask me the same question?'

'As many times as it takes until we can finally believe you and therefore exclude you from our enquiries. That's the way a murder investigation tends to work.'

Mr White shook his head, his earlier anger having now seemingly subsided. 'I can't believe this is happening to me. It could ruin my life.'

'But not as much as Mr Burton's,' replied Milner.

Chapter 34

'How did it go?' asked Milner.

DC Bennett had returned to the station from his visit to speak with Mrs White. 'She did confirm everything that her husband had told us. Her husband was at home when she got back, at seven o'clock, from visiting her sister. Although she was a bit puzzled when I asked her how he seemed, she did confirm he appeared to be upset about something. When she asked him if he was okay, as far as she could remember, he replied that he was supposed to have met someone from the club but that the person did not arrive. I asked if he mentioned the reason for the meeting. Again, she said she asked but he just answered something about it being a golf club matter.'

'Did you believe her?'

'I did, yes,' he answered, a touch of disappointment clearly evident in the tone of his voice. 'There was none of the hesitation you would normally see if a person is not telling the truth. All I can say is if she was lying then she deserves an Oscar. What about your interview with Mr White?'

'Like you said about his wife. He didn't give the impression he was lying. There was the anger and indignation that you would expect when questioning someone's honesty, especially relating to a murder investigation.' He paused briefly before continuing. 'I haven't, though, completely ruled him out yet. We do need to try and track his movements before we can finally do that. He's still one of our prime suspects. Any success yet with CCTV coverage?'

'I'm still looking through it all. As you can imagine there's a lot to go through, so I've steered a few other officers into helping out.'

'What have you told them to look out for?'

'Either Mr Burton's car or Roger White's, on any route close to the quarry. They have the descriptions and registration numbers of their cars. At the moment they are reviewing any public CCTV that is available. If that doesn't throw up any sightings then we'll start including footage on commercial properties. As I said, it's a big job.' As Milner did not immediately reply, DC Bennett continued. 'What do you think we should do next?'

Milner walked towards the chart featuring all of the names. 'Let's take a look,' he said. 'DCI Stone has ruled out Tony Cook. I don't think Mike Preston is our murderer. Jonathan Mercer was not even in the country at the time of the death, and, until CCTV footage proves otherwise, it looks as though Roger White is also unlikely to be the one. And we are all agreed it's highly unlikely to have been one of the women.'

'So that leaves Craig Blackwell,' DC Bennett said, with undisguised enthusiasm. 'It can't be anyone else. Why don't we bring him in?'

'On what basis?' asked Milner. 'We can't accuse him of murder simply because he withdrew some money from his own company. I know it's quite a lot of money to you and me, but, frankly, to men like him and Glyn Burton, it's not that big.'

'But he doesn't have a cast-iron alibi for the day Mr Burton disappeared. Surely that's enough for us to legitimately ask him a few more questions? It might help him to remember if he's here, at the station.'

Milner, clearly considering what DC Bennett had just suggested, took his time before he answered. 'Okay. Give him a call and ask him to come in.' Knowing the bad feeling between the two of them, he added, 'But don't antagonise him. We don't want him arriving here in a belligerent mood. We want him as relaxed as possible. That way we are more likely to catch him out if he is lying.'

'Don't worry, sir, I'll be as nice as pie.'

Milner, giving him a slightly sceptical look, simply said, 'Just don't make him angry, that's all.'

'Have we heard from the boss yet?' asked DC Bennett, changing the subject.

'Nothing so far,' answered Milner.

'He won't be able to resist calling in to see how we are getting on. Just mark my words,' DC Bennett said, with a light laugh. 'Have you any idea what he's doing?'

'No idea at all. You know what he's like. He only ever tells you anything if he thinks you should know. He obviously doesn't think we should know about this.'

'Do you think it might have something to do with the other investigation? You know, the one involving Commander Jenkins.'

'I did think that myself,' said Milner. 'I hope not, but you saw for yourself just how much it has affected him.'

'I agree. And that's only what he allows you to see. I'm sure there's more going on than his appearance suggested. He's not the type of person to so readily accept something, especially if it's something he feels so strongly about.'

'Anyway,' Milner said, 'I'm sure, sooner or later, we'll find out what he's been up to. In the meantime, we keep our focus on this case. As agreed, arrange for Craig Blackwell to come in. See if you can get him in later today. Before he gets here, though, we review everything he's told us. If he is lying then we need to be able to identify when he's doing it. Let's see if we can get this resolved before DCI Stone contacts us.'

DC Bennett was to be proven correct; Tom would be in contact before long. What neither of them could possibly foresee, however, were the circumstances of that contact.

Chapter 35

At about the same time Milner was finishing his interview with Roger White, Tom and Mary were on their way to meet Paul and his family. Mary had earlier received a call from Paul to confirm where they would be for their meeting. It had been decided they would meet in the reception area of their hotel. Fortunately, the hotel was located on the western edge of London and so it wasn't too much of a journey for Tom and Mary. The problem, though, as usual, was finding somewhere reasonably nearby to park. In the end they chose one of the numerous underground car parks operated by a well-known national chain. This, however, had its own drawbacks – certainly as far as Tom was concerned.

'I can't believe how much they charge to park for just a few hours,' muttered Tom. 'It's legal robbery. You also need to have taken an advanced driving course just to be able to park your car. It's so narrow down there. If they don't bankrupt you with the parking fee, your insurance company will, after you scraped it just trying to get in and out.'

Mary chose not to argue the point, suspecting that part of Tom's anger was probably due to his increasing anxiety. Instead, she simply said, 'Well, at least we are close by.'

After parking the car and emerging into the daylight they made the short walk to the hotel. As they approached the entrance, Mary said, 'Okay?'

'I'm fine,' he simply replied. Nonetheless, Mary took his right hand in her left one and gave it a slight squeeze of encouragement.

As soon as they entered the hotel, they both spotted a man and woman, along with two children, seated in the far corner of the reception area. It was equally obvious that they too had been noticed, because suddenly the man stood and walked towards Tom and Mary.

'Hi, I'm Paul,' he said, 'I'm guessing that you must be Mary and you must be Tom.' He was quite a bit taller than Tom and, even having just spoken those few words, clearly had a distinctive Australian accent. Although he was only in his early thirties he was totally bald, but this, combined with his clear blue eyes and slightly tanned complexion, gave him a very striking appearance. The type of appearance which would get you noticed every time you walked into a room.

Tom had wondered what Paul would call him and had come to the conclusion that he would most likely use his Christian name. He therefore found it quite reassuring when he did exactly that. The other worry that he'd had was what to do after the initial introduction. He knew this was likely to be the most awkward moment. Should he hug his son or just shake his hand? In the event, he realised it was a bit of a non-choice. He was not a natural hugger anyway, and had personally always felt slightly uncomfortable on the admittedly few occasions he had been greeted with a hug. So he had simply decided to take his lead from Paul.

'It's great to see you both,' said Paul. He hugged Mary. 'We've all been excited about meeting you.' He then held his hand out to Tom. 'I don't know about you, but I've been really nervous about this moment.'

Tom took his hand. 'I know what you mean,' he replied.

'Right,' said Paul. 'Why don't I introduce you to the family?' He led them back in his family's direction. 'This is my wife, Kerry.'

'Great to meet you both,' she said, hugging Mary and then doing the same with Tom.

'And these,' Paul said, 'are Sam and Emily.'

Mary, clearly more comfortable when talking with children, leant forward, whilst stooping slightly so that she was nearer to their height. 'You must be so excited about coming all this way. I've never travelled as far as you both have.'

It was now Tom's turn and he felt that all eyes were on him. He had no experience of talking to young children and his awkwardness was becoming apparent.

Fortunately, he was saved by Sam. 'Are you the famous detective? Daddy has told us all about you. You must have solved lots of murders. Do you have your gun with you?'

Tom found himself laughing. 'I'm afraid I don't carry a gun. Only special policemen have those.'

Sam frowned, clearly disappointed with Tom's answer. 'But you have solved lots of murders, haven't you?'

'Well, not lots, but a few,' he replied.

It was Emily who next put him on the spot. 'Are you my real granddad? Daddy says you are, but I think that Granddad Jack loves me the most, especially since Nanny Anne died.'

'Emily,' said Kerry. 'We all love you the same.'

'It's not a problem,' answered Tom, before turning to face Emily. 'I'm sure Granddad Jack is the best granddad in the whole world. You are so lucky to have someone like him who loves you.'

Mary gave him a smile, suggesting she was proud of the way he had handled that potentially embarrassing situation.

'Why don't you join us for a meal? We've booked a table at the hotel restaurant,' said Kerry. 'We thought we'd have something to eat and then get the tube and go into central London. The kids especially can't wait to see the Tower of London. Is that okay with you, Tom?'

'Sounds like a great idea,' he answered, with the same level of enthusiasm shown by Kerry.

Sam, once again looking at Tom, was clearly not going to let his favourite subject drop. 'Are there any murderers in the Tower of London? Will we be able to see any?'

'They stopped locking people up there many, many years ago. But I agree with you that they should still be kept there. I know the head of the police in London. I'll speak to him about that the next time I see him.'

Clearly impressed with Tom's answer, Sam simply said, 'Cool.'

*

Tom and Mary sat at the places which had been reserved for them. Tom found himself seated between Paul and Kerry, whilst Mary was seated next to Kerry. He suspected some thought had gone into the seating arrangements.

'You must all be very tired,' said Mary. 'After such a long journey.'

'Yes, it was a long way,' said Paul, 'but at least the delay wasn't too bad. Sam and Emily, fortunately, slept for quite a long time on the plane. I must have slept for some of the time, but I suppose it will be later when it starts to catch up to all of us.'

'So, what is your job in Australia?' asked Tom.

'I work in real estate,' he answered. 'I have a small business which buys and sells property in and around Melbourne. Jack – that's Mum's husband – introduced me to it. He had his own business, and I worked for him for a few years before setting up mine.'

'Were you then in competition with him?'

'Not really. His business focussed on the lower-value end of the property market, whilst mine is at the higher end.'

'Is it successful?' asked Tom. 'Not that I know a lot about the property market, but isn't it very dependent on economic conditions? It must have its ups and downs.'

'That's certainly true and we've had a few tough times, but right now things are very positive.'

'I have a house which I've been trying to sell. Perhaps you could help out?' Tom said, with a light laugh. 'Although I wouldn't describe it as at the top end of the property market.'

'Yes, Mary mentioned you were living at her home. Does that mean you are planning to get married soon?' Paul asked, with a directness which Aussies are renowned for.

Tom, out of the corner of his eye, just caught Mary looking in his direction. 'That's certainly the plan, but we haven't set a date yet,' he answered, as diplomatically as possible.

Recognising that now might be as good a time as any to broach the subject, he immediately carried on, although this time in a quieter voice. 'I was so sorry to hear about Anne. It must have been so upsetting for everyone.'

'Yes, it was,' Paul replied, suddenly struggling to keep his emotions in check. 'We all thought that she had managed to get through it, but the cancer suddenly returned and ...'

'I understand,' Tom said. 'She must have been so proud of you.'

'Yes, I think she was. And, of course, she loved all of her five grandchildren.'

'I didn't know she had five,' Tom replied, before falling silent.

'Mum and Jack had two children. Jamie is now twenty-six and has two children, whilst Lauren is twenty-four and had her first not long ago.'

'It seems there's a lot I don't know,' Tom said, reflectively.

Paul, recognising that, perhaps, this wasn't the time or place to have this discussion, diplomatically tried to change the subject. 'I'm sure we'll get the chance to speak later about this. But what about you? Believe it or not, your exploits in that murder case you were involved in even made Aussie television. In fact, it was when you were giving some sort of statement to the press that Mum recognised you and then told me who you were. To say I was surprised would be the understatement of all time. I did know from Mum that you were a policeman, but I'm afraid that's all I knew. I understand from Mary you are a detective chief inspector with the London Metropolitan force? That must be exciting.'

'It has its moments,' he answered, thinking of the time, not that long ago, when he had been shot. 'But mainly it's lots of admin and paperwork.'

'Are you investigating anything at the moment?' Paul asked. Realising his question might have placed Tom in a potentially compromising situation, he quickly added, 'I'm sorry. I shouldn't have asked.'

'That's okay. Coincidentally, we are currently in the middle of a murder investigation.'

The mention of the word *murder* prompted Sam to speak. 'Wow. When will you catch them?'

'Well, hopefully soon, but sometimes it takes a bit longer.'

'Does that mean you should still be working on it, instead of being here?' asked Paul.

'I have a good team of officers,' he answered. 'I'm sure they can cope without me being there for a few days.'

'Well, please don't feel as though you have to spend all of your time with us. I'm sure there will still be plenty of time for us to spend together.'

'What are your plans whilst you're in the UK? I understand from Mary you are travelling up to the Midlands next week to visit your mum's brother.'

'That's right. Uncle John lives in Sutton Coldfield. He came over for the funeral and that's when we decided we'd like to visit the UK, now that the kids are a bit older. Do you remember him?'

'Yes, I do,' replied Tom. 'He was Anne's younger brother, if I remember correctly. He came to our wedding. When did you and Kerry marry?'

'About nine years ago. We first met when she came to work

at our company, and things sort of moved on very quickly after that.'

Just then the waiter arrived with the menus, and the next few minutes were spent making their choices. After the waiter had taken their orders, the conversation returned to their plans for the visit.

'If you get the time,' said Mary, 'you are very welcome to stay with us. Even if it's just for the day.'

Mary's suggestion took Tom a bit by surprise, especially as she'd told him not to get ahead of himself when he'd asked her about their lodging plans. Nonetheless, he thought it best to endorse her invitation. 'I know you've planned a busy schedule, but it would be really nice if you could.'

'Where exactly do you live?' asked Kerry.

'It's in a place called Bagshot,' she replied. 'By car, it's less than an hour away from here. That depends, of course, on the time of day. Getting in and out of London can be a bit of a nightmare sometimes.'

'Is it anywhere near where Paul lived?' asked Kerry.

'Not too far away. We lived in Sunbury then,' replied Tom.

'Perhaps we can all go and see it, then,' Kerry suggested. 'It would be good for the children to see where their dad used to live.'

'That's arranged, then,' said Mary, before anyone else could say anything, leaving Tom slightly taken aback by this sudden turn of events.

Chapter 36

The rest of the day was spent visiting some of the attractions in London. Although this was not something that Tom would normally want to do, nonetheless he found himself actually enjoying the experience. In particular, he surprised himself with how much pleasure he got from Sam and Emily's excitement. By the time they returned to the hotel it was after six o'clock.

'The children look tired,' said Mary.

'They are not the only ones,' added Kerry. 'The time difference, and all of the walking we've done this afternoon, is beginning to hit me.'

'We should start making our way back home, then,' Mary said.

'Why don't we have a drink together?' suggested Paul, looking at Tom.

Kerry, picking up on Paul's suggestion, said, 'Mary, why don't you come up? I'd really appreciate your help in putting the kids to bed.'

'That's a good idea,' she answered. 'If we left now, we'd only get stuck in the traffic.'

Tom, so far, hadn't said a word, as the conversation happened around him. 'That seems to be agreed, then,' he said now. 'It looks like we have been given approval to go to the bar. It would be rude not to do so.' He laughed.

Mary gave him a fleeting smile, before taking Emily's hand and, along with Kerry and Sam, heading towards the hotel lift, leaving Tom and Paul in the reception area.

'I assume that was planned,' said Tom.

This time it was Paul's turn to laugh. 'Well, yes, we did speak about it as a possibility.'

'Anyway, whoever's idea it was, it was a good one.'

They both walked towards the bar, which, at this early time of the evening, was almost deserted.

'What's your poison?' asked Paul.

'I'll get these,' Tom replied.

'I'll get them. It's the least a son can do for his dad.'

Tom found himself moved. 'Thank you for saying that. I never thought I'd hear those words said to me.'

Paul suddenly moved forward and hugged him. 'And I never thought I'd get the chance to say them to you.'

It was, without a doubt, the most emotional Tom had felt for a very long time, and he was surprised by just how difficult he was finding it to keep those emotions in check.

'Let's get a drink,' said Paul, recognising the suddenly dramatically heightened emotion of the moment. 'What do you suggest?'

Tom looked at the selection of draught lagers and beers at the bar. 'Normally I would have a red wine, but I think this time I'll have this one,' he said, pointing at one of the beers.

'I'll have the same, then,' Paul said, before ordering them.

The barman poured their drinks and they took them to a corner of the bar area where, even if more people suddenly arrived, they were guaranteed some privacy.

'I really enjoyed today,' said Tom, once they were seated. 'I have to be honest, though: walking around the middle of London would not normally be my preferred way to spend an afternoon. In fact, I can't remember the last time I actually did that. But, then again, I've never done it with you and your family.'

'I couldn't help noticing, though, that you were walking slightly uncomfortably, especially later in the day,' Paul said. 'Just to let you know, I did ask Mary about it.'

Tom suddenly sat up straight. 'And what did she say?' he asked, with a degree of sudden defensiveness.

'She told me how you'd been shot in your right leg, not that long ago, and that it was still affecting you.'

'Well, yes, it's still a bit sore, but it's a lot better than it was and it's getting better every day.'

'Why didn't you tell me?'

'It's not something I now regularly think about. As I said, it's a lot better than it was.'

Paul, sensing that this was a subject that Tom didn't want to discuss, paused briefly before he next spoke, this time in a tone that lightened the mood. 'Sam would have been really impressed. I think you missed a trick there.'

'Maybe next time, then,' replied Tom, with a small smile.

Both Paul and Tom took a sip of their beer.

'Why did you and Mum split up?' Paul suddenly asked, quickly bringing Tom back to reality. It was a question – perhaps, *the* question – that Paul had every right to ask and Tom had been expecting. Nonetheless, the suddenness of it still took him by surprise.

'It's a question I have asked myself many times over the years,' he replied. 'I think – no, I'm sure – it was because I put my career ahead of my family. It's certainly not an excuse, but being a young policeman trying to make his mark in the force, and especially back in the eighties, was all-consuming. With hindsight, of course, it's easy to see, but at the time you just seemed to get caught up in it all. The job controlled you. You were often judged by the number of hours you put in rather than the quality of those hours or even, sometimes, the results you achieved. I remember working a crazy number of hours when, in truth, I really didn't need to. But you ran the risk of being seen as some sort of lightweight if you left at anything like a normal time.' He fell silent for a moment, before adding, 'But, as I said, it's not meant as an excuse. At the end of the day, it was my decision. It's not something I'm proud of.'

'How did Mum react to that?'

'At the beginning, she seemed to accept it as part and parcel of being a police officer, but later, especially when she became pregnant and then you were born, it became more of an issue. After that, things between us deteriorated rapidly. When she told me she was leaving, to be honest, I wasn't that upset. Perhaps if I had then shown more commitment to our marriage, things might have worked out differently and you'd be speaking with an English accent, not an Aussie one.'

'Except, of course, I wouldn't have met Kerry and had Sam and Emily.'

'That's very true,' replied Tom. Sensing that now might be a good time to ask some of the questions he was interested in, he said, 'Jack seems a really good man. Sam and Emily obviously love him a lot.'

'Yes, he is. Jack and Mum were so happy together. When they married, I was about five years old, but, right from the start, he treated me as his own son, and, over time, I came to see him as my own father.' He hesitated. 'I'm sorry.'

'You don't need to be sorry about anything,' answered Tom. 'In fact, I wish I could, one day, meet him so that I could personally thank him for raising such an impressive son.'

Paul, not feeling able to respond to Tom's compliment, said, 'He was an absolute rock when Mum got ill and it broke his heart when she died, and I'm not sure he'll ever get over it. Fortunately, though, the kids have helped to fill the void, at least partly.'

'How did he feel about you all coming over here to meet me?'

'He was fine about it. No problem at all. In fact, he encouraged us to do it. But what about you?' he asked. 'Did you ever think about getting married again? Before Mary, I mean?'

'Not really. I had a couple of semi-serious relationships, but I knew I wouldn't be able to put any marriage ahead of my career. I know that sounds incredibly selfish – and, of course, it is selfish – but that's how I felt at the time. As the years went by, I suppose I became too set in my ways and marriage became an even more unlikely prospect.'

'So, how did you get together with Mary? What changed?'

'That's what I often ask myself,' he said, laughing. 'You might find this hard to believe, after what I just told you, but we met via an internet dating site. It was actually called, er, *You're Never Too Old for Love* ... and, as the name suggests, was aimed at ... well, let's say the older generation.'

'You're joking,' Paul replied, matching Tom's earlier laughter. 'Somehow I can't see you being on a dating site.'

'I did say you might find it hard to believe. It was at a time when my career was at, probably, its lowest point and I was seriously thinking of taking early retirement. Anyway, I think it must have affected my brain because, one night, I suppose when I was going through one of my self-pitying moments, I suddenly decided to sign up.'

'And that's when you met Mary?'

'Well, not initially, but, eventually, yes.'

'So, Mary wasn't your first choice?' Paul asked.

'Well, she wasn't my first date, but she was certainly my first choice,' he replied.

'Good answer,' Paul said. 'She seems a really nice lady.'

'She is. As I said, I was at my lowest point when I met her. It's not an exaggeration to say that, since we met, my life – personally and professionally – has changed for the better. I'm a very lucky man.'

'And you think you will get married?'

'I think so,' he replied, before correcting himself. 'I hope so.'

'Well, good luck with whatever you two decide to do.'

'Thanks,' Tom said, before changing the subject. 'Apart from work, what other interests do you have? Don't all Aussies spend all their time outdoors, or is that just a myth?'

'It's definitely true that our weather encourages you to go outdoors, although sometimes it's just too hot. I play golf, and we usually smother ourselves in the highest factor sun protector. Plus I always have to wear a cap.' He gestured to his bald head.

'So you play golf?' asked Tom, immediately recalling the circumstances of the current investigation.

'I do, yes. In fact, Sam is now getting interested in it as well. I'm really looking forward to the time when we can play together. What about you? Do you play?'

'I don't, I'm afraid. I think I'd only be any good as your caddy.'

'That's agreed, then. If we can ever arrange it, you can push my golf trolley for me.'

Just then, Kerry walked into the bar with Mary in tow. 'The kids are settled now and so I thought I'd come down, while I've got a couple of minutes, to see you before you leave.'

'I mentioned to Kerry,' said Mary, looking at Tom, 'that, if they wanted to, they could come over to our house tomorrow. I said, if they got the train to Egham, I could collect them at the station. Then you could show them where Paul used to live.'

Tom, recognising that Mary was looking for his agreement, was happy to oblige. 'That's a good idea. Just let us know when you've set off.'

A short while later Tom and Mary were driving back home. Mary had clearly been itching to ask the obvious question but had, to now, resisted. Finally, though, she said, 'So, how did it go with Paul?'

'Much better than I dared to think,' he replied.

'And what did you talk about?'

'We did discuss why Anne and I divorced, although, to be fair, it wasn't something which dominated the entire time. He was interested in my time in the force, where we met and if we were planning to get married.'

'And what did you say?' she asked. 'About getting married, I mean.'

'I said that I hoped we would.'

Mary squeezed his hand. 'I'm so glad it went well for you,' she said.

So was he. In fact, he couldn't remember the last time he'd enjoyed being in the company of a group of people so much, as normally he much preferred his own company.

That night, as he lay in bed, despite being quite physically tired, he was finding it difficult to sleep. His mind was still buzzing with the events of the day, not aided by the fact he couldn't help trying to go over his conversation with Paul *verbatim*. So much had happened, during the day, that he was struggling to remember everything which had occurred. Soon, though, he would recall something which would have a direct bearing on the investigation into Glyn Burton's murder.

Chapter 37

'Thank you for coming in,' said Milner. 'Especially as it was at such short notice.'

'It was made clear to me that I didn't really have a choice,' Mr Blackwell said, looking towards DC Bennett. 'This is now the fourth time I've spoken with the police. What is it you want to talk about this time?'

'Mr Blackwell. The last time my colleagues DCI Stone and DC Bennett spoke with you, they asked where you had been between 3 pm and 8 pm on the day Mr Burton disappeared. I understand, at the time, you couldn't remember. You've now had the chance to remember. So perhaps you could now tell us?'

'As I told your colleagues at the time, I couldn't exactly remember because it was over two weeks earlier.'

DC Bennett interrupted him. 'Actually, what you said was that you couldn't remember at all. You did not say you couldn't *exactly* remember. That would have been a perfectly understandable answer. But you didn't say that.'

'Exactly or not exactly, at the time I couldn't immediately remember. Is that okay for you?' he asked, directing his question towards DC Bennett.

DC Bennett didn't respond and it was Milner who, again, took up the questioning. 'So, can you remember now?'

'I went back into the office around three thirty and was there for a few hours. I can't remember exactly how long, but I think I got home just after seven. If you speak to my wife, she will confirm that.'

'We will speak to her. Thanks for your suggestion,' said DC Bennett, in his most sarcastic tone.

'What were you doing in the office on a Sunday afternoon?' Milner asked. 'Do you often go in then?'

'Sometimes,' he answered. 'It depends on what I have to do. On this particular Sunday I had to finish a presentation. I told you that's why Glyn called me. We were pitching for some new business and Glyn wanted to discuss what progress I was making. Although it was my role to find new clients, he wanted to get an update from me.'

'Who was the prospective client?' asked Milner.

'I've provided the information to you already,' Mr Blackwell replied, making his annoyance clear.

'It would help if you could let me know, though,' suggested Milner.

'His name is James Wilton. He's a broker who has quite a large client list. We have been trying to get his business for some time.'

'So, when was the presentation?'

'It was the following day, on the Monday afternoon, at our offices. Glyn was due to attend but, of course, didn't.'

'You must have been concerned that he didn't attend, especially as it was such an important meeting,' suggested Milner.

'I would say surprised more than concerned,' he answered. 'I was the one who was presenting, so it wasn't really a problem Glyn wasn't there.'

'Why, then, were you surprised?'

'Mainly because, when we'd spoken the day before, Glyn gave every impression that he would be there. And, anyway, James Wilton was someone who could bring us more business.'

'I assume, later, you called Mr Burton to tell him how the meeting went.'

'Of course I did,' he answered. 'But his phone seemed to be dead.'

'Did you then try his home number?'

'No, I didn't.'

'Why not? Surely that would have been the logical thing to do. After all, by your own admission, Mr Burton had taken a keen interest in the presentation to Mr Wilton. He would at least have wanted to know how it went.'

He didn't immediately reply, and when he did it was in a significantly quieter tone. 'I thought he might have been with Mrs Mercer.'

'And, if he was, you didn't want to raise Mrs Burton's suspicions. Is that right?' asked Milner.

'Yes, that's right,' he simply replied.

Another brief silence followed.

'So,' said DC Bennett. 'Just to be clear. You went into your office at about three thirty, stayed there for a few hours and then left for home, arriving back around seven. And you didn't go anywhere else during that time?'

'I've told you where I was,' he answered, in a tone which now suggested his rising annoyance. 'How many more times do I need to tell you?'

'Thank you. That's clear,' said Milner, aware of the sudden increased tension. 'Could I just ask if you called anyone, or anyone called you, whilst you were away from your home on that Sunday afternoon?'

There was a slight hesitation before he answered. 'I think I might have called Susie, my wife, to let her know what time I would be home.'

'And that's all?' Milner asked.

'I think so,' he replied, before adding, 'Yes, I'm sure.'

'One final question, Mr Blackwell,' said Milner. 'Do you have any idea who would want to murder Mr Burton?'

'As I've said before, I have absolutely no idea.'

'Thank you again, Mr Blackwell, for coming in. If you do think of anything else which you feel might be important to our investigation, please contact us. I believe you have my colleagues' contact details already, but here are mine,' said Milner, handing him his card.

'Is that all?' he replied, either surprised or relieved that their discussion had finished.

'That's all,' said Milner, 'although it's always possible we will want to have a discussion with you again.'

For a brief moment it looked as though Mr Blackwell was about to say something else. When he didn't, Milner said, 'DC Bennett will show you out.'

A short while later, when Milner and DC Bennett were both together again, DC Bennett said, 'I still think he's lying, sir. I can tell. There's something about him which isn't right.'

'If that's the case, then you need to find out what it is. We can't go around accusing someone of murder just because we don't like them.'

DC Bennett didn't respond, and so Milner continued. 'What we can do, though, is check out his alibi. Let's talk to his wife to see if she confirms what he's just told us. Also, have you had the chance yet to speak with Mr Wilton?'

'Not yet, sir. He's been away for a few days but is due back tomorrow. I've left a message for him to ring me back as soon as he returns.'

'Good,' he said, before adding, 'Why don't you also get hold of Mr Blackwell's phone records for that Sunday?'

'What about CCTV, sir?' asked DC Bennett. 'Why don't I check to see if there is any which would show him entering and leaving his office when he said he did?'

'Okay. Get on to it straight away, then,' answered Milner.

'Any messages from the boss?' asked DC Bennett.

'No, although I'm sure there will be.'

'I wonder what he's been doing.'

'I've learnt not to speculate,' answered Milner. 'What I do know, though, is that, whatever it is, it will be a surprise to us.'

Chapter 38

It was late afternoon, the following day, and Milner and DC Bennett were reviewing the latest information they had obtained.

'So, it wasn't just his wife who he spoke with when he was in the office,' said Milner. He was studying an A4 sheet of paper which listed all the calls Craig Blackwell had made and received on that particular day.

'And that's not all,' said DC Bennett. 'I've just taken a look at the CCTV coverage, which shows him leaving the building where his office is located at 4.32 pm. If you remember, he said he was there for a few hours and arrived back home around 7 pm.' He sounded as though he were enjoying himself. 'I've checked to see how long it would take to drive from his office to his home. Even accounting for a few delays, it wouldn't have taken more than forty minutes. That would mean, then, that he would have left past six, whereas the CCTV shows him leaving at 4.32 pm. So, where was he between that time and 7 pm? And that's not all,' he said, an almost triumphant air now in his voice. 'I also checked to see if the timings would allow him to leave the office, meet with Mr Burton, murder him, dispose of the body and then arrive back home for 7pm.'

'And do they?' asked Milner.

'It's tight but possible,' he answered.

Milner didn't immediately respond, as he considered what he'd just heard, and so DC Bennett carried on.

'I think we should bring him in again. There are so many holes in his alibi that he's got to be our main suspect now.'

'We can't keep bringing him in without formally charging him. If we do then we will need a lot more than what we've got at the moment. Let's review what we do have. We know he took a call from Mr Burton on the Sunday. His explanation for that call is perfectly logical. You told me earlier he did have a business meeting with Mr Wilton the day after Mr Burton disappeared. It's reasonable, therefore, for them to have a discussion about that meeting. He then says that he was in his office most of the Sunday afternoon, preparing for the meeting. Again, all very logical. He did leave earlier than he said, but he could claim that he just got the times wrong. There are no forensics at all to link him with the murder. As far as I can see, it's all just circumstantial. As DCI Stone would say ... his defence lawyer would have a field day.'

'But he's lied all through this,' replied DC Bennett, trying to maintain his earlier enthusiasm. 'And you are forgetting the cash he drew out. I just don't buy his explanation that he needed the money for a new car.'

'You might be right, but, again, we can't charge him solely on the basis that he's spending his own money. No, what we need is at least some evidence placing him near the scene of the crime. It's a bit of a long shot, but why don't you see if any CCTV has his car close to where the body was found?' He looked at the A4 sheet again. 'These other numbers. Have you been able to trace them yet? They might give us another lead.'

'I'm on it already, sir,' DC Bennett answered, albeit now with considerably less enthusiasm.

'Good. Let's see what comes back and then we'll review again,' Milner said, handing the sheet to DC Bennett.

'Why don't I just go and talk to him about the timings and see how he reacts?' DC Bennett asked. 'You never know; it just might throw him enough that he lets something else slip.'

Milner looked directly at DC Bennett. Although DC Bennett had far more experience as a police officer, the reality was that Milner was the senior officer in the relationship. Even so, he didn't want to totally dismiss DC Bennett's theory. 'Gary,' he said. 'I know you feel strongly about this and, I agree, there's something not quite right about all his explanations, but let's do this by the book. If it is him who murdered Mr Burton, then we are only ever going to get one chance to charge him. So let's make sure that, when we do, the charge sticks. We need hard evidence, not circumstantial evidence. Agreed?'

'I suppose so,' answered DC Bennett.

'Why don't you go home? We'll review things again in the morning. A good night's sleep for both of us might help.'

After his meeting with Milner, DC Bennett began to review the existing CCTV footage. This time, though, he was looking to see if Craig Blackwell's car had been anywhere near the quarry where Glyn Burton's body had been discovered.

After a while, and as he'd had no success so far, he decided to continue with it in the morning and leave for home.

As he got into his car, and started the engine, he suddenly had a thought. If he was to prove Craig Blackwell's guilt, then he had to take decisive action, and he now knew what he should do. It was a decision which would prove to have totally unforeseen and ultimately fatal consequences.

Chapter 39

'Thank you for a lovely day yesterday,' said Mary.

Mary had collected Paul, Kerry, Sam and Emily from Egham station and then driven back to her home in Bagshot. Tom had stayed behind, not least because Mary's car could only fit five people into it. Even so, it had apparently been a bit of a squeeze, but, fortunately, the journey back had been a relatively short one. They were now all seated in Mary's front room.

'You don't have to thank us,' answered Paul. 'We also had a great day, didn't we, kids?'

'It was mega,' said Sam. 'I've only seen Buckingham Palace and Big Ben in photos. I can't wait to tell all my mates about it, and especially that I now know a real-life London detective.'

Tom laughed. 'As long as they aren't expecting Sherlock Holmes.'

'I thought, after we've finished our drinks, we could set off to see the house where you used to live,' Mary said. 'After that, perhaps we could have a pub lunch and then maybe walk around Virginia Water. But it's really up to you. You are the ones on holiday.'

'Sounds good to me,' said Kerry. 'A British pub lunch will be another first for Sam and Emily.'

'We'll also take Tom's car. Perhaps all the boys could go with him and the girls with me?'

Tom could see that Mary was really enjoying herself making the arrangements. He had quickly realised, not long after they had first met, that organising things like this was something she was actually not only very good at but, perhaps more importantly, had fun doing.

'Are you sure?' asked Paul. 'We don't want you to go to a lot of trouble.'

'It's no trouble at all,' said Tom. 'And anyway, I wouldn't dare to go against what Mary suggests.'

About thirty minutes later they had parked their cars and were standing immediately outside a small house, close to the middle of a row of terraced houses.

'I don't expect you can remember it, can you, Paul?' asked Kerry.

'Not really. I was only about two years old when we emigrated. Mum did, though, have an old photo of all of us standing outside.' He pointed to the front door. 'We were all standing just there.'

'Do you still have the photo?' asked Mary.

'Yes, I do, somewhere back at home. I suppose I should have tried to find it so that I could bring it with me.'

'Actually, if it's the photo I'm thinking of,' said Tom, 'it was taken when you had just started to walk. So you must have been just over a year old. I think one of our neighbours took it.'

'It's really small,' Emily suddenly said, far from impressed. 'Did you really live in such a tiny house, Daddy?'

'I really did, yes,' he replied. 'When I was young, we didn't have all of the things you have today.'

'You're starting to sound like Tom,' said Mary. 'Sometimes I think he's at his happiest when he's telling me about all of the things he *didn't* have when he was young. Why don't I take a photo of you standing outside the house?'

'That's a good idea,' replied Paul. 'But the owners might not like a group of strangers standing at their front door, having their photo taken.'

'I'll go and talk to them,' suggested Tom, before walking down the short path and knocking on the door. Almost immediately the door was opened by a young woman. Although the others couldn't quite hear what was being said, they did see Tom pointing towards them. He then walked back and rejoined them. 'Yes, she's fine with that. In fact, she said that she would take the photos if we liked.'

They all headed towards the front door and stood there whilst she took a number of different photos of them in various combinations, including one just of Tom and Paul where Paul, as he was taller, had his arm around Tom's shoulder.

They had the promised early pub lunch afterwards, and then spent a couple of hours walking around Virginia Water.

Although it was beginning to get quite chilly, Sam and Emily seemed immune to this. Once again, their walk gave Tom and Paul the opportunity to spend some time together. What was becoming obvious to Tom was the fact that, as they spent more time together, he was finding himself less and less on edge in Paul's company. By the time they had returned to the car park, the tension he had felt the previous day, when they had first met at the hotel, had all but disappeared, to be replaced, to his relief, by something more natural and relaxed.

'Why don't you come back to our house?' suggested Mary. 'I'm sure you need a hot drink after being outside for all of that time.'

'Are you sure, Mary?' asked Kerry. 'We don't want to put you out. I'm sure you have other things you could be doing.'

'It really isn't a problem,' she answered. 'I can run you back to the station a bit later.'

'Wasn't that the Wentworth Golf Club I saw on the way here?' Paul asked as he got into Tom's car, alongside him. 'It's a course I've always wanted to play. I didn't realise it was so close to where you live.'

'Why don't we drive in, so that you can at least take a look at it?' suggested Tom.

'Are you sure?' he asked. 'Have we got time? It's starting to get a bit dark. But it would be great if we could.'

Tom then got out of the car and walked towards Mary's to speak to her.

'That's sorted, then,' he said when he returned. 'Mary will go straight back home whilst we go there.'

Just a few minutes later they had turned off the A30 and down the long drive which led to the clubhouse. Tom parked the car and they took the short walk towards the final hole, where a group of four golfers, despite the fading light, were just finishing their round.

'I can't believe anyone would want to play at this time of year,' said Tom. 'I thought you only played golf when the weather was nice and warm.'

'Committed golfers will play in any weather,' Paul replied, with a slight laugh. 'You can see that they're all still wearing caps, probably in the hope that the sun would appear.'

Tom continued to study the golfers as they walked past him, each of them pushing their trolley.

'So I couldn't encourage you to take up the game, then?' asked Paul, when they had returned to Tom's car.

'I think it will need more than encouragement to get me to play. It looks like an expensive hobby,' he answered.

'It can be, but you don't need to spend a lot of money and, anyway, golf is a great way to make lots of new friends.'

As he heard this, Tom immediately thought of Mr Burton and the less-than-welcoming reception he had received when he'd joined his own golf club.

*

Later that evening Tom and Mary were alone again, each with a glass of wine in hand.

'I think it's been a really enjoyable couple of days,' she said. 'You must be really pleased.'

'Relieved, really,' he answered. 'But you're right; it all went off far better than I expected and, I have to say, it was great to be able to spend time with Paul and Kerry. It was also fantastic seeing Sam and Emily enjoying themselves so much. They are really nice kids.'

'They are,' she said. 'Did you agree when we would see them again?'

'Yes, the day after tomorrow. I thought it would be good, tomorrow, to let them have some time together, as a family. Paul will call me tomorrow night so that we can arrange something.'

Mary squeezed his hand. 'I told you it would all work out well, didn't I?'

'You did, yes. As ever, you were right,' he replied, with a slight chuckle. 'I should listen to you more in future.'

'It will be a bit of a blow when they return home,' she said, this time in a more serious tone. 'How do you think you will handle that?'

'Yes, I've been asking myself that question as well. The honest answer is that I really don't know. Let's face it; I've never been in this position before.'

'By the way,' said Mary, 'Paul has already emailed me the photos of us standing outside your old house. I'll print them off tomorrow.' She paused. 'I think I'll get the one of Sam and Emily put into a nice frame. What do you think?'

'That's a good idea. We can put it alongside the one of your grandchildren, over there,' he suggested.

Mary finished the last of her wine and said, 'I feel really tired. I think the last couple of days have suddenly caught up with me. I think I'll go up.'

'I'm feeling tired as well,' he replied. 'You go up, then. I'll just drink this and then I'll be up.'

After Mary had left, he poured what was left of the wine into his glass. Instinctively, he then looked at his phone, half-expecting there to be a message from Milner. When he saw there wasn't any message, he couldn't help feeling a twinge of disappointment. Even so, his thoughts returned, once again, to the murder investigation.

Suddenly, he leant back. He'd always thought that the answer was within touching distance. What he hadn't expected, though, was just how close it had actually been.

He immediately picked up his phone and made a call. It rang a few times and then was answered.

'Yes, sir?' said Milner. 'I wasn't expecting a call from you, especially at this time of the day.' Tom suspected he didn't entirely mean what he was saying. 'I thought you were taking a few days off.'

'Never mind that,' answered Tom, in a characteristically brusque tone. 'I want you and DC Bennett in the office at seven thirty, tomorrow morning.'

Milner, recognising the urgency of what he had just said, now replied in a similar vein. 'What is it, sir? What's happened?'

'I'll tell you tomorrow,' he answered.

Chapter 40

After his meeting with Milner, instead of driving back to his home in Feltham, DC Bennett headed towards the home of Craig Blackwell, in Hampstead, North London. He knew it was a long shot, but experience had taught him that, sometimes, long shots did come off.

In truth, he didn't really know what to expect or even what he was looking for. All he knew was that he had to do something. Whilst he had to admit that any evidence they had was circumstantial, he remained convinced it was Craig Blackwell who had murdered his business partner. And he was going to provide the evidence that would prove this.

The journey from the station in West London to Craig Blackwell's home in Hampstead was never a straightforward one, and it was almost 8.30 pm before he got there. Mr Blackwell's house, just like Mr and Mrs Burton's in Richmond, was both impressive and expensive, once again confirming the fact that their business was an extremely successful one.

Although the house was slightly set back from the road, DC Bennett managed to find somewhere reasonably close by, which still gave him full sight of the driveway, and then switched off his engine. He suddenly felt much better, sensing that he had made the correct decision. Just being able to see for himself where Craig Blackwell lived somehow made him feel as though he was now doing something positive and was, as a result, just that bit closer to getting to the truth.

An hour later, though, and his enthusiasm and positivity had started to wane. A little earlier, having received a text from his wife, Julie, he had texted her back to let her know he would be home by about eleven, and so had told himself he would stay until 9.45 pm before heading back home. It had been a long day and, in the warmth of the car, he had found himself feeling quite tired, and so opened the driver's window to let in some fresh air.

It was almost at the time he had set himself when, suddenly, a car – Craig Blackwell's car – emerged from the driveway. DC Bennett immediately started the engine, closed the window, pulled out into the road and began to follow him. At this time of night there wasn't a lot of traffic about, and so he took care not to get too close, in case he raised his target's suspicions. He knew it was highly unlikely that Mr Blackwell expected to be followed but, nonetheless, he wasn't taking any chances.

After a while Mr Blackwell turned on to a road which took him immediately due east of the heath, and so it looked as though he might be heading northwards. DC Bennett continued to follow, at a distance. At the northern end of the heath, Mr Blackwell indicated left for a road which, DC Bennett could see on his sat nav, would eventually lead onto the A1. This road was only partly lit, made darker by a line of trees on either side of it. Some distance before it joined the A1, Craig Blackwell indicated right and turned into an adjoining road.

DC Bennett could see from the sat nav that the road was not very long and eventually came to a dead end. He decided, because of this, not to directly follow him. Instead, he slowed down so he could get a better view as he passed by.

In that short time, he could make out that Craig Blackwell's car had stopped, about one hundred metres along the road. He could also make out another car, and Mr Blackwell's car was now alongside it. On the opposite side were a couple of properties, both set well back from the road.

Fortunately, a short distance beyond the *cul de sac* was a lay-by. DC Bennett pulled into it, switched off the engine, quickly got out of his car and then started to walk back towards where the two cars were parked. He realised he needed to get as close as possible to them but without revealing himself. So, rather than try to walk down the short road, he went into the wooded area immediately before the road and worked his way carefully to a spot which, despite the darkness, was close enough for him to see what was happening but not so close that he would be spotted.

He quietly settled himself behind a gorse bush, which gave him some extra cover. Here he could clearly spot Mr Blackwell, who appeared to be in animated discussion with two other men. DC Bennett took out his phone and began to video their meeting. Although he could only make out the odd word, their body language suggested it was now becoming more heated.

Suddenly, one of the other men tried to grab Mr Blackwell's coat, causing Mr Blackwell to push him instinctively away and attempt to get back into his car. Before he could do this, however, the other man made a grab for him and, together with the first one, managed to drag him away from his car and then throw him onto the ground. As Mr Blackwell tried to get up one of them kicked him in the side, and then the other began repeatedly hitting him in the face, before pulling out what looked like a knife and pinning him down.

'Pay up or you'll get some of this!' he shouted, loud enough for DC Bennett to catch the words. By now the man with the knife was kneeling on Mr Blackwell's chest, the knife pressed against his throat.

'Where's the money?' the other man shouted.

When there was no answer, he again kicked Mr Blackwell in the side.

Once DC Bennett had taken in everything that was happening, and realised the seriousness of the situation, he put his phone into his pocket and ran around the bush, towards them. 'Police!' he shouted.

Taken by surprise, both men moved away from the semi-conscious body of Craig Blackwell and faced DC Bennett. By now, though, both men were holding knives, and, when they realised that it was just one man, their earlier confidence now restored, both ran towards DC Bennett. Although he managed to step to one side, avoiding a knife thrust, one of the men got behind him and caught him in a headlock.

Despite his injuries, Craig Blackwell had somehow managed to get to his feet and, in an attempt to help, tried to pull the man away from DC Bennett. This loosened the man's grip just enough for DC Bennett to push him away slightly. Whilst he was doing this, however, the other man suddenly thrust his knife into DC Bennett's midriff. He withdrew the knife and then stuck it into him once again.

Although DC Bennett could instantly feel the warm ooze of his blood beginning to run down his lower abdomen, he didn't, at least initially, feel any pain and, in fact, he tried to grab hold of his assailant. It was at this point, however, he realised his strength was ebbing rapidly and the attacker was easily able to shove him towards the ground, before, for the third time, thrusting his knife into DC Bennett. By now it was obvious DC Bennett's resistance had totally disappeared and he lay there whilst one of the men continued to kick him.

'What have you done?' shouted Craig Blackwell.

'Let's go,' said one of the assailants.

'What about him?' asked the other, looking at Mr Blackwell.

'Okay, let's do him as well,' he answered, excitedly. 'He knows who we are,' before walking towards him, knife held out in a menacing manner.

Just then, a woman emerged from one of the nearby houses. 'What's going on? Who are you?'

Hearing this, the two men suddenly turned away from Mr Blackwell. They jumped into their car, started the engine, quickly turned it round and sped off towards the main road.

'We need an ambulance, quickly,' shouted Mr Blackwell. 'This man is a police officer and he's just been stabbed.'

The woman immediately turned and ran back towards her house, whilst Mr Blackwell held DC Bennett's head off the ground. He could see an ever-increasing bloodstain spreading over DC Bennett's clothes and onto the ground. 'Try not to move,' he said quietly. 'An ambulance will be here shortly. You'll be all right,' he added, although, as he continued to look at the blood seeping from his clothes, this was more in hope than expectation. He paused. 'Thank you. You saved my life.'

There was no response.

A short while later the woman had returned, along with a man from another house on the road. 'The ambulance will be here soon. I've also called the police.'

The two of them then went to take a closer look at DC Bennett and, seeing for themselves the blood now beginning to flow over the ground, immediately recognised the seriousness of his condition. They could also see that Mr Blackwell was in a serious condition of his own.

'Are you police as well?' the man asked.

'No,' he replied. 'Just this man.'

'Who were they?' asked the woman.

Before he could answer, however, the sound of an emergency siren could be heard in the distance and it wasn't long before an ambulance pulled into the road, almost immediately followed by two police cars.

One of the paramedics urgently began to check DC Bennett's injuries, in order to make a quick assessment as to their seriousness, whilst the other one did the same with Mr Blackwell.

The first paramedic carefully cut away some of DC Bennett's clothing in order to have a closer look at his injuries. 'We need to get him to hospital quickly,' he said, the concern in his voice confirming the seriousness of DC Bennett's condition.

Although Mr Blackwell's injuries were also serious, a quick examination by the other paramedic had confirmed that they were not life-threatening.

One of the police officers, looking from DC Bennett to Mr Blackwell, said, 'Do you know who he is?'

'His surname is Bennett and he's a detective constable with West London police.'

When he heard this, the police officer carefully felt inside DC Bennett's pockets and eventually pulled out his identification card. 'Did you see who did this?' he asked.

Once again, Mr Blackwell didn't answer as suddenly one of the paramedics, increasing concern clearly in his voice, said, 'We need to get both of these men to hospital as quickly as possible. I suggest you ask your questions later.'

'Will he live?' asked Mr Blackwell.

'I don't know,' answered the paramedic. 'But, as I said, we do need to get him to hospital straight away.'

After both men had been carefully wheeled into the ambulance, it immediately set off for the hospital, leaving the police behind to secure the crime scene and begin to take statements from the two witnesses.

Chapter 41

After his phone call with Milner, Tom had not immediately gone to bed. Instead, he remained where he was, as he thought through all the implications of what he had suddenly realised. This realisation had, as is often the case when there is a sort of epiphany, made sense of other events that had previously happened. More importantly, it had also provided a much clearer picture as to who might have murdered Mr Burton, although what Tom still didn't know was why he had been murdered.

When he did finally decide to go to bed, he found it impossible to sleep and simply lay there, alongside Mary, staring at the ceiling. As he often did in such circumstances, he used the time to review everything he now knew, trying to put it into some sort of order. Eventually, though, he must have drifted off, but it couldn't have been much later when his phone began to ring, and he was once again suddenly fully awake.

He picked up his phone and could see it was Milner.

'Sir?' said Milner, after Tom had pressed the answer button.

'Yes? What is it?' he asked, the tone of his voice clearly reflecting his concern. He knew Milner would not call him in the early hours of the morning unless it was something very important.

'Gary has been stabbed,' Milner simply replied.

'Stabbed?' Tom repeated, not quite able to fully take in what Milner had just told him. He hesitated. 'How is he?' he asked, with a degree of trepidation.

'Not good, I'm afraid. He's in theatre at the moment.'

'Where are you?'

'I'm on my way there right now. I got a call from the North London police a short while ago. Apparently he was attacked late last night, not far from the A1. I called you straight away as soon as I was informed.'

'What was he doing there?' asked Tom.

'I've got no idea, sir,' he answered quietly.

'Okay, I'll be there soon. Which hospital is he in?'

After Milner had given him the details, Tom quickly started to get dressed.

'What is it, Tom?' asked Mary, having been woken by the phone call and then worried by the tone of his brief conversation.

'That was Milner,' he replied, as he continued to get dressed. 'Gary – DC Bennett – has apparently been attacked and is in hospital. I need to get there as soon as possible.'

'It he okay?' she asked, now sitting upright.

'All I know is he has been stabbed and is currently in theatre. Other than that, I've got no idea.'

'Oh my God,' she said. 'How did it happen?'

'I don't know,' he simply answered.

By now Tom had finished getting dressed. He leaned over and kissed Mary on the cheek. 'I'm not sure how long I'll be, but I'll try and call you when I get the chance.'

'Don't worry about me.' She hesitated. 'I hope Gary is okay.'

*

By the time Tom arrived at the hospital, Milner had already been there for some time.

'How is he?' asked Tom. He could hear the anticipation of bad news in his own voice.

'He's still in theatre. I got the impression, though, that he's in a pretty bad way. It seems that he was stabbed multiple times.'

This prompted something in Tom's mind. 'Has anyone spoken with Julie? She needs to be told what's happened.'

'She's already on her way. I called her earlier. One of the station's uniformed officers has gone to collect her and bring her here.'

'What did you say to her?'

'Only what I know. That Gary had been attacked and was in a bad way and was currently in the operating theatre. There wasn't much more I could tell her.'

Both men remained silent, each deep in their own thoughts. After a short while, a uniformed police officer approached them. 'I'm PC Peter Howlett. I was one of the officers who got the call about the attack on DC Bennett.'

Tom shook his hand. 'What can you tell us?' he asked.

'We were in the area when we received a call about a stabbing. When we arrived the paramedics were already there, but we could immediately see that DC Bennett was in a bad way. There was blood seeping from his clothes and spilling onto the ground. The other injured man told us that the person with the knife wounds was a police officer. It was then that I took out his ID and confirmed who he was.'

'Did DC Bennett say anything?' asked Tom.

'I'm afraid not, sir. As I said, it was obvious he was in a bad way and, anyway, we wanted to let the paramedics do what they could for him.'

'And what about the other man?' asked Milner. 'Did he say anything else?'

'He said that, if it hadn't been for DC Bennett, he would almost certainly have been killed.'

'So he was able to speak clearly.'

'More or less. Although he had clearly sustained quite a few injuries, and there was a lot of blood on his face, it didn't look as though he had also been stabbed.'

'Did he say anything about who attacked them?

'Yes, sir, he did,' he answered. 'From what he was able to tell us, it seems he was being attacked by two men when DC Bennett suddenly appeared and confronted them. It was then they turned on DC Bennett and stabbed him.'

'Do we know who this man was?' asked Milner. 'The one who was initially attacked.'

PC Howlett referred to his notebook. 'His name is Craig Blackwell.'

Both Tom and Milner's expressions clearly betrayed their astonishment. 'Craig Blackwell?' repeated Tom. He turned to face Milner. 'Did you have any idea about this?'

'None at all, sir,' he answered, his own disbelief obvious.

'So where is Craig Blackwell now?' asked Tom.

'He's also in surgery, although his injuries are not considered to be life-threatening,' replied PC Howlett.

Neither Tom nor Milner, still digesting the information that Craig Blackwell had been there, seemed able to ask any follow-up questions, so PC Howlett carried on.

'We don't have any idea, yet, as to who the two men who carried out the attack were.' He quickly added, 'Well, no names, anyway, but there were a couple of witnesses. They live in the houses which were closest to the attack. It's a very quiet road – just a few houses on it. One of them heard some shouting and came out to investigate. She called out and her shouting seemed to distract them, and that's when they ran away. Although it was dark, and her road is unlit, she managed to get a brief look at the two men, and she was able to give us a statement. It's highly likely, if she hadn't come out to investigate, that things might have been even worse.'

'And what about the other witness? You said there were two.'

'Yes; although he came out later, he managed to get a look at them through his window.'

'Thank you,' answered Tom, before adding, 'I assume North London will be investigating. Who is the SIO?'

'Not sure yet, sir,' he replied. 'It's still early days, but I suppose it could be DCI Chapman. If there is nothing else, sir, I think I should be getting back to the station to write my report.'

'Yes, no problem, and thank you for everything you did for DC Bennett.'

'I hope things work out well for him,' PC Howlett said, before walking away.

Chapter 42

Tom and Milner were now both seated on the plastic chairs in a small waiting room, immediately outside one of the operating theatres.

'What the hell was Gary doing there at that time of night?' asked Tom. 'And why was Craig Blackwell with him?'

'I've got no idea, sir,' answered Milner, almost despondently. 'We'd met yesterday afternoon to review the latest evidence relating to Mr Burton's murder. At no stage did we discuss meeting up with Craig Blackwell.'

'What latest evidence?' asked Tom.

Milner quickly updated him on their interview with Craig Blackwell and the subsequent follow-up action they had agreed on. 'Do you think he decided to do a bit of freelancing?' he then asked. 'You know how he felt about Craig Blackwell.'

'That's what I was just thinking as well,' replied Tom. 'As you say, he was absolutely convinced it was Mr Blackwell who'd committed the murder.'

Before either of them could take the conversation any further, the double doors opened and a tall, middle-aged man, clad in blue hospital scrubs, walked directly towards them. It was immediately obvious from his facial expression and overall body language he was unlikely to be bringing good news.

Tom and Milner both stood.

'DCI Stone?' the man asked. 'I'm James Keegan, one of the consultants here. I'm afraid it's not good news. Your colleague, DC Bennett, died a few minutes ago.' He paused briefly, and then carried on. 'I'm truly sorry. His injuries were extremely severe. He had sustained numerous deep stab wounds, one of which pierced his heart. I'm afraid there was nothing we could do.'

Both Tom and Milner were stunned, unable to quite take in what they had just been told. Finally, though, it was Tom who managed to speak. 'Thank you for all of your efforts. I'm sure you did everything possible. I assume, then, that Gary was still alive when the paramedics got him here?'

'He was, yes, but only just. As I say, his injuries were extremely severe. Frankly, it was a miracle he was still alive.'

'He was never one to give up easily,' was all that Tom could think to say in reply.

After Keegan had left, they both sat down again, each deep in thought. This time it was Milner who broke the silence. 'I can't believe it,' he said, his voice suddenly breaking with emotion, causing Tom to look at him. 'I should have made sure he didn't do it. After all, the signs were there.'

Tom reached over and took hold of his arm. 'You have nothing to feel guilty about. We don't fully know what happened yet. Gary was an experienced officer, and I'm sure he had his reasons. Let's wait until we have all the facts. It's probably no consolation right now, but let's not forget that if he hadn't been there, then Craig Blackwell would almost certainly have been killed. Whatever Gary thought of him, it seems as though he still, instinctively, went to his assistance.'

If Tom's remarks were intended to offer some degree of reassurance to Milner then they had not succeeded, as he could now see Milner's eyes beginning to well up. He knew that any additional words he might say would be unlikely to have any effect on how Milner currently felt, and, as the ensuing silence was only broken by the occasional quiet sob from Milner, it simply reinforced his own personal feeling of total helplessness.

They remained seated for a while longer, each still trying to collect their thoughts. Suddenly one of the doors opened and Julie entered, accompanied by a female member of the hospital's staff. Both men stood. As soon as she saw them, she began to cry. 'Is Gary dead?' she asked, almost beseeching them to reply in the negative.

'Julie, I'm so sorry,' answered Tom. He moved forward, and, putting his arms around her, simply repeated what he had just said. 'I'm so sorry.'

Tom held her tightly, feeling her sobs reverberating through her body. No one said anything until finally she pulled away from him and turned to face the hospital staff member. 'Can I see him?' she asked, in a surprisingly clear tone.

'Let me just go and check,' the staff member replied, before walking towards the doors where, earlier, the surgeon had appeared from. She opened the doors and disappeared.

'How did it happen?' asked Julie, somehow managing to control her emotions.

'We are not too sure yet,' answered Tom. 'All we know is that he went to help someone who was being attacked by two men. It seems as though they turned on Gary. It was then he was stabbed.'

'Stabbed?' repeated Julie, her voice rising, reflecting her increased emotions. 'Oh my God.'

Tom held her tightly, once again, feeling her rhythmic sobbing. Just then the doors opened again, and the woman reappeared, along with the surgeon.

'Mrs Bennett,' he said. 'I'm really sorry. We did everything we could to save your husband.' He fell silent for a moment, allowing Julie some time to try to regain her emotions. 'I understand you would like to see your husband. Is that correct?'

Julie, now not even able to speak, just nodded.

'Please come this way, then,' he said. 'If you don't mind, my colleague will also be with us.'

The woman gently took hold of Julie's hand, and the three of them walked back through the double doors to the operating theatre. After they had disappeared, both men once again sat down.

'I can't believe I allowed this to happen,' said Milner. Although his own earlier sobs had now stopped, his face, nonetheless, still conveyed his heightened emotions. 'I should have realised that Gary might have done something like this.'

'David?' replied Tom, quietly. 'We've had this conversation. I've told you already. You have absolutely nothing to blame yourself for. Gary would have known what he was doing. The best thing we can do now is help find the people who did this. Let's also remember we've got our own murder investigation to resolve. We spoke last night about this. Craig Blackwell's involvement is a common link in the investigation, so we should start by talking to him.' He paused. 'Agreed?'

Milner could hardly bring himself to look at Tom. Nonetheless, he replied, albeit in a quiet voice, 'Agreed.'

Chapter 43

'We can only allow you to speak with Mr Blackwell for a few minutes. His injuries are quite severe, and we are still concerned he might have incurred some internal damage. So, please, keep your questions as brief as possible. If he is to recover quickly then rest is what he needs right now.'

Tom and Milner were standing outside a side room where Craig Blackwell had been placed. One of the doctors treating him had been called, by a nurse, to speak with them, after they had requested some time with Mr Blackwell.

'We understand,' answered Tom. 'We will keep it as brief as possible. What injuries has he sustained?'

'Multiple injuries to his face. He has a broken nose and cheekbone, both of which will require corrective surgery. We are monitoring the sight in one of his eyes. He also sustained some broken ribs. Our main concern, though, is that he might have damaged some of his internal organs. At the moment it's a bit too early to tell. In the meantime our priority is to stabilise him before he goes back into theatre.' He finally added, to further underline his concern, 'Mr Blackwell's beating was very severe.'

The doctor nodded to the nurse, who then led Tom and Milner into the room.

Tom was deeply shocked when he saw Craig Blackwell. He had heard what the doctor had said about his injuries, but it was only when he saw them for himself that he could comprehend their full seriousness. He had expected to see Mr Blackwell attached to a saline drip, as well as the usual monitoring devices. What he hadn't expected, however, was the severe bruising on his face. There were a couple of medical dressings on other parts of his face, which, Tom realised, probably protected some deep lacerations. One of his eyes was also covered by a bandage. Although he was sitting upright his body looked very stiff and rigid, probably due to the broken ribs.

There was only one chair in the room, and so both Tom and Milner remained standing.

'Please don't be long,' said the nurse, before leaving the room and closing the door behind her.

'How is he?' asked Mr Blackwell, in such a quiet voice that, initially, Tom had trouble understanding what he had said.

Tom had assumed – wrongly, as it now obviously transpired – that Mr Blackwell would have known about Gary's death. But, logically, of course, there was no reason he would already have been told.

'I'm afraid DC Bennett died a short while ago,' answered Tom.

Despite his condition, Mr Blackwell seemed to display genuine shock and, if possible, his body became even more rigid. Initially, he didn't verbally respond, but eventually he said, 'He saved my life. If he hadn't suddenly appeared I'm certain I would be dead.'

'Are you able to tell us what happened?' asked Milner.

He simply nodded and then, in the same quiet voice, said, 'I was meeting some people who supplied me.'

'With drugs?' asked Tom.

'Yes. Cocaine,' he replied, in a surprisingly matter-of-fact manner.

'Is that why you needed the cash?'

'Yes,' he simply replied. 'After Glyn's death I had decided to try and stop. I was meeting to tell them, but they said I still owed them money and had to pay it. I knew I didn't, but they tried to blackmail me. They said they knew where I lived and could afford to pay. They made threats against my family.'

'Physical threats?' asked Milner.

'Not directly. Just that I should take special care of them. That type of thing.'

'Then what happened?'

Suddenly he appeared to find renewed energy. 'That's when they attacked me. I'd tried to get back in my car, but one of them pulled me back and started kicking and hitting me. The other one had a knife at my throat. That's when DC Bennett suddenly appeared. He just ran out from the bushes at the side of the road and tried to get the knife off the man.' He paused briefly, as he tried to recover from his exertions. 'I've got no idea why he was there, but if he hadn't appeared just then I'm sure they would have killed me,' he said, repeating what he had told them a short while earlier. 'When they saw him, they, briefly, left me alone and ran straight for him. I got up and tried to help him, but I didn't have the strength to do much. The side of my body was very painful, and I was struggling to breathe. I don't exactly know what happened next. All I could see was he'd fallen to the ground. They then started on me again, and it was at that moment that someone else appeared and started shouting. I think it was the owner of one of the houses on the road. Anyway, it was just enough to distract them, and they got into their car and drove away. A short while later an ambulance arrived, and then the police.'

'Do you know who the two men were?'

'Yes,' he answered, before quickly adding, 'Well, I know what they called themselves and I have their mobile number.'

Once again, no one spoke for some time, before he resumed. 'I wish I had told you the truth,' he said, 'but I am now.'

Before anyone could say anything else, the door opened, and the same nurse reappeared. 'I think you need to leave now,' she said firmly. 'As the doctor told you, it's important Mr Blackwell gets some rest.'

'Just one last thing,' said Tom. 'You mentioned a mobile number for the men who attacked you. Do you have it on your phone?'

'Yes. It's in my phone contacts under *Sugar*,' he replied. 'I think the phone is in the drawer by the side of the bed.'

Milner opened the drawer, took out Mr Blackwell's phone and scrolled through the contacts section until he came across the details he was looking for. He wrote down the number in his notebook and put the phone back in the drawer.

As they were leaving the room, Mr Blackwell suddenly said, 'I'm so sorry.'

Chapter 44

Although it was still early morning, they had headed straight back to the station after leaving the hospital.

'What do you want to do next, sir?' asked Milner, still clearly deflated.

'See that there?' Tom asked, looking at the chart showing all the main suspects in the Burton murder investigation. 'We are going to get it resolved, and then we can all grieve for Gary. First, though, I need to make a call.'

He checked the contact numbers in his phone, found the one he was looking for and pressed the call button. Due to the early time of day, he expected it to go to voicemail. After just a couple of rings, however, it was answered.

'Tom,' said DCI Jack Chapman. 'I was somehow expecting you to call.'

DCI Chapman was part of the North London force and was the SIO who, as it had happened in his area of responsibility, would be investigating DC Bennett's murder. A few years ago, Tom had been assigned to North London, reporting directly to DCI Chapman, to help with an investigation into a series of murders: the high-profile case that had dramatically resurrected both Tom's career and his personal enthusiasm as a DCI.

DCI Chapman's tone became more sombre. 'I'm sorry to hear about the death of DC Bennett. It must have been a real shock for you all.'

'It was,' replied Tom. 'Gary and I went back a long way. He was one of the best.'

'I understand, from our officers, there were witnesses.'

'Yes, fortunately there are. Two, to be precise. We have just returned from the hospital, where we also spoke with the other person who was assaulted. He was able to provide us with some information on their attackers.'

'That's good. Did he provide you with descriptions?'

'Better than that. He gave us a contact number.'

'How did he have that?' asked DCI Chapman, clearly slightly puzzled.

'They were his dealers,' replied Tom. 'They'd supplied him with drugs previously. He says he arranged to meet to inform them he wanted to stop. It was then that they got nasty. They demanded money and, when he refused, they attacked him.'

'Do you believe him?'

'Well, he has lied to us previously, but this time I believe, yes, he's telling the truth.'

DCI Chapman then asked the most obvious question. 'So, why was DC Bennett there? It's quite a way from your patch. I assume you know it's normal procedure to inform the other force if any cross-area operations are taking place.'

So Tom told him. He told him about Glyn Burton's murder and his business and personal relationship with Craig Blackwell. He told him how Gary had been convinced that it was Craig Blackwell who had murdered his business partner. And finally, he told him how Gary, of his own volition, must have followed Mr Blackwell to the meeting point, seen the attack, and then tried to protect him.

DCI Chapman didn't immediately respond. After a while, though, he said, 'That would explain the video.'

'What video is that?' asked a surprised Tom.

'An officer found what turned out to be DC Bennett's phone near to where the attack took place. He must have started recording the meeting before he went to Craig Blackwell's defence. You can just about make out the assailants, but it's not very clear. Certainly not clear enough, by itself, to get a conviction. That's why the contact number will be very useful.'

'I'll text you it straight away. Hopefully, your tech boys should be able to put a name to the number.'

'Thanks, Tom. Rest assured if we can get a name we will pick him up immediately.' He paused. 'As a police officer was murdered there's bound to be a lot of media interest in this. You probably haven't had time to give this any thought yet, but, at some stage, we should decide who should front any press conferences.'

'You're right. I hadn't even considered that. I think the main priority, though, is to get the two people who carried out the attack into custody as quickly as possible. At least, if we can do that, it will provide Julie – Gary's wife – with a bit of comfort, knowing that whoever did this is now off the streets.'

'I agree,' said DCI Chapman. 'If you can text me that number I'll get on to it immediately. I'll also make sure I keep you posted on developments. One other question. Did you know DC Bennett was following Craig Blackwell?'

'I didn't, no,' answered Tom, in a now very subdued tone. 'As I said, it seems as though he took it upon himself to do it. Nonetheless, I should have considered it as a possibility. In retrospect, there were a number of clues which suggested something like this might happen. But, unfortunately, I didn't spot them. It's something I'll have to live with for the rest of my life.'

Chapter 45

'Are you sure about this, sir?' asked Milner. It was later that same morning and, as the gates were closed, they were parked on the road, a short walk from Mrs Burton's house in Richmond.

After Tom's conversation with DCI Chapman, they had refocussed their attention on their own murder investigation. Before they had left, Tom had asked Milner to set up the CCTV footage relating to the time when Mr Burton had left his house on the Sunday afternoon, the day he had disappeared. As they had reviewed it, Milner had seen DCI Stone paying particular attention to the footage showing Mr Burton driving away from the house.

'Are you looking for anything in particular, sir?' Milner had asked.

'Sort of, but I just wanted to double-check something,' he had replied. 'As I told you last night, I'm sure about who didn't do it, and I'm almost sure now about how and where Mr Burton was killed. What I still don't know, though, is exactly why he was killed. But that's something, hopefully, we will find out soon. In the meantime, I think it's important we keep Mrs Burton updated on developments. After all, it's some time since we last spoke with her.'

'And what about who killed him?' Milner had asked, not unreasonably. 'Do you have a theory on that as well?'

'I do, yes, but that's all it is at the moment.'

'And are you going to share it with me?' Milner had asked, the tone of his voice betraying his growing annoyance.

'Not just yet,' Tom had answered. 'But rest assured I will when I'm certain.'

Now the two of them got out of their car, walked towards the gates of Mrs Burton's house and then pressed the button by the side. Almost immediately they could hear Mrs Burton's voice. 'Hello. Who is this?'

'It's DS Milner and DCI Stone,' answered Milner. 'I spoke with you earlier.'

'Just a minute. I'll open the gates.'

The gates slowly began to open, and Tom and Milner walked towards the front door. Just as they were about to ring the bell, the door was opened by Mrs Burton.

'Thank you for seeing us at such short notice,' said Tom.

'Why don't you come through?' she replied, before leading them into the main living area. 'Why do you want to see me?' she asked. 'Have you found something?'

'We are making progress, although, if you are asking if we have found out who killed your husband, then I'm afraid the answer is no.' Tom paused. 'Would you mind if we sat down?'

'Sorry,' she answered. 'Please do.'

'I'm returning this to you,' said Tom, holding out the photograph of her husband and the three other golfers. 'Thank you for letting us keep it for a while.'

She took the photograph from Tom, and placed in on the small table in front of her. 'If you don't yet know who did it, why are you here?' she asked.

'Last night, your husband's business partner, Craig Blackwell, was attacked. He sustained serious injuries and is currently in hospital. I wanted to make sure you heard this directly from us, rather than hear or read about it via the media.'

'Oh my God,' she said, with genuine shock. 'You said *serious injuries*. Just how serious are they?'

'They are very serious but, thankfully, not life-threatening. The doctors say, with rest and time, he is likely to make a full recovery.'

'Poor Susie,' she said. 'I must call her to see if there's anything I can do.' She went straight on, although now with a different level of concern in her voice. 'Why was he attacked? Is this anything to do with Glyn's death?'

'That's what we are currently trying to find out,' answered Tom. 'The attack only happened last night and so it's still very early in the investigation. But,' he added, 'it is a bit of a coincidence.' He paused momentarily before continuing. 'How are you, Mrs Burton?'

She looked at him quite suspiciously. 'How do you think I am? My life has been turned upside down. I'm a nervous wreck. I can't sleep at night and keep thinking he will still walk through the door.'

'I'm sorry,' he said. 'If there is anything I can do to help, you only have to ask.'

'What can you possibly do? I just want to somehow be able to turn back the clock and live my life again. At the moment I feel as though I'm in some sort of permanent limbo. So, unless you can do that for me, there's nothing you can do.'

Tom stood up, quickly followed by Milner. 'Thank you again for seeing us. We will let you know if there are any further developments.'

Instead of walking towards the door leading out of the living room, Tom walked towards the cabinet where the photographs of their children were. 'How are your children coping? It must be very difficult for them,' he said, picking up one of the photos.

'It has been, yes,' she answered. 'Especially for William. He seems to be the one who is struggling most to cope. I hope, though, that eventually they will both come through this.' As she finished saying this she suddenly began to cry.

'I'm sorry,' said Tom. 'I didn't mean to upset you.'

'It's just that,' she said, before stopping. 'It's just that I don't know if I'll ever recover from this.'

Just as they reached the front door, Tom suddenly said, 'There was one other thing. Would you mind showing us where your husband kept his golf clubs?'

'His golf clubs? Why?' she asked, her face betraying her puzzlement.

'We were expecting to find them in the boot of his car, or somewhere close, but didn't. We just need to check where they are, that's all,' he answered.

'They are in the garage,' she simply replied. 'You can get in this way.'

She led them through the kitchen and towards a large utility room, which housed a washing machine, drier and large freezer. On the outside wall was a door which accessed the garage. She opened the door and switched on the interior light. It was a sizeable garage, although without any cars in it. Mr Burton's car was still with forensics, whilst Mrs Burton's was parked on the drive.

In one corner, Tom could see two sets of golf clubs, alongside which was a substantial powered golf trolley. 'Would you mind if we took a photo?' he asked.

'I suppose not,' she answered.

Tom turned to face Milner. 'DS Milner? Would you mind? Make sure you get everything in. The trolley as well as the clubs.'

Milner took out his phone and took a few photos. 'Are these okay?' he asked, showing them to Tom.

'Perfect,' replied Tom. He turned back to Mrs Burton. 'It's possible, though, we will need to come back and carry out a more thorough examination.'

'Really?' asked Mrs Burton. 'Haven't you got enough information? What more could you possibly need?'

'I understand that it's unsettling,' answered Tom, 'but we need to be as thorough as possible, otherwise we might miss some crucial evidence.'

As soon as they were outside, Milner stopped walking and turned to face Tom. 'What was all that about? Would you please, sir, tell me what the hell is going on?'

So Tom told him.

Chapter 46

'Tonight?' asked Milner. 'Do you think something will happen that quickly?'

'I really don't know,' answered Tom, 'but it's definitely possible.'

It was early afternoon and they had both arrived back at the station, where the atmosphere, given DC Bennett's death, was unsurprisingly extremely sombre. Many of the officers there had known or worked alongside him over many years. Inevitably rumours were swirling around the station relating to just why he had been killed, but no one actually approached either Tom or Milner for clarification or explanation. Everyone knew that to do this would not only place Tom and Milner in a very difficult position, but would also potentially compromise any subsequent convictions. Nonetheless, this didn't preclude many officers approaching them in order to offer any help they might need as well, of course, as to offer their sympathy.

'How do you want to handle it, then?' asked Milner. 'Given the short notice, we might have problems getting the necessary resources.'

'Somehow I think that will be the least of our problems,' answered Tom. 'We only have to mention that it was the investigation that Gary was involved in and there will be no shortage of volunteers.'

They spent the next thirty minutes discussing what they would do as well as the resources needed to carry out their plan. Just as they were finishing there was a knock on the door and Howard Birch, the station's superintendent, entered. He closed the door behind him.

'Tom. David. I'm so sorry,' he said. 'I heard you were here – although, given the circumstances, I'm surprised you *are* here. I understand you have both been at the hospital since the early hours. Given everything you've been through, you must both be exhausted. Wouldn't it be better if you went home and at least tried to get some rest? I'm sure whatever you are involved in can wait a bit longer.'

In truth, Tom had lost track of time and only now, when it was mentioned, realised how little sleep he'd had. As he heard this he found himself looking at Milner and suddenly realised that Milner must have had even less, as it was he who had taken the initial call informing him that DC Bennett had been admitted to hospital. Superintendent Birch was correct, of course, and Tom knew that adrenaline could only last so long. Given the new developments relating to the Glyn Burton murder, the timing, however, was especially unfortunate.

'Thank you, sir,' answered Tom. 'DS Milner and I were just discussing what we were planning to do next with regard to the investigation into the murder of Glyn Burton. It looks as though there has been a significant breakthrough.'

'Really?' Superintendent Birch replied. 'Is it related in any way to DC Bennett's death?'

'Indirectly, yes. But only in the sense that Craig Blackwell – that's the person who Gary was following – was the business partner of Glyn Burton.'

'I don't understand, then, why DC Bennett was following this Craig Blackwell if he was just his business partner. Did he suspect he might have been involved in Mr Burton's death?'

So Tom told him about DC Bennett's strong suspicions that Craig Blackwell was involved in his business partner's murder and how, last night, DC Bennett had, for some as yet unknown reason, decided to follow him. He then told Superintendent Birch about the attack on Craig Blackwell and how DC Bennett had gone to his assistance, which had led to him also being attacked.

'Was Craig Blackwell also injured?'

'Yes, he was, sir. The doctors say he sustained quite serious injuries, although not life-threatening.'

'And DC Bennett's wife? I assume we have people looking after her,' Superintendent Birch said.

'Yes, sir,' answered Tom. 'A liaison team are with her right now.'

'Good. Just make sure she gets all the help she needs.'

There then followed a brief silence, as they all took in the awful consequences of DC Bennett's death.

It was Superintendent Birch who eventually broke the silence. 'So, tell me about this significant development.'

Tom spent the next few minutes updating him. After he had finished, Superintendent Birch said, 'I'm sure you don't need me to tell you, whilst it is compelling, the evidence is still basically circumstantial. But, if there is anything else you need from me, just ask. Anyway, good luck.'

'Thank you, sir,' replied Tom.

After Superintendent Birch had left, Tom said, 'How are you? You look exhausted.'

'I'm okay,' Milner answered, his defiant tone betraying his true feelings.

'Well, you don't look okay to me,' said Tom. 'Why not, as Superintendent Birch suggested, go and get some rest? Nothing is likely to happen in the next few hours, and there's probably going to be another long night ahead of us tonight.'

'Are you planning to get any rest?' asked Milner, still defiant. 'And anyway, do you really think I'll be able to rest after what has happened?'

Tom knew he was right, of course. Despite their fatigue, being alone would almost certainly simply mean they had even more time to relive the events of the last few hours.

'Well, in that case, go and catch up on a few things. I find it helps if I'm kept busy. You could chase up that search warrant, for example. I'm sure there are lots of other things you need to catch up on as well. Let's meet again at 4.30 pm and be ready to brief the team at 4.45 pm.' He paused. 'But first, go and get something to eat. It must be a long time since you ate. As I said, it could be a long night for you.'

This seemed to at least partly placate Milner, who simply said, 'I know you are right, but I really don't feel like eating anything right now.'

'Well, at least try.'

After Milner had left the office, Tom immediately picked up the phone and called Jenny, who was Milner's girlfriend as well as Superintendent Birch's PA.

'It's DCI Stone here,' he said. 'You've no doubt heard about Gary. I can't tell you the full details right now, but David seems to have taken it really badly. Do you think you could come down and make sure he gets something to eat and drink? There's that coffee shop just around the corner. We will be out again tonight, and I'm concerned he hasn't eaten anything substantial so far today.'

After his conversation with Jenny, he suddenly remembered he had promised to call Mary and so, once again, picked up his phone and made a call.

Mary immediately answered. 'Tom? I was starting to get really worried about you. Is it true that it was DC Bennett who was murdered?'

'It is, yes,' he simply answered. 'But how do you know?'

'It's just come up on the television news. They mentioned that a forty-year-old detective constable had died of knife wounds. Although they didn't give a name, I guessed it might be DC Bennett.'

'As you can imagine, there's a lot going on here at the moment. I'm not too sure when I'll be back, but I'll try and ring you when I get the chance. It could be late, though, so don't wait up for me.'

'How are you?' she asked in a subdued tone.

'I can't deny that Gary's death has really affected me,' he answered, in an uncharacteristic moment of emotional honesty. 'I should have anticipated something like this might happen. All the signs were there; it's just that I chose to ignore them.'

'Tom,' she replied, 'I know you must be very upset, but you mustn't blame yourself. I didn't really know DC Bennett, but, from what you have told me, it seems he was an experienced officer. I'm sure he knew what he was doing.'

Even if Tom accepted Mary's explanation, he couldn't yet bring himself to say so, such were his feelings of personal guilt. Instead he made do with, 'I have to go. I'll call you later.'

Chapter 47

Tom and Milner were, for the second time that day, parked close to Mrs Burton's house. Although they were not immediately outside, they had still managed to park in a spot which gave them an unrestricted view of the front of the house. Immediately behind them was another unmarked car with three uniformed officers sitting in it.

'Jenny told me you had called her,' Milner said. 'Thank you, sir, for that. I didn't realise just how hungry I was until we had something to eat. I have to admit, though, when she told me, I wasn't exactly happy that you'd called her.'

'I don't blame you,' answered Tom, with a light laugh. 'Given the circumstances, I would have felt exactly the same. Sometimes, believe it or not, even I'm wrong and too stubborn to accept advice when it's offered.'

'Really?' replied Milner. 'I can't believe that, sir. You are well known for always taking advice.' He laughed a little himself.

'Yes, well, just make sure you don't tell anyone about it. I don't want people to think I'm starting to get touchy-feely. That wouldn't do my hard-earned reputation any good at all.'

This brief conversation seemed, as much as possible given the circumstances, to lighten the mood. Whilst it was impossible to entirely forget about the circumstances of DC Bennett's death, at least for the moment they could discuss other things.

It wasn't too long, though, before their conversation was interrupted. The front door opened and Mrs Burton emerged, got into her car, started the engine and drove out into the main road.

Tom picked up the radio. 'Okay, looks like we are ready to go. As agreed, we'll start to follow and then let you through after a mile or so. We'll then drop in behind you until it's our turn to follow again.'

By now both cars were following Mrs Burton, and after a

couple of minutes Tom, closely examining the sat nav map in the middle of the dashboard, said, 'It looks like she's heading towards Richmond Park.'

A short while later and they had entered the park.

'There's a lay-by just ahead,' Tom reported. 'We'll pull in there and you take over.'

Milner pulled into the lay-by, allowing the other car to over-take, before immediately rejoining the road behind it. Not long afterwards, Tom could see the car in front of them was now indicating right and Milner slowed down to follow. Tom could see, from the map, that this part of the park was very isolated.

The narrow road went on for less than a mile before it joined one of the main roads which ran through the park. However, just before they reached this road, the radio suddenly came to life. 'Target indicating immediate left. Repeat, immediate left,' said an officer, with sudden urgency. 'We will carry on.'

Tom quickly glanced at the map but couldn't see any lay-by or turning indicated on it. Milner slowed down but, despite this, they were soon at the place where she had turned. Although it was dark, Tom could easily spot Mrs Burton's car, which had now stopped. He could also, however, make out another car alongside hers, before they had driven past.

'Just stop up here,' said Tom. 'I'll get out and try and get a better look. If I'm careful they shouldn't spot me out here. There's another place to pull in about half a mile along the next road. Stop there and wait until I call you. So keep your mobile handy.'

Milner stopped the car. 'Why don't I do it, sir?' he suggested.

But, before Milner could say anything else, Tom had opened the door and got out of the car. 'Just keep your mobile on,' he repeated.

Tom walked back towards where the cars had parked. Fortunately, there were no other cars coming down the road and so he was able to get there quickly. It was a dark night and so there was little chance he would be spotted, but he still took extra care to remain concealed.

There was a large, mature oak tree not far from the parked cars, and so he slowly walked towards it. He crouched down behind it, confident that he would not be spotted. After a short while, his eyes had attuned just enough to the darkness for him to pick out two people now seated in the back of Mrs Burton's car. One, clearly, was Mrs Burton. The other was a man, and they were currently embracing each other.

Whilst this was happening, Tom concentrated his focus on the other car and, in particular, the number plate. He took out his notebook and wrote down the time, then the make and registration number.

After a short while, as he continued to crouch behind the tree, he could hear the sound of an approaching car, which almost imperceptibly slowed down as it went by. Although he couldn't see the driver he could, nonetheless, see that it was the car which Milner had been driving. He took out his phone and called Milner, making sure that his voice didn't carry.

'I assume that was you who just drove past,' he said quietly.

'It was,' replied Milner. 'Are you okay, sir? I thought that I'd better check.'

'I'm fine,' he answered, before giving him a brief summary of what was happening. 'I don't know how long they are likely to be here, so just make sure you aren't spotted. I'll call you again when I think they are leaving.'

He then settled down, focussing his eyes on Mrs Burton's car. After some time, both doors suddenly opened, and the two got out. They embraced again before Mrs Burton got into the driver's side of her car, whilst the man got into his own car.

Tom called Milner. 'They are just about to leave. Let them get away and then pick me up. I'll be standing just by the entrance. We'll then follow them. Same procedure as before. So let the other officers know.'

'Do you know who the man is?' asked Milner.

'I've got a pretty good idea,' he simply answered.

Both cars then drove out of the place where they had been parked. Tom, having been picked up by Milner, followed the two cars, with the other police car immediately behind them.

Tom got back onto the radio. 'Let's take it easy. No mistakes. We don't want them to spot us now. It looks as though they are both heading back towards Richmond. It might be that they are going to Mrs Burton's house. If that is the case, then park up where we were earlier. If they split up, however, then Milner and I will take the car which the man is driving. Understood?'

'Understood,' came the quick reply.

Once they got to the outskirts of the town, Mrs Burton's car signalled left, as though she were indeed heading home, whilst the other one kept going straight on, towards the town centre. The traffic was a bit heavier now and so Milner had to be careful that he didn't fall too far behind or get held up by a red traffic light. Eventually, they arrived at a main road, where the car indicated left, heading west along the A316. It wasn't long, however, before it turned left again. A short distance along the road, the driver indicated right and then immediately left before finally coming to a stop in a resident's parking spot. Milner slowed down, allowing them both to see the man entering one of the terraced houses.

'Did you get that, sir?' asked Milner.

'Why don't you turn around and stop close to the house? We'll be able to get a better look that way.'

Milner managed to turn around and then come to a stop almost directly opposite the house.

Tom made a note of the address. 'Okay, let's go,' he said.

'Don't you want to question him? After all, you seem pretty sure he was involved,' said Milner.

'Not yet,' he replied. 'Anyway, what am I supposed to ask him? Why was he parked up, at night, in the middle of Richmond Park, with someone whose husband had recently been murdered? Let's wait until we have all of our evidence lined up. I don't think either of them is going anywhere any time soon. In the meantime, though, let's just get 100% confirmation as to who our mystery man is.'

He made another call and passed over details of the car's registration number, as well as the address of the house that the man had just entered. It wasn't long before his phone rang.

'Are you absolutely certain?' Tom asked. Clearly receiving the reply he had hoped for, he then said, 'That's good. Thanks.'

'Well?' asked Milner.

'It's definitely our man,' answered Tom, unable to disguise his feeling of satisfaction. 'We are in business.'

Chapter 48

By the time they arrived back at the station it was starting to get late, but waiting for them was Superintendent Birch.

'How did it go?' he asked, even before Tom had reached his office.

'He's definitely who we thought he might be,' Tom answered. 'So that's a relief.'

Milner then appeared, a polystyrene cup in each hand. 'Sorry, sir,' he said, seeing Superintendent Birch. 'I didn't know you were here. I'd have brought you a cup as well, if I had.'

'Don't worry,' he answered. 'I think your needs are greater than mine. And anyway, I'm used to the proper coffee that Jenny makes for me. I don't think my taste buds would survive the stuff that comes out of the machine.'

There was just a hint of sudden redness appearing on Milner's face when he heard this reference to Jenny. He was just relieved DCI Stone didn't tease him – something, under normal circumstances, he would have taken great delight in doing. Instead, DCI Stone said, 'All we need to find out now is *why* Mr Burton was killed.'

'When do you plan to bring them in, then?' asked Superintendent Birch.

'Tomorrow morning. There's not a lot more we can do tonight, anyway. Tomorrow morning will give us the opportunity to make doubly sure that all the paperwork is in place. Especially as there are now two locations.'

Superintendent Birch's tone had changed when he next spoke. 'Tom, you may have heard that Gary's death is now out in the open and I've received many requests for us to make an official statement. Sir Peter called me just before you got back. He thinks, as it's not going to go away, we should do it sooner rather than later. So it's been arranged for 1 pm tomorrow, outside the station. The question is "who should do it?" Sir

Peter will be there, and will say something, but he's keen for someone from here, closer to Gary, to be the main person. I'm happy to do it but, as Gary was in your team, I wanted to give you the option first.'

This was not a surprise to Tom, especially after Mary had mentioned hearing about an officer's death on the news. Nonetheless, during the past few hours, he had been able to put it to the back of his mind. Now that option was no longer available. 'I think I should make the statement, sir. As you say, he was in my team, but, more importantly, I've known Gary for many years. I think it's the least I owe him.'

'I suspected that might be your answer, so I've put the force's media team on standby. They've already been working on the logistics. They are just waiting for you to call them. Here are details of your main contact. She's the media relations manager.' He handed Tom a small slip of paper.

Tom glanced at the name and telephone number on the slip. 'I've worked with Jane before. You might remember she arranged the press interview on the Aphron case.' It was during this particular press conference that Tom had begun to strongly suspect there was a concerted campaign to discredit him at play. 'Let's hope it's more successful than that one, although, to be fair, it wasn't her fault.'

He looked up from the paper, suddenly concerned. 'Has anyone spoken with Julie about this?' he asked. 'She's going through enough right now without switching on the television and listening to people talking about her husband.'

'All done,' answered Superintendent Birch. 'Her police welfare officer has spoken with her already. She understands the need to make an official statement. In fact, she would like to attend it.'

There was a brief silence before Superintendent Birch spoke again. 'As I said earlier to you both, it looks as though you could do with some rest. You've been on the go for a long time now. I'm sure you'll agree the last thing we need now is a cock-up because you've missed something due to being dog tired. Why don't you both go home and try and get some sleep?'

After the excitement of the preceding few hours, and now that they were back in a warm office, Tom, not for the first time today, suddenly felt very tired. It was the type of tiredness that often caused a nagging headache and could, as his concentration levels diminished, result in errors.

Tom and Milner spent the next half-hour or so discussing the following day's arrests plan. They then went home to try to get some rest, recognising that the following day would be one of the most important and emotional days of their careers.

Chapter 49

It was late when Tom arrived home. Despite his suggestion that Mary should not wait up for him, she was in the lounge, watching TV, when he got back.

As he entered the room she immediately stood up and put her arms around him. 'I'm so sorry,' she said. 'I can't begin to imagine how his wife must be feeling.' She pulled away and, looking directly at him, said, 'That could easily have been you or David. I just feel sick every time I think about it.'

Tom, not being able to think of any words which would offer any degree of reassurance, instead said, 'What I really need, right now, is a proper cup of coffee.'

'Why don't you sit down whilst I make you one?' She then added, as an afterthought, 'Have you had anything to eat today?'

'A couple of sandwiches, that's all. But I'm really not hungry.'

'Are you sure? I could quickly make you something.'

'Thanks, but, as I said, I'm really not hungry.'

As she walked towards the kitchen, Tom followed her. The last thing he needed right now was to be alone, and, anyway, now would be a good time to update Mary, not only on what had happened – that much she deserved – but, also on what was likely to happen tomorrow. So he briefly told her of the planned arrests, but he mainly wanted to forewarn her about the impending press conference.

After he had finished, she said, 'What will you say? It must be incredibly difficult, when you've known someone for so long.'

'I don't know, yet, what I will say. All I do know is that I owe it to him and Julie.'

Tom could see that Mary was now beginning to get emotional herself, and so he pulled her towards him and, for a while, they remained that way with nothing being said between them. Eventually, he released his hold on her. 'I know the plan for tomorrow was to spend some more time with Paul and his family. Could you call him first thing? The next few days are likely to be very busy and so I can't really commit to anything just yet. But tell him I'll somehow find time so that we can all meet up again.'

'Of course I will,' she replied. 'Why don't you go to bed now? It's getting late and you look exhausted. I'll sleep in the spare room, so that I'm not disturbing you.'

Even though it was late, and he was tired, he felt as though he had almost gone beyond the point where sleep would come easily. 'You are probably right,' he simply answered, knowing there was a good chance that he would just lie there, looking at the ceiling.

Mary kissed him and said, 'Try and get some sleep. What time will you be leaving?'

'Early,' he answered. 'I'm meeting with Milner at 7 am. So I need to leave here no later than, say, six thirty.'

'I'll make you some breakfast, then, before you leave.'

'You don't need to do that. I can always get something at the station.'

'Tom,' she said, in her most assertive voice, 'I am making you some breakfast. The least I can do for you is make sure you have eaten something. And anyway, knowing you as I do, there is a strong chance you'll forget. You're not leaving until you've eaten it. I suspect you'll need as much energy as possible tomorrow.'

Chapter 38

'Okay, that's agreed, then,' said Tom. It was the following morning, and Tom and Milner had met earlier to finalise their plans. He was now addressing the other members of the team. 'We don't need any drama with the arrests. We'll read out the charges, and their rights, and bring them both back here to the station. Although I don't expect any physical stuff, let's not take any chances. You never know, so be prepared. Any questions?'

'Are there likely to be any children there?' asked one of the uniformed officers.

'We don't think so,' answered Milner, 'but, just in case there are, we have child support officers on standby. DCI Stone and I will call them in if required.'

When it was obvious there were no more questions, Tom nodded. 'Right, let's go. Good luck.'

Not long afterwards, Tom and his team were outside Mrs Burton's house. The gates were open, allowing them unrestricted access to the property. They'd agreed Tom would bring in Mrs Burton whilst Milner would carry out the arrest at the other address.

It was just after 8 am when Tom pressed the doorbell, and he had to repeat it a couple of times before the door opened. Mrs Burton was wearing her dressing gown and was clearly shocked when she saw the group of officers standing there.

'Would you mind if we came in, Mrs Burton?' asked Tom.

'Why? What do you want?' she replied, still unable to take in what was happening.

'I can tell you when we are inside. It will be much better than doing everything stood here.'

Mrs Burton stood back, allowing everyone to enter.

'Thank you,' said Tom, before following her into the large living area.

'Why are you here?' she asked, once everyone was in.

'This is a warrant for your arrest,' answered Tom, holding up a piece of paper.

'My arrest?' she repeated, before sitting down. 'I don't understand.'

'Mrs Burton. We are arresting you for being complicit in the murder of your husband, Glyn Burton.' He read her her rights, after which he said, 'If you could please now get dressed and accompany us back to the station, where you will be formally charged.'

Mrs Burton began to sob, before eventually saying, 'I knew this would happen. You can't believe what I've been through over the past few weeks. It's been an absolute nightmare.'

'Are you admitting to being involved in the death of your husband?' asked Tom, seizing the opportunity just presented.

'Yes,' she answered, before finally breaking down. Between sobs, she added, 'But I didn't mean to kill him. I didn't know what I was doing.'

'I think it would be better if we continued this conversation back at the station. Why don't you get dressed? One of my female officers will help you.'

After Mrs Burton had left the room, Tom turned to one of the other officers. 'When we have left, get hold of forensics and let them know they can start. Tell them to concentrate, initially, on this room. I know it's a few weeks now since it happened, but they might still be able to find some evidence.'

He then walked towards where the photograph frames were, took out his mobile and took a photo of them.

Whilst this was happening, Milner's arrest was not going quite so smoothly, as the man had become increasingly aggressive as he began to understand what was happening. In the end, Milner took the decision to handcuff him.

It wasn't long after, though, that both people were back at the station and seated in adjoining interview rooms, along with their legal representation.

Tom had decided it would be best to first interview Mrs Burton as, given her current emotional fragility and earlier admission, they were more likely to make significant progress.

It was Milner who started the interview. 'Mrs Burton? Do you know why you are here?'

She simply nodded.

'Just for the record,' said Milner, 'Mrs Burton has indicated that she does know why she's here.' He carried on. 'Mrs Burton? Earlier you indicated to my colleague, DCI Stone, that you were involved in the death of your husband, Glyn. Do you still agree that was the case?'

'Yes,' she immediately answered, before her legal representative even had the chance to advise her. She caught the look he gave her. 'I don't care any more,' she said, clearly unwilling to take any advice he was about to offer. 'I just want it to be over.'

'It would help if you could tell us what happened on the day your husband disappeared,' said Milner.

By now Mrs Burton was surprisingly composed, almost as though it were a relief she could, at last, tell the truth. 'Glyn arrived home early from golf. We weren't expecting him back that soon. It was then it all happened.'

'What exactly did happen?' asked Milner, in an almost sympathetic tone.

'He caught us together, and that's when he suddenly attacked Jim.'

'Jim?' asked Tom, speaking for the first time. 'Do you mean Jim Mason, the man he used to golf with?'

'Yes,' she answered.

Chapter 50

'Why did Mr Mason come to your house?' asked Milner.

'I'd called Jim the previous night,' she answered, 'after Glyn and I had argued, and told him I'd decided to leave my husband. He could hear just how upset I was. He said he'd come round to the house early the following morning. He knew Glyn would be playing golf and got there just after Glyn had left.'

'So, when your husband unexpectedly arrived home early, he found you both together and presumably wanted to know why Mr Mason was there?'

'Yes,' she simply replied. 'It was then I told Glyn about Jim and myself and that I was leaving him. He completely flipped and went for Jim.'

'What happened then?'

'Glyn had pushed him to the floor and was hitting him. Although Jim tried to hold him back, he was not able to force him away completely. I thought Glyn was going to kill Jim. That's when I hit him. I just wanted to get him away from Jim. I didn't mean to kill him.' She began to cry as the memory of that fateful day came back to her.

Tom stood and went to pour a glass of water from the cooler before placing it in front of her. 'Please take your time,' he said.

They waited patiently until she had, once again, stopped crying, before gently resuming their questioning.

'If it's any consolation, I'm certain you didn't mean to kill your husband,' said Tom. 'Did you hit him with the frame that had the photograph of your son in it?'

'Yes,' she answered. 'How did you know that?'

'Well, the first time I came to your house, I noticed there was only one photograph of either of your children. That was the one of your daughter. It was in a very distinctive frame. I thought it a bit strange, especially when I heard you speak so movingly about them, that you would only be displaying one of them, not both. But it was when we found a small, broken piece of the same type of frame in the boot of your husband's car that my suspicions were confirmed. We found a slight trace of your husband's DNA on it, suggesting it was what had killed him. And then finally, when I came to visit you at a later date, I couldn't help but notice you had replaced it with the very same type of frame.'

Mrs Burton remained silent for a while, before finally speaking again. 'It was the first thing that I could grab. It was only when we saw the blood we realised just how serious it was.' Once again she began to sob. 'Oh my God. I can't believe that I'm even talking about this. It's a nightmare.'

'Would you like to take a break?' asked Tom.

When she just shook her head, Tom carried on, gently trying to prise out the full story from her. 'Do you mind if I ask how long you have been in a relationship with Mr Mason?'

'You make it sound so sordid,' she immediately answered.

'I'm sorry,' said Tom, 'I didn't mean it to sound that way. I'm just interested to understand everything, that's all.'

'I knew, of course, Glyn was seeing other women. To begin with, though, I just seemed to close my eyes to what was going on, reassuring myself that, whatever he was doing, it was not serious and that he would never leave me. After all, he always came back home. But it was his affair with Mike Preston's wife that changed everything. I knew Amy. Well, I'd met her a few times at golf club functions. Funnily enough, she was one of the few people there who I did get on with. That's why I refused to go to any more of them. I felt humiliated, with everyone at the club knowing what had been going on, and I didn't want people to start feeling sorry for me.'

'So you knew your husband and Mike Preston had been involved in a fight in the club car park?'

'Eventually, yes. It was Jim who mentioned it to me.' She paused briefly and then continued. 'And, to answer your previous question, it was just after that we began to realise we had feelings for each other. One morning, we bumped into one another in a supermarket. To be honest, it was a bit difficult at first, because Jim and Mike had been friends for a long time, and I'm sure Jim didn't know where his sympathies lay, with him or me. We finished up having a coffee together and, well, suddenly found ourselves meeting quite regularly for a coffee. It was a short time afterwards that things became more serious.'

Once again, she paused momentarily before continuing, this time with genuine defiance. 'I do not feel guilty about what I did. Jim was no longer married, and I had, by then, passed the point of trying to save my marriage. The children were now old enough to understand that there were problems with our marriage. I just wanted some happiness and to be able to share my life with someone who loved me.'

'Why didn't you call for an ambulance, or the police? It sounds as though what happened to your husband, at least partly, could be explained as being in self-defence. Why, then, did you decide to try and cover up his death?' Tom asked. 'Was it Mr Mason's idea?'

For the first time during the interview, Mrs Burton displayed some anger, rather than the contrition that had characterised her statements thus far. 'I know what you are trying to do. You want me to say that it was all Jim's fault. But it wasn't and I'm not going to do that. Whatever was agreed was done together.'

As he heard this, Tom couldn't help but feel real sympathy for her. Even in the depths of this ultimate nightmare situation, she was still unwilling to blame someone else exclusively for what happened.

The irony of the situation suddenly struck Tom. On the very day that Glyn Burton was planning to leave his wife, for Caroline Mercer, his wife was planning to leave him for Jim Mason. If the weather had been kinder that particular day, and Mr Burton had not returned home early, then their complicated personal relationship difficulties might have been resolved. And two people would still be alive.

'So, instead, why don't you tell us what you did next?' asked Milner.

So that was exactly what she did.

Chapter 51

After their session with Mrs Burton, they took a short break, rather than going straight on to interview Jim Mason.

'I just can't believe Gary died as a result of all of that,' said Milner, as they sat in Tom's office, each of them holding a drink. 'It just seems so unfair.' His emotions were quite obvious.

'I agree,' answered Tom, 'but life, especially when you are investigating crime, is full of unfairness. At least, finally, Mrs Burton was honest with us.'

'It's just a pity she wasn't honest with us some time ago. If she had been, Gary would still be alive now.'

Tom knew Milner was right but just couldn't bring himself to say so. The situation was difficult enough without having to talk about *if*s and *but*s. He had always been of the opinion that what was done was done. Until someone invented a time machine, it would always be impossible to change the past. Sometimes, though – and this was one such occasion – he couldn't help questioning his own principles.

'Knowing what we now know, how would you suggest we tackle Jim Mason?' asked Tom, keen to move the conversation on to more practical matters.

'I think we should approach it as if we don't know the full story. That way, at least we will soon find out if their stories are consistent. Mrs Burton was clearly still very supportive of him. It will be interesting to see if he's as supportive of her.'

'I agree.' Tom stood up and placed his empty cup in the bin. 'Okay, let's go and speak with him.'

*

As soon as they entered the interview room, Mr Mason said, 'Where's Jane? Can I see her?'

'I'm afraid that's not possible. Mrs Burton has been arrested and charged with being complicit in the murder of her husband. She has also been charged with perverting the course of justice.'

'That's crazy,' he replied, his voice rising in anger. 'She had nothing to do with it. It was me who killed Glyn.'

'And how did you do that?' asked Tom.

'We were fighting, and I just grabbed whatever was closest and hit him with it.'

'And what was it you hit him with?'

'I can't remember. All I was thinking at the time was to get him off me.'

'Let me help you, then,' said Tom. 'It was one of these, wasn't it?' He showed him a photograph of the framed pictures, which he'd taken earlier that morning at Mrs Burton's house.

'I don't know,' he answered. 'It might have been, but I can't remember.'

'If it had been you who had used it, then you would have had to have very long arms,' suggested Tom. 'The frame was higher up, on a cabinet. At the time, you had Mr Burton pinning you down on the floor.'

When he didn't respond, Tom continued. 'We found a small piece of the frame in the boot of Mr Burton's car. It was marked with his DNA and matched the small incision close to his temple.'

As before, Mr Mason remained silent.

'I have to tell you that Mrs Burton has already told us what happened, as well as admitting to striking the fatal blow, using the picture frame.'

Mr Mason's earlier confidence now seemed to totally disappear, and when he next spoke it was in a very subdued tone. 'It was an accident. Jane didn't mean to kill him. She was just trying to protect me from Glyn. At first it looked as though he had been knocked unconscious when his head hit the floor, but then we saw blood appearing.'

'Let me ask you the same question I asked Mrs Burton,' said Tom. 'Why, if you say it was unintentional, didn't you call for an ambulance?'

'I don't know,' he answered quietly. 'We were both totally shocked and I think we just panicked. We started to clear up the blood and things just seemed to develop from there. We just wanted to be together, and so, before we knew it, we had …'

'You had what, Mr Mason? Hatched a plan to cover up his death?'

'Yes,' he answered, before putting his head in his hands. 'I can't believe we did it.'

'I'll tell you what I think happened,' Tom said. 'Let me know if I get anything wrong.' He carried straight on. 'After you'd cleared up some of the mess, you carried his body out and placed it in the boot of his car. Incidentally, that must have been quite difficult as Mr Burton was quite a big man. I assume Mrs Burton helped?'

He simply nodded in agreement.

Tom continued. 'You first, though, had to take out his golf clubs and golf trolley to make room for him. You put these in the garage, alongside some of his other golf equipment. We have forensics examining them right now. I don't know whether we'll find any of your prints on them, but I suppose there's a chance.' He paused briefly. 'You then had to decide where to take him. Was that your idea or Mrs Burton's?'

'That was mine,' he quickly replied. 'I knew the place. We'd taken some of the kids from the school I work at there on a beginner's sailing course, about six months previously, so I knew where it was.'

'When you were ready, you then put on some of his golf clothes, got into his car and drove out. In order to try and pass yourself off as Mr Burton, you also put on a golf cap and pulled it down so that your face was not one hundred percent visible. That was a mistake, though. We have CCTV footage of you driving away from the house, wearing the cap, whereas, when he arrived home earlier that morning, Mr Burton was not wearing one. Something nagged away at me about this right from the start. Also, I knew I'd seen it, or something like it, previously. This bothered me, and it was only when someone I know – a family member, in fact – mentioned golf caps, and then later someone else mentioned photographs, that I finally put the two together. After that, everything else fell into place.'

'So you've known for a while it was me?' Mr Mason asked.

'Yes, I did suspect. I also had my suspicions about where Mr Burton had died. What I didn't know with any certainty, though, was why he died. Well, not until last night, that is.'

'Last night?' he repeated. 'What happened last night?'

'Last night we followed Mrs Burton, when she met you in Richmond Park.'

Mr Mason looked completely deflated. 'How did you know we would be meeting there?'

'I didn't know *where* you would be meeting, but I strongly suspected that you *would* be meeting. Mrs Burton had, no doubt, called you, as soon as she could, to say we'd been to visit her earlier in the day and that we had been particularly interested in Mr Burton's golf equipment. She did seem very unsettled by all of this, and so we knew it was highly likely she would want to discuss it with you. We were then able to confirm it was you from your car's registration number. To double-check we even followed you home, so that we had an address.'

As Mr Mason had heard this, he had become increasingly agitated, but it was just one part of all of this which, when he spoke, appeared to concern him the most. 'You say you followed her. Were you there all the time we were together?'

'Yes,' he replied.

'Does Jane know about this?' Mr Mason asked, with genuine concern, almost as though he were trying to protect her.

'We did not feel the need to tell her,' answered Tom.

He took out, from a file he had brought into the room with him, a still from the CCTV footage showing Mr Burton arriving home, and placed it on the table in front of Jim Mason. 'You can see that he's not wearing a cap.' He then took out another photograph, this time from the footage taken when he was, apparently, leaving his house, later that same afternoon. 'This one, though, clearly shows Mr Burton – or, actually, you, pretending to be Mr Burton – now wearing a cap. Incidentally,' he said, looking directly at him, 'we checked with some of the people he regularly played golf with, and none of them could remember Mr Burton ever actually wearing one.' Finally, he took out a copy of a photograph. It was the one he had first seen in Mr Burton's office at his home: the one featuring Glyn Burton, Roger White, Mike Preston and Jim Mason. 'I understand this was taken a couple of years ago, when you all went on a golf holiday to Portugal.

As you can see, Mr Burton is the only one not wearing a cap. More importantly, however, the cap *you* are wearing seems to be the same one you were wearing when you drove away from Mr and Mrs Burton's home.'

'I can't believe it,' he replied. 'All because of a golf cap.'

'Well, it certainly helped, but that wasn't the only thing that worried me. For example, I got the opportunity to look at some texts on Mrs Burton's phone. It was at the time she told us that her husband had texted her at 4.30 pm, that afternoon, to say that he would be late home. Obviously, he didn't send the text. I suspect it was you who sent it, in order to help with your story about him leaving the house earlier. It was picked up by one of the masts not too far away from where his body was later found, but the phone went dead not long afterwards. Was it then that you destroyed it?'

'Yes. I thought it would buy me a bit more time.'

Now Milner spoke. 'So, what happened then? After you'd got rid of the phone.'

'By then it was starting to get dark. I waited a bit longer and then drove the car closer to the quarry, which I thought would be a good spot. I knew the water was quite deep. I hadn't realised, though, there was a fence all the way around the quarry. After a while I found a place where the fence had been damaged by a falling tree. So I drove the car through it. I was still expecting it to be quite difficult, but I was more worried about the noise it might make. Fortunately, though, the car got through at my first attempt. Then I drove it as close as I could and pushed it in.'

'Weren't you worried you might be seen or heard?' asked Milner.

'Yes. That was my biggest fear, but I didn't see even one person, either when I was driving in or afterwards, when I walked away.'

'Did you walk back, then?'

'I did, yes. Actually, it wasn't that far from where I live, although I probably took a lot longer by not using the most direct routes.'

'You didn't go back to see Mrs Burton, then?' asked Tom, interested to hear as much as possible.

'No. It would have been too risky.' He then paused and, when he next spoke, his earlier matter-of-fact narrative style had been replaced by something with far more concern. 'I was really tempted, though, as I was worried about Jane. She was there all by herself, in that big house. We'd agreed that, although we had spent quite a while together cleaning up, it was important she went over it all again whilst I was out.'

'And, presumably,' added Tom, 'you made sure of what she was going to say to the police?'

'That was, I suppose, my biggest concern. As you can imagine, Jane was very upset and, although we had agreed what she should do and say, I was worried, because of her emotional state, she wouldn't be able to do it.' He paused for a brief moment. 'I felt terrible that she was there by herself and I wasn't able to support her. But I just couldn't take the risk of being seen with her there.' He finally added, 'So you can see it was me, not Jane, who did all of this. I'm the one who should be punished, not her.'

Chapter 52

'I know I shouldn't have,' said Milner, 'especially given everything else that has happened as a direct result of this, but at one point I started to feel some sympathy for both of them, especially Mrs Burton.'

'That does sometimes happen,' replied Tom. They had arrived back at his office. 'Especially when the culprits are as willing as they both were to admit their guilt. You'll find, though, as your career progresses, and you make more arrests, you'll come across many more who not only lie through their teeth, but show absolutely no remorse or contrition for what they have done.'

Just then Superintendent Birch knocked on the door. 'Okay to come in?' he asked politely.

'Come in,' replied Tom. 'DS Milner and I were just having a quick debrief.'

'Yes, I heard they had both confessed to the death of Mr Burton. Congratulations. You must be very pleased with your work.' Realising the potential insensitivity of what he'd just said, he quickly corrected himself. 'I'm sorry. I didn't mean it to come across quite like that, especially today of all days.'

'It's not a problem, sir,' answered Tom. 'We all still have a job to do, although, of course, it would have been better if DC Bennett had been here as well, to enjoy the success.' This brief conversation had the effect of immediately bringing him back to the event which was now just over an hour ahead of him. 'Do you have any idea what the Commissioner intends to say? I don't want to end up saying the same things.'

'I do, as a matter of fact,' he answered. 'That was another reason why I wanted to see you. He simply intends to say a few words and then hand over to you, if that's okay. Have you thought about what you might say?'

'That's all I have been doing, apart from, of course, the

moments when DS Milner and I were tied up with Mr Burton's murder investigation.'

'Will you be okay?' Superintendent Birch asked, with a degree of concern and anxiety.

'I've got no idea,' he answered.

Just then, any further conversation was interrupted when Tom's office phone rang. It was Jenny, Superintendent Birch's PA. After a brief, mainly one-way conversation, Tom replaced the phone and said, 'That was Jenny, to let you know Sir Peter has arrived. He's in your office.'

'Thanks.' Superintendent Birch started to make his way out of the office, before suddenly stopping. 'I'll see you downstairs,' he said, before adding, 'and good luck.'

For a while, after Superintendent Birch's departure, both men remained quiet, each deep in his own thoughts. After a while, Milner said, 'Should I remove the chart?'

Tom glanced up at the chart listing the people associated with the Glyn Burton case, then stood and walked towards it. He removed the copy of the photograph featuring the four golfers. 'Ironic, really,' he said.

'What do you mean, sir?'

'Well, the person who committed the murder was literally staring us in the face all along. What's more, he was the one person, amongst all the people here, who we didn't interview. That's a lesson, Milner, for both of us. Check everything and then check it again.'

Before Milner could respond, however, they were interrupted. Jane Perkins, the media relations officer for West London police, knocked lightly on the door and said, 'Am I interrupting something? I can always come back.'

'No, that's all right,' answered Tom. 'Please come in. We were just taking a few minutes.' He paused. 'I think you've met DS Milner before.'

She walked towards Milner and they shook hands.

'I'm truly sorry about the death of DC Bennett,' she said, looking from Milner to Tom. 'It must be extremely distressing for everyone who knew him.'

'Apart from being a vital part of the team he was also a friend,' Tom said. 'So, yes, it's very tough, right now, for everyone.'

She waited for a moment, until she felt the time was right to continue. 'As it's a dry day, I suggest you make your statement just outside the main entrance. Quite a few of the news stations are already arriving and setting up. I don't want to tell you your job, but my advice would be to keep whatever you are going to say reasonably short. By the way, DC Bennett's wife and two children have just arrived. One of the station's welfare officers is looking after them.' After a brief moment, she continued. 'I understand Sir Peter is proposing to say a few words before you.' She looked at her watch. 'It's now ten past twelve. The press have been told that the statements will be made at 1 pm. So I suggest we all meet in the ground floor conference room at ten to one. I'm sure you still have a few things to do, so I'll leave you to it. I'll see you again at ten to one.'

After she had left, Milner said, 'Is there anything you'd like me to do, sir?'

'Thanks, but I probably need a bit of time to myself right now. What I would suggest, though, is that you go and meet Julie and let her know I'll be there shortly.'

Notwithstanding everything that had happened over the past couple of hectic days, Tom had, when the opportunity presented itself, given some thought to what he might say, and so he spent the next twenty minutes writing down a few of these thoughts. When he had finished, he read through what he'd written a couple of times, until it was clear in his mind. He then picked up the sheet of paper, put it into his pocket and was just about to leave his office when his mobile rang. He could see that it was DCI Chapman.

'Tom. I'm glad I managed to get hold of you. I understand you will shortly be making a statement regarding DC Bennett's murder.'

'Yes, I was just about to make my way there,' he answered.

'I won't keep you, then, but I thought you'd like to know that this morning we arrested the two men who, we believe, were involved. It's still early days, of course, but I'm confident we have enough evidence to get a conviction.'

'Thanks, Jack, for taking the time to let me know. I'm sure that will be a great boost for all the officers here. It might also be some consolation to Gary's family.'

After his conversation he immediately made his way to the conference room, on the ground floor, where everyone was assembling.

As he entered the room he could see Sir Peter and Superintendent Birch were both speaking with DC Bennett's wife, whilst Milner and a female welfare officer seemed to be in discussion with her two children. Jane Perkins was talking to a small group of other people who Tom didn't recognise, but he suspected they might be from the media. Along one wall was a table, upon which was a selection of sandwiches and various other snacks. It looked as though they were still untouched.

Tom made his way towards Julie and, without saying anything, put his arms around her. After a short while, he pulled away from her and said, 'I know it's a stupid question, but how are you?'

'I'm not too bad,' she answered. 'It's the kids I'm worried about, though.'

As Tom looked at her, he could see, in her face, all the tell-tale signs of lack of sleep. There were dark marks under her eyes, which her make-up couldn't entirely conceal.

'Are you okay to do this?' he asked. 'You don't have to do it.'

Now it was her turn to look at him closely. 'What do you think? We all want to do it, however difficult.'

Tom, once again, hugged her close and whispered, 'Gary would be proud of you all.'

Just then Jane Perkins approached him. 'I'm sorry to inter-rupt, but, just to let you know, everything is ready.' She looked towards the group of people she had just been speak-ing with. 'They are keen that we stick to the agreed time, otherwise it might not make the midday news.'

Tom took hold of Julie's hand, gave it a gentle squeeze, and, along with Sir Peter and Superintendent Birch, they made their way outside, where a large number of cameras were waiting for them. Jane led them to a pre-agreed position. A line had been drawn on the ground indicating where they should all stand. Sir Peter stood in the centre with Superintendent Birch to his right. Tom, together with Julie and the two children, was on his left.

'Is everyone ready?' Jane asked, directing her question at the newspeople. After they had all given her the thumbs-up, she turned towards Sir Peter and simply said, 'Sir Peter.'

'Good afternoon, everyone,' he said, reading from a statement. 'Two days ago, one of my officers was killed when carrying out his duty. Detective Constable Gary Bennett joined the Metropolitan force almost twenty years ago, and in the time since then he always sought to uphold the values which characterise each and every one of our officers: professionalism, integrity, courage and compassion.' He paused and then, looking directly at the cameras, said, 'His death has, once again, brought home to us how those values sometimes come at a high price. At this distressing time, the thoughts of myself and all of my officers in the Metropolitan police force are, of course, with his wife and family.'

A short silence ensued, and Tom took this as his cue. 'Good afternoon. I'm Detective Chief Inspector Tom Stone, and DC Bennett was a key part of my team. I personally have known Gary for many years, both as a colleague and, in recent times, as a friend. Like most people here today, I have many regrets, but, without a doubt, one of the biggest ones is the fact it took me so long to count him as a true friend.' He paused. 'Sir Peter just mentioned the key values to which we all aspire, but no one really knows if they would be able to meet those values until the situation arises. I can tell you that DC Bennett not only subscribed to those values but also applied them when the situation demanded. He died when, despite he himself being unarmed, he unhesitatingly went to the assistance of a member of the public who was being viciously attacked by two men, both of whom were wielding knives. He knew the odds were not in his favour, but, in that split-second moment, he still decided, without regard for his own personal safety, to go to someone's assistance. That is the true meaning of courage.

'DC Bennett will be sadly missed, not only by myself and the other members of my team, but also by all his friends and colleagues here at West London police. But, of course, none of that can compensate for the loss which his wife, Julie and their two children, Karen and Peter, are feeling.' He then turned away from the cameras and, looking directly at Julie and the two children, said, 'But you should be hugely proud of what Gary did.'

Chapter 53

It was later that same afternoon and Tom was just arriving back home. After everything that had happened, he was, unsurprisingly, once again feeling both physically and mentally exhausted. The adrenaline that had carried him through the previous twenty-four hours had now expended itself.

After the official statements had finished, they had all gone back into the conference room at the station. Although some people had eaten some of the food provided, he, personally, hadn't. He just didn't have any appetite at all and made do with a cup of coffee.

He had spent most of his time there with Julie and her two children. After a short while, though, she had decided to leave and return home. She had told Tom how she was struggling to handle all the nice things that people were saying about her husband. She said, despite everyone's best intentions, all it was doing was reminding her of how Gary was no longer around.

As he parked his car on the drive, the front door suddenly opened. He got out of the car and walked towards Mary, who, without saying anything, put her arms around him. When she finally pulled away from him she said, 'I'm so proud of you. That was so lovely, what you said about DC Bennett.'

'You saw it, then?' he asked.

'It was on the news. We all saw it.'

'All?' he asked.

'Yes. Paul and his family are all here. As you suggested, I let him know you wouldn't be able to meet up, so he suggested that they come over here.' She paused briefly. 'I think they wanted to support me.'

'Are they still here?' he asked.

'Yes. They are inside.'

He followed Mary into the house and then into the main living room, where they were all seated. Both Paul and Kerry stood as he entered the room.

'This is a pleasant surprise,' said Tom, unable to think of anything else to say.

'How are you?' asked Kerry, in a way which suggested genuine concern for him.

Before he could reply, Sam, in an obviously excited tone, suddenly said, 'Granddad! We saw you on TV. I can't wait to tell all my mates about it.'

Paul, looking towards Tom, simply raised his eyebrows, as if to say, *That's kids for you.*

It was the first time Tom had been called *Granddad* by either Sam or Emily. Mary, suddenly conscious of the effect this was having on him, said, 'Why don't we let Granddad Tom take off his coat, and then we'll decide what everyone wants to do?'

Taking this as his lead, Tom took off his coat and walked towards the kitchen.

Paul followed him. When they were alone, he said, 'Are you sure you're okay? You look totally whacked.'

'I'm not sure,' Tom answered. 'It's all been a bit hectic over the last day or so. It's probably only now catching up to me.'

'I'm not surprised. Mary mentioned to us how you've been involved in a murder investigation and that it was all coming to a head. Are you able to tell me what the outcome was?'

'Well, we've made arrests and they have admitted their guilt. We just need due process to now take its course. You won't know this, but you actually helped in solving it.'

'Really? What did I do?' he answered, a look of puzzlement on his face.

'It was when you mentioned that you always wore a cap when playing golf.' He then explained how Glyn Burton never wore a cap when playing golf, but was apparently suddenly wearing one when he was supposedly leaving his house on the day he disappeared.

'So you were able to prove who did it just on that basis?'

'Well, not just on that, but, in cases like this, it's important to try and find an anomaly or discrepancy. Something which doesn't fit in with what you already know. That then makes you think about alternative scenarios.'

'And what about the murder of your colleague? Was that related or a separate investigation?'

Tom hesitated before answering. 'I can't really go into detail about the specifics, but, again, arrests have been made, so I'm hopeful that justice will be served.'

'That's good news, then, especially for his wife and family.' He paused. 'By the way, I was really proud of you today. It can't have been easy,' he said, with what was clearly genuine feeling.

'No, it wasn't, but I appreciate you saying that.'

'We were thinking of having dinner together later, but I would imagine, after the day you've had, that's the last thing you want to do.'

'I'm sure I can keep going for a bit longer yet,' Tom answered, with a slight laugh. 'Where did you have in mind?'

'Nothing too flash. We passed a family steak restaurant not too far from here. I think the kids would like that. We are planning to travel up to the Midlands tomorrow. It's a bit earlier than we had originally planned, but Uncle Ray called to say something had cropped up – someone who he knew has died and their funeral is next week – and so it would be better if we could come up a day or so earlier. It does mean, though, that we will be returning a bit earlier. Anyway, I just thought it would be nice to spend some more time together before we travel up there.'

'Good idea,' Tom answered. 'Just give me a few minutes to change into something else and I'll be ready.'

It wasn't long after that that they were all seated in the restaurant. After the combination of some food and a few drinks, Tom suddenly began to feel tired again. He had declined to have a dessert, but the kids were tucking into their chocolate sundaes with real gusto. Suddenly Emily began to giggle and point at Tom.

'Look, everybody, Granddad Tom is asleep.'

Chapter 54

The following morning Tom had woken early and, realising that he would find it difficult to get back to sleep, had decided, rather than just lying there, to get up and have an early start at the station. When he arrived, Milner was already there.

'Could you not sleep either?' Tom asked, half-jokingly.

'Not really,' replied Milner, unwilling or unable to respond in kind to Tom's attempt to lighten the situation.

'Is there anything I can do to help?' Tom asked.

'Not really,' he again replied, and Tom took this as a sign that Milner didn't want to talk about what was clearly bothering him. So they spent their time tying up all the loose ends with regard to the arrests of Mrs Burton and Jim Mason.

In truth, apart from ensuring all their evidence and statements were in order, it was one of the more straightforward conclusions to an investigation Tom had been involved in, not least because of their readiness to admit their guilt. But Gary's shadow still hung heavy over the entire station and Milner, in particular, seemed to be affected by his death.

As the morning progressed, Tom had tried, on a couple of occasions, to speak with Milner about it, but had met a bit of a brick wall every time. He recognised, though, that perhaps, given his own personality, he wasn't the most qualified to initiate this type of discussion. He made a mental note to speak with Jenny about it. It might be a good idea if Jenny and Milner took some time off together. Just getting away from the station for a few days, and from all of the memories that it held, might help Milner's mental state. Tom suspected, due to some earlier conversations, that Milner was taking some personal responsibility for Gary's death, and his current behaviour seemed to reinforce that feeling. He'd decided, therefore, that what Milner probably needed was some time and space in order to finally come to terms with what had happened. But that strategy was just about to be blown out of the water.

'Are you serious?' asked Tom, with undisguised incredulity in his voice. 'You and I both know that is absolute rubbish.'

Tom was now seated in Superintendent Birch's office, on the fifth floor.

'I couldn't believe it myself,' Superintendent Birch answered. 'When I found out about it I called DCS Small straight away. Unfortunately, his hands, like mine, are tied on this. You know there's an independent internal investigation whenever a police officer dies whilst on duty. I must admit, I simply thought it would be a fact-gathering exercise with conclusions as to the lessons learnt. Not for a single moment did I think DS Milner would be personally subject to investigation.'

Tom didn't immediately respond as he thought through all of the implications of such an investigation for Milner, and an uncomfortable silence followed.

Finally, Tom said, 'Has it started yet?'

'No, not yet,' replied Superintendent Birch. 'I only received the email this morning. It simply says that an investigation will start shortly, at which point DS Milner will be suspended from all duties until the investigation has been completed.'

'And what has he actually done to warrant this? What are they looking for?'

'It doesn't mention any specifics, just that it will involve his suspension.' Superintendent Birch hesitated, his face now betraying his concern. 'In the past, when this type of internal investigation has occurred, the investigators have usually been looking for any procedural errors or even some degree of negligence in the way the case has been executed.'

'Negligence?' repeated Tom, his voice rising in step with his anger. 'How on earth could DS Milner be accused of negligence?'

'Tom,' replied Superintendent Birch. 'At this point, I'm only speculating. Let's wait and see what happens before jumping to any conclusions.'

Rather than having the effect of providing reassurance for Tom, all this did was reinforce his anger. 'Well, I'm not going to accept this. I will speak to the Commissioner if I have to.' He shook his head. 'If anyone should be suspended then it should be me. After all, I was the SIO on this case.'

'Tom, I know you are angry – and you have every right to be – but that is only likely to make things worse. You were on official holiday. You had assigned responsibility, whilst you were away, to DS Milner, and DC Bennett reported directly to him. If we follow your logic then it should be me who ought to be suspended, as it was me who agreed to you taking a few days' holiday.'

Tom's earlier anger had surprisingly abated when he next spoke. 'I hear what you are saying,' he said, making it clear that he didn't agree, 'but I'm not going to let this go.'

By the time Tom had returned to his office on the second floor, he had already decided what he would do, and that was why, later that same afternoon, he was standing outside Metropolitan Commissioner Sir Peter Westwood's office.

'You were lucky to get hold of him today,' said Sir Peter's PA. 'He is at a chief constables' conference in Manchester tomorrow and not back until later in the week. Can I get you a coffee whilst you're waiting?'

'No, thanks,' he answered. His intention was to make this as brief as possible.

'I saw you on television, the other day, with Sir Peter. That was just so sad,' she said.

'Yes, it was. It's not something I would ever want to repeat.'

Just then the door opened and Sir Peter was standing there. He offered his hand to Tom, who reciprocated.

'Tom. Good to see you again. How are things back at the station?' Sir Peter asked, with genuine concern in his voice.

'It's early days yet, sir, and emotions are still quite raw. Some officers are keen to talk about DC Bennett, and remember things he was involved in, whilst others are still finding it difficult to even mention his name. I'm sure, though, given time, the cloud will start to lift.'

Sir Peter followed Tom into his office and closed the door, before speaking again. 'And how about you? How are you feeling?'

'I have good days and bad days. Sometimes I forget that Gary is dead. At other times it seems like everything I'm doing simply reminds me he is no longer around.'

Sir Peter didn't immediately reply, recognising that Tom, perhaps, needed a little more time. Finally though, he felt he could continue. 'I never really got the opportunity to congratulate you on the successful conclusion of the investigation you were working on. Superintendent Birch mentioned it to me when I was at the station. Anyway, many congratulations.'

'Thank you, sir,' Tom replied. 'But, as usual when there's a successful result, it's due to teamwork.' He took this as the opportunity to raise the issue concerning Milner. 'That's why I wanted to meet with you, sir. I understand Superintendent Birch has been informed that there will be an investigation into DC Bennett's death.'

'Yes, I was aware of that. As you know, it's standard procedure when an officer is killed on duty.'

'I understand that, sir,' he answered. 'But I didn't know it was standard procedure to automatically suspend the officer involved whilst the investigation was taking place.' He carried straight on, not allowing Sir Peter to reply. 'I can't believe, at all, there is any reason for suspending DS Milner. On what possible basis could that be justified?'

'Obviously I'm not aware of the specific details for this particular case, but I'm sure the investigating team have their reasons. And anyway, just suspending an officer doesn't imply guilt. It's simply to ensure that the investigation can be carried out in an independent and impartial manner.'

Tom could see, expressed this way, the logic in what Sir Peter was saying. What hadn't been factored in, however, was Milner's current state of mind. 'If that's the case, sir, then it should be me who is suspended. As I said to Superintendent Birch, I was the SIO. It was my investigation and DC Bennett died on my watch. So suspend me, not DS Milner.'

Sir Peter looked intently at Tom before responding. 'Tom, it's not my decision. That's why it's an investigation run by an independent third party.'

'I'm sorry, sir, but I can't believe you have no influence whatsoever.' He then tried another approach. 'Suspending a young officer such as DS Milner at the start of his career can only be counterproductive. I have no doubt, if he stays in the force, he will go on to become one of the force's most successful senior officers. I wouldn't be at all surprised if one day he works from this office. The alternative is that he becomes so disillusioned with the way he has been treated, he decides to leave. What possible benefit is that to the force or the country?'

If he had hoped his appeal would succeed, he was quickly disappointed. 'I'm sorry, Tom, but, as I said – even though you might not believe it – I have no influence over how the inquiry is conducted. And anyway, the only way in which these inquiries can operate successfully is if they are totally independent and not subject to any third-party influence.'

Tom's earlier relative equanimity had now disappeared. 'So it's acceptable for two senior figures – and let's face it, current establishment figures – to be quietly retired, on their gold-plated pensions, and with their reputations intact, whereas a young police officer will be subjected to the most public personal and professional scrutiny. Where's the fairness in that?'

'Tom, I know you are upset and angry, but that type of comparison is not going to help. And, anyway, we've already had this discussion.'

But Tom was not about to let it drop. 'So you're saying that an instance where two people have been, at best, involved in the cover-up of the deaths of an innocent man and woman, or, at worst, actually complicit in their deaths, should not be subject to *any* investigation.' He paused momentarily, as he tried to put all of the thoughts swirling around in his head into words, before continuing. 'Whereas the involvement of a young police officer, who is not even leading the murder investigation, should be subject to the full force of an internal inquiry regarding his behaviour, with the possibility of it ending his career.'

Sir Peter, probably wisely, treated this as rhetorical and remained silent. So Tom continued. 'Of course I'm upset and angry. I'm sure you would be as well, if you were in my shoes. What do you expect me to do? Just accept that one of my officers will possibly be sacrificed on the altar of police procedure?'

Tom fell silent as he, once again, gathered his thoughts. When he next spoke it was without any of his earlier anger. 'I'm sorry, sir, but I'm just not willing to accept this. If anyone has to be suspended then it should be me. If it's still decided that DS Milner will be suspended, then I will seriously consider tendering my resignation.'

Chapter 55

It was later that evening and, after his meeting with Sir Peter, Tom had driven straight home. As so often happened when he had things on his mind, he arrived home without remembering the actual drive. Under normal circumstances, by now, his earlier anger would have been reduced somewhat. This time, though, if anything, it had actually increased.

Of course, he understood the need for such an inquiry. It was the only way in which any mistakes could be identified and procedures put in place in order to minimise the risk of them ever happening again. He also understood the importance of any such inquiry being carried out in a totally independent manner. What he couldn't understand, though, was why Milner should be the focus of the investigation.

Despite what Sir Peter had said about it not implying any guilt on Milner's part, Tom knew the way things like this worked and how it was likely to be perceived by colleagues and associates. The very fact Milner had been suspended would, in the minds of some people, still imply at least a degree of culpability. There would always be a hint of suspicion following him wherever his future career took him. What was also true was that, even if he was eventually fully exonerated, it would still be a matter of record that he had been suspended.

There was also the issue of how Julie, DC Bennett's wife, would react when she found out Milner had been suspended. It wasn't difficult to imagine how she might begin to blame Milner for her husband's death. Tom also knew that, for someone like Milner who set himself high standards, the suspension would be something he would, undoubtedly, struggle to come to terms with.

And there was another thing. Whilst Tom's involvement in the Glyn Burton murder investigation had provided some short-term distraction, in truth, the situation regarding

Commander Jenkins and Charles Cope had continued to nag away at him. The events of the past twenty-four hours had simply brought this inner turmoil to the surface once again.

'They are such a lovely family,' said Mary, not for the first time.

'Yes, they are,' agreed Tom, although he couldn't help thinking that it had nothing to do with him.

Paul, Kerry and the kids had now travelled to Birmingham in order to visit Paul's uncle. Last night they had agreed, when they returned, to meet up with Tom and Mary again before they flew back to Australia.

Later, after Tom and Mary had had something to eat, they settled down to watch a programme that both of them particularly enjoyed. Tom, though, just couldn't relax, and this was not lost on Mary.

'Are you all right?' she eventually asked. 'You don't seem to be yourself.' Before he could say anything, though, she continued. 'I'm not an expert in these things, but I would imagine it does take some time before the full impact of what's happened really starts to sink in. Is there anything I can do?'

'It's not just that,' he answered. 'Although, of course, it is a factor. But there's something else.' Even as he said those words, he wondered whether he would regret saying them. Under normal circumstances, it was not something he would have shared with anyone. But these were not normal circumstances, and one thing he had learnt during his time with Mary was that not only was she a good listener, but she also somehow managed to provide the right advice. He'd often thought how, if she had been around earlier in his life, perhaps he might not now be so reluctant to share or even show his emotions.

A look of puzzlement appeared on Mary's face. 'What is it, then?'

'It's related to DS Milner.'

'I know you said he'd taken it especially badly, and was really struggling to come to terms with Gary's death, but isn't that quite normal?'

'I'm sure it is, but there's something else,' he answered. Before Mary could ask what that something was, he began to tell her about his conversation with Superintendent Birch, who'd informed him of the likelihood of DS Milner being suspended. He then told her about his subsequent conversation with Sir Peter.

'So you've resigned?' she asked, her voice reflecting her astonishment.

'No,' he answered. 'I haven't resigned. Well, not yet, anyhow. What I did was inform the Commissioner that I would consider resigning if they go ahead with Milner's suspension.'

'How likely is that?' she asked.

'What? Resigning or Milner being suspended?'

'I suppose both, actually.'

Tom hesitated briefly before replying, knowing the likely impact his answer would have, not just on his career but almost certainly on their relationship as well. 'The more I think about it, the more I'm convinced I should resign if he is suspended.'

'You're not just making that decision because, right now, you are angry?' she asked. 'Wouldn't it be better not to make any decision until a day or so after you know what will happen?'

Tom knew she was right. As a rule of thumb, it was best – particularly for someone like him, with such a calculating personality – to wait until emotions had subsided. On the other hand, he'd also, throughout his career, trusted his instincts. Sometimes, however high feelings are running at the time, your immediate response is the correct response. 'I know you are right, but I just feel so strongly about this.'

'But what about if they decide to suspend you instead? Won't that also affect your career?'

'I'm sure it would, but, frankly, I'm at the point where I don't really care any more.'

Mary fell momentarily silent. Eventually, though, she said, 'Whatever you decide to do, you know, don't you, that I'll be here to support you?'

A thin smile appeared on Tom's face, and then he took hold of her hand. 'I know that,' he simply answered.

Chapter 56

The following morning, Milner visited Tom's office.

Almost as soon as he was seated, Milner said, with a degree of enthusiasm which had been missing in his recent demeanour, 'I just received a call from a contact of mine at North London. He told me the two men arrested after Gary's death have been formally charged with his murder, together with the attack on Craig Blackwell. They've also obtained more evidence linking them to drug dealing.'

'That's good news,' answered Tom, unable to quite match Milner's obvious positivity.

'They are also considering charging Craig Blackwell with possession,' Milner added.

'I would imagine that's the least of his problems right now.'

'What about all the secrecy regarding the sale of land at the golf club? Do you think it will still go ahead now?'

'That's a good question,' answered Tom, pleased that Milner was, once again, showing a bit of his normal enthusiasm. 'I'd forgotten all about that. It must be all they are talking about at West London Golf Club. Anyway, that's one for the lawyers, I suppose.'

Tom was still very concerned for Milner, certain that he would react badly to any suspension. All he could do in the meantime, though, was try to carry on as normal – well, at least, as normally as anyone could after the death of a close colleague – and be there for him if it did happen.

'Have you heard yet when Gary's funeral is likely to be?' asked Milner.

'I haven't, no,' replied Tom. 'It will depend on when the PM can be done. I hope, for Julie's sake, that it's soon.'

Just then, Tom's phone rang.

'It's Jenny,' said the voice on the other end of the phone. 'Are you able to come up to see Superintendent Birch?'

'When?' replied Tom.

'Well, he did say to ask if you are available right now.'

'Okay. I'm on my way.'

As he made his way up the fifth floor, he had a strong sense of foreboding. Jenny was not her usual chatty and friendly self and he had picked out clear concern in the tone of her voice. When he arrived this feeling was further confirmed when she simply said, 'Superintendent Birch is waiting to see you.'

As soon as he entered the room, Superintendent Birch, discarding the usual pleasantries, said, 'Tom, I have bad news. I've just learnt DS Milner will shortly be informed of his suspension whilst the investigation into the circumstances of DC Bennett's death continues.'

Although this news still hit Tom hard, deep down he was not especially surprised. He had been able to sense, from his previous conversations, which way this particular wind was blowing.

'How did you find out?' he asked.

'I've just received a call from the Commissioner.' But, before Tom could ask any follow-up questions, Superintendent Birch continued. 'If it's any consolation, he did mention that he had made a case for DS Milner *not* to be suspended whilst the investigation was ongoing. He spoke personally to the head of the inquiry team. Unfortunately, he wasn't successful.'

'You said DS Milner will be informed shortly. Just how shortly will that be?' asked Tom.

'I believe he will receive an email later today informing him that he will be suspended. He will then have a meeting with the head of the inquiry team, off site, tomorrow morning.'

Tom remained quiet as he tried to take on board the full implications of what Superintendent Birch had just told him. Finally, he spoke again. 'Would it be possible for me to speak with him before he receives the email? It's likely he will want to discuss it with me anyway, as soon as he gets it.'

'I'm afraid that's not possible, Tom,' Superintendent Birch quickly answered. 'You – or anyone else, for that matter – cannot be seen to be involved at this stage. If you were, then it's possible it could be construed as applying undue influence. Frankly, the last thing DS Milner needs is for the inquiry to be compromised – albeit with the best of intentions.' There was even more bad news to come. 'It will be explicitly stated, in the email, that DS Milner should not discuss this with anyone

– and that includes you – whilst the inquiry is being carried out. It's likely, of course, you will be called to give evidence, but, unless and until that happens, you should make it crystal clear to DS Milner that, if he does want to discuss it with you, you are not able to do so.' He paused briefly. 'Tom? Do you understand that?'

After another brief moment of silence Tom simply answered, 'Yes.'

'Look, Tom, we both know DS Milner did absolutely nothing wrong and in no way contributed to the death of DC Bennett. I'm sure the inquiry will also come to that conclusion and he will be totally exonerated. The best way we can help DS Milner is to follow the procedure to the letter. I'm sure you will get your chance to speak on his behalf when they call you. I'm fully expecting that I will also be called. That will be our opportunity.'

As Tom left the office, Jenny looked up. 'Is everything okay, sir?'

Tom, whilst trying to sound as positive as possible, could only bring himself to say, 'I'm sure it will be.'

*

It wasn't long after Tom's discussion with Superintendent Birch that an ashen-faced Milner appeared in Tom's office. In his hand he was holding a single sheet of paper. Tom didn't need to guess why Milner was here.

'I've just received this,' Milner said, handing over the sheet to Tom. Given his appearance, together with what the sheet was likely to contain, the tone of his voice was surprisingly calm.

Tom took the sheet and quickly read through it, before handing it back. 'Why don't you sit down?'

'You don't seem surprised,' said Milner.

'No, I'm not, although I only found out yesterday that this was being considered.' He immediately carried on. 'David, I know you are bound to be upset, but it is standard procedure to carry out an independent inquiry under these circumstances. That usually involves the temporary suspension of the senior investigating officer until the inquiry delivers its findings.'

'But weren't you the SIO?' asked Milner.

Tom didn't immediately respond. Milner's question was perfectly logical and one which, although he'd anticipated it, he had not been looking forward to replying to.

'I was, at least until I vested that authority in you, when I took a few days' holiday. I know it's of little consolation right now, but I have already made the point, to both Superintendent Birch and the Commissioner himself, that it should be me who is suspended, not you. Unfortunately, the matter is out of their hands. The decision is that of the independent police inquiry.'

Now it was Milner's turn to remain silent. Tom, for once, decided to fill that silence.

'I have to tell you, officially, I am not allowed to discuss any of this with you whilst the inquiry is in progress. Unofficially, however, I want you to know that, should you wish, I will be here and available.' It was a decision he had taken after his last meeting with Superintendent Birch. Whatever the consequences for Tom personally, he wasn't about to abandon Milner.

'Thank you, sir. I appreciate that,' replied Milner, albeit in a discernibly downbeat tone. 'I'm sure you have already done everything possible.'

'My immediate suggestion is that you should consult with your union representative,' Tom said. 'You will be interviewed and it might be useful to have representation during this. What's also important is for you to refer to any notes you took at the time, as well as writing down anything you can remember that was discussed with Gary during the period immediately prior to his death.'

It was at this point the seriousness of the situation suddenly seemed to hit Milner. 'I can't believe this is happening. What am I supposed to have done wrong? Surely I can't be blamed for Gary's death?'

'I know it's not easy right now, but you should know that you have the full support of Superintendent Birch and Sir Peter, as well as mine. I'm sure the inquiry team will quickly come to the conclusion that Gary's death could not have been prevented.'

Something else suddenly came to Milner's mind. 'What will Gary's family think when they hear this?' he asked, with increased concern.

'Gary was an experienced officer who died whilst bravely

carrying out his duty. Julie and her family understand that and this inquiry will not alter the way they feel.'

Both men remained quiet for a while, until Tom broke the silence. 'David, I really do think it would be best if you went home. It will only make things worse if you hang around here. You know the way the grapevine works in a station. It won't be long before rumours start to spread. Someone will have heard something from someone else, who thought they'd over-heard something being said.'

'I suppose you're right,' Milner answered in a matter-of-fact manner, before turning and heading towards the door.

'There's one other thing,' said Tom. 'You will have to hand over your warrant card and any other police ID.'

For the first time, Tom really did think that Milner was about to break down. But, with almost supreme willpower, he somehow held himself together, handed over all of his ID cards and then walked out of the office.

Chapter 57

'I'm really glad we were able to spend some more time together before we flew home,' said Kerry. 'It's been wonderful meeting you both.'

'Well, we've both enjoyed it as well,' replied Mary. 'I'm so happy it worked out well for everyone. You never really know with this type of thing, do you?'

Mary and Kerry, along with Sam and Emily, were seated together in a coffee shop at Heathrow airport, waiting for the family's return flight to be called. Tom and Paul were at the counter, ordering some drinks.

'Yes, I do know what you mean,' Kerry said. She looked in the direction of her husband. 'You wouldn't think so, looking at them right now, but he was so anxious about meeting Tom.'

'If it's any consolation, Tom was exactly the same.' Mary paused momentarily. 'He's had a lot to contend with recently at work, and meeting you all has, I'm sure, been just what he needed.'

'Yes, I've heard about some of it, but it's only when you know the person involved that you fully understand what they have to go through.' After a moment Kerry added, with increased concern in her voice, 'Do you think he will be okay?'

'To be honest, I don't really know,' answered Mary. 'As you've probably realised already, Tom is not the type of person who wears his heart on his sleeve. He tends to keep those feelings to himself. Even though we've been together for a while now, I still can't really tell how he is truly feeling. We have discussed this a few times in the past, but it just seems so difficult for him to really admit how he feels. In fact, this last week or so, whilst you've all been here, he's been as open as I've ever seen him. I think it's helped that Sam and Emily have been around.'

'Yes, I can see that. To be honest, we weren't quite sure how they would react when they met him. But I suppose we shouldn't have worried.'

'Tom's not naturally comfortable in the company of young children. But,' Mary said, 'I know he's really enjoyed seeing them.'

Before Mary could expand on this, they were interrupted when Tom and Paul returned with the drinks.

'You two look very serious,' said Paul.

'Not really,' Kerry quickly replied. 'We were just saying how lucky we both are to have such wonderful partners.'

As Tom gave Mary a quizzical look, Paul simply said, 'Yeah, right.'

A short while later, and after they had all finished their drinks, Sam came running towards them and excitedly said, 'Our flight is on the board. It says we have to get on now.'

They all stood, and Kerry first embraced Mary and then Tom. 'It's been great meeting you both. We've had a wonderful time. I'm sure it's something Sam and Emily will always remember.' She looked in the direction of the two children. 'Why don't you give Granddad Tom and Mary a hug?'

After they had done just that, Paul embraced Mary, and then it was the turn of Tom.

'It's been great being able to spend time with you,' Paul said. 'And remember what I said about coming over to Oz to visit us. You never know, I might even teach you how to play golf.'

'I'm not sure about the golf part,' answered Tom, with a light laugh. 'I think I've had enough of golf recently. But we'll definitely think about coming to visit you.'

Paul and his family then picked up their luggage and began to walk towards the check-in area. Just before they turned a corner, they all stopped and waved to Tom and Mary, before disappearing out of sight.

Mary took hold of Tom's hand. 'How are you feeling?' she asked.

'I don't know. I suppose it will be later when I start to miss them.'

'Were you serious about going to see them?'

'Why not?' he answered. 'I'd hate to think I won't see them again.'

Mary squeezed Tom's hand. 'You see, there is, after all, life after the police force.'

Chapter 58

It was a few days later and Tom was seated in one of the interview rooms at the station. Also in the room were another man and a woman. They were leading the inquiry into the death of DC Bennett. It was the woman who, looking directly at Tom, spoke first.

'Thank you for attending today, DCI Stone. My name is DCS Janet Colley and this is my colleague, DCI James Russell. Just to let you know, as this is a formal inquiry, our meeting today is being recorded.' She then looked down at a sheet of paper set on the table in front of her, and began to read from it. 'So that everyone is clear, the main purpose of this inquiry is to investigate the circumstances which led to the death of DC Gary Bennett and recommend any procedural changes which could minimise the chance of similar outcomes happening again. If, after this inquiry has concluded, it is our considered opinion that poor leadership or non-compliance with relevant procedures contributed to DC Bennett's death, then we will, of course, be suggesting appropriate action. Is that all clear?'

'Perfectly,' answered Tom.

'Why do you think DC Bennett decided to follow Mr Blackwell, on the night he died, without informing DS Milner that he was planning to do so?' she then asked, without any further preamble.

'I really don't know,' said Tom. 'There could have been lots of reasons.'

'Such as?' she asked.

Tom had been notified of the meeting the previous day. As was his usual custom, he had spent quite a while anticipating their likely questions, together with the key points he felt he needed to get across. He had also decided that, however difficult, he would not fall into the trap of being too defensive.

'DC Bennett was an extremely conscientious and dogged

police officer,' he said. 'He had been in the force a long time and, no doubt, during that time had developed a copper's natural instinct to know when something was not quite right. He felt strongly Mr Blackwell was a key suspect in the murder of Glyn Burton. I suspect, although I cannot be certain, of course, that he simply decided, on the spur of the moment, to drive to Mr Blackwell's house in order to see if he could find out anything else about him.'

This time it was DCI Russell who spoke. 'And it was that *spur-of-the-moment* decision which ultimately cost him his life.'

'And, without a doubt, saved the life of Mr Blackwell,' said Tom. He paused briefly before continuing. 'Mr Blackwell has already confirmed, without DC Bennett's personal intervention, he would certainly have been killed himself.'

'That's entirely possible, DCI Stone, but this inquiry has a clear brief, as just outlined by DCS Colley, and that is to investigate the circumstances leading to the death of DC Bennett.'

DCS Colley then spoke. 'We have a number of statements, from other officers, which suggest that DC Bennett was almost fixated on proving Mr Blackwell's guilt. Your loyalty to him is to be commended, but isn't it the truth that this clear fixation was allowed to develop at the expense of standard police procedures, and it was this lack of proper supervision which ultimately was the cause of DC Bennett's death?'

'No, it wasn't,' answered Tom. 'It was the fact that an unarmed police officer, without regard for his own safety, went to protect a member of the public. Can I just remind you it was the two men who attacked him that "*ultimately*" led to his death?' Despite his good intentions not to become defensive, he instantly realised this was exactly what he had just done. Surprisingly, though, he didn't regret it.

'But *you* knew DC Bennett felt strongly that Mr Blackwell was central to the murder investigation and that, in his opinion, Mr Blackwell was probably the person who had murdered Mr Burton. That's correct, isn't it?'

'Yes, it is,' he answered.

An uneasy silence followed, before DCI Russell said, 'You just mentioned how DC Bennett had been a serving police officer for a long time. Wouldn't it have been normal, given his length of service, for him to have moved beyond a DC?'

'Not everyone has aspirations to become a DCS or DCI. In my experience it's always better to have a square peg in a square hole. Over the years I've seen too many examples of officers being promoted beyond their level of competence.'

They both chose to ignore Tom's last comment.

'So you wouldn't describe DC Bennett as being particularly ambitious?' DCS Colley asked.

'Not especially, no. But you shouldn't confuse ambition with competence and determination.'

Once again not responding to Tom's comment, DCS Colley decided on a different line of questioning. 'I understand, at the time of DC Bennett's death, you were on holiday. Is that correct?'

'Yes, that's correct.'

'Isn't it a bit unusual to take a holiday during a murder investigation? Especially one which, as subsequent events confirmed, was rapidly coming to a climax?'

'I took a few days off for personal reasons,' he answered, as matter-of-factly as possible. 'And, anyway, you are wrong when you say the investigation was coming to a climax. At that time we still did not have any hard evidence. We had some circumstantial evidence but no evidence on which we could make an arrest.'

'And it was then, just before you took some days off, that you appointed DS Milner as acting SIO. Is that also correct?'

'Yes, it is,' he answered.

'What briefing did you carry out with him at the time?'

'A verbal brief. Mainly to go back over all of the evidence to see if there were any discrepancies. I also said to contact me should there be any major developments.'

'So, nothing in writing?' asked DCI Russell.

'No. As I just said, it was a verbal briefing.'

'I understand it was your recommendation that DS Milner should be promoted from acting DS to full DS. On what basis did you make that recommendation, given DS Milner's relative inexperience?' asked DCS Colley.

'It was my judgement that he was ready to be promoted. To my mind he had shown he had all the necessary attributes and was ready to take on the role.'

'And how did DC Bennett react to DS Milner's promotion? As you have already said, he had considerably more experience than DS Milner. It wouldn't have been a surprise if there was at least some resentment.'

'At no stage did I see any resentment on DC Bennett's part. In fact, it was a great pleasure to see just how well they worked together.'

'But, obviously, they didn't work *that* well together. If they had, then surely DS Bennett would have felt he could inform DS Milner of what he planned to do on the day he died,' replied DCS Colley.

'As I've already told you, I suspect it was a spur-of-the-moment decision.'

Once again, they all fell into an uneasy silence. Eventually, DCS Colley spoke. 'DCI Stone, if you could turn the clock back, would you have done anything differently when you briefed DS Milner?'

Tom hesitated before answering. 'It's a hypothetical question, but I might have briefed both DS Milner and DC Bennett together.'

DCS Colley started to put the sheets of paper immediately in front of her into a neat pile. 'Thank you very much, DCI Stone, for your time. Just to let you know, timing-wise, we intend to publish our findings and recommendations a few days from now. In the meantime, I would remind you that, until then, you should not discuss any aspect of this inquiry with anyone. Is that clear?'

'Perfectly,' he simply replied.

Chapter 59

'I'm sorry, sir,' said Milner. 'You didn't have to do that. It was all my fault.'

Tom and Milner were alone in Tom's office. Tom had just announced to the other officers on the second floor that he would be taking immediate retirement.

The previous day he had met with Superintendent Birch, who had informed him of the results of the inquiry. The main finding was that, although it was unlikely that DC Bennett's death could have been prevented, its likelihood could at least have been reduced with clearer and more effective supervision from Tom, and especially from Milner. On this point, the inquiry concluded that both Tom and DS Milner *should* have provided that increased supervision. As a consequence, the recommendation was that they should both be demoted. In Tom's case, his demotion would be to Detective Inspector, whilst Milner would be demoted back to Detective Constable. Surprisingly, though, Tom had also been given the option of taking early retirement.

After his interview with DCS Colley and DCI Russell, Tom had become convinced some form of disciplinary action would be taken. His inclination had always been to fight such a verdict, but he soon realised that any appeal was likely to be unsuccessful, and would only prolong all of the uncertainty. Better to take whatever sanctions were handed out and move on. Except, whilst he could come to terms with this, he doubted very much whether Milner could.

What he hadn't expected was the option to take early retirement, based upon his current DCI salary. Superintendent Birch had informed him that it was the Commissioner himself who had pushed for this. When Tom had discussed it with Mary, the previous evening, she had been unequivocal that he should take up this offer. What had been surprising was that it hadn't taken too much persuasion on her part for him to also come to that conclusion. It was an odd way to end his career, but, strangely, he didn't feel any great sadness or resentment. In fact, once he had made the decision, he had almost instantly felt a great surge of relief flowing through his body.

'David,' said Tom, 'please don't blame yourself. You've known me long enough now to know I don't tend to make decisions simply based upon emotion.'

'That's true,' he answered, with a light laugh, and the first time Tom had seen him smile in a few days.

'And anyway,' said Tom, 'this will give me more time to spend with my grandchildren.' He paused. 'I've already spoken with DCI Shaw and he says he is more than happy to have you on his team. He's a good DCI and knows how these things work. I'm certain it won't be too long before you are being considered for promotion again.'

Once again Milner began to laugh. 'You didn't always speak so highly about DCI Shaw.'

When Milner had first joined the team, Tom had made it clear that DCI Shaw was one of the new breed of career officers who stood for everything he, as one of the 'old school', hated. Over time, though, Tom's opinion had changed to such an extent that here he was now, actually extolling DCI Shaw's virtues.

'Well, everyone is entitled to change their mind once in a while,' Tom said. 'Even me.'

Whilst all of this did help, temporarily, to ease the tension, Milner's tone betrayed his inner feeling of despondency when he spoke again. 'I don't think I could do that. How will other officers perceive me? *That's Milner,* they will say. *He was once a DS, but screwed up, and one of his officers died as a result.* It will be impossible for me to gain any respect.'

Tom deliberately left it a while before he replied.

'David,' he said. 'Do you remember the discussion we had with Mr Sax?'

This was a reference to an earlier investigation they had worked on, involving the murder of a prominent Jewish man. During the course of their investigation they had spent time speaking to Mr Sax and had both heard what he had personally endured and seen, at first hand, during his time imprisoned in Auschwitz.

Tom carried straight on. 'He mentioned how one day you

could become this country's top police officer. Mr Sax is an excellent judge of character, because he was right. I've got absolutely no doubt that, if you want to, you could go all the way. But to get there you will certainly have to overcome many more setbacks along the way, just like Mr Sax did during the horror years he endured in Auschwitz. Just treat this as one of those setbacks. You can respond in one of two ways. React negatively, walk away and forever resent the force, or react positively, seeing this as something which will make you stronger. Which option do you think Mr Sax would have taken? I think we both know the answer to that.'

9 780956 979889